Dedicated to my own personal demons.

Had you not been there to give me dark moments of my own, it might not have been quite as easy to write the torments and horrors in this story.

Hopefully, this dedication will encourage you to take it easy on me in future…

With love,

Cam

Content Warning

Please be aware that this book contains strong adult themes, including, but not limited to:

⇨ Graphic & Sexual Violence

⇨ Self Harm

⇨ Alcoholism

⇨ Hateful Language

"While I feel these things are necessary in the context of the story, it's important to me that my readers understand what they're in for.
- Cam W."

WELCOME DESCENT

CAM WOLFE

Cover art — SwerklStudio

Cam Wolfe Publishing
Brisbane, QLD 4000, Australia

This book published 2021

Cam Wolfe asserts the moral right to be
identified as the author of this work
www.camwolfebooks.com

Table of Contents

Prologue

How should he be punished?

Storm clouds grew in the distance, creeping over the horizon like a blanket of dark foam. Joseph watched from the floor-to-ceiling window of his office, running a finger around the rim of his scotch glass.

How should he be punished? Joseph thought to himself again.

'Sir?'

Joseph sighed and turned to face the intern, his expression placid.

'You fucked up.'

The intern's already ghostly face went a shade paler.

'I'm sorry, sir.'

'No. Not good enough, I want you on the phone with the accounts team. Fix it.'

'My shift finished twenty—'

'Now.'

The intern looked down at his feet and his chest deflated. He turned to leave, hands stuffed into his pockets and then he stepped back. Joseph looked up from his glass with a glare that could cut stone, but the intern was still staring into the floor.

'Oh, someone from Valley South Acquisitions is on the line for you as well. A Mr. Bub?'

'Bub?' Joseph snorted and sat down. 'Don't know him. Send him to one of the others, Peter maybe.'

The intern nodded and scurried off as quickly as their feet would take them. Joseph watched until they vanished from sight, his lips curled into a smile. That intern—*Jake? John?*—could not have been more than five years his junior, and yet they were running errands and Joseph was here; drinking nine-hundred dollar scotch and wearing a suit that would cost nearly ten intern's pay checks. How wonderful it was to be at the top.

Joseph ran a hand through his thick black hair and looked at the spot where a photo frame would usually rest. Truth be told, Jake's mishap was as minor as they come; it would be fixed with a five-minute phone call. However, Joseph had no plans to tell the intern this, there is little fun to be had in that. He would torture poor Jake for a little while, make him work a little harder than the rest—maybe fetch a few more coffees. After a week or so he would ease off, that was usually enough time to leave an impression. The

2

impression was all that mattered. If you show people you're not to be fucked with, they won't.

It was late and the storm was thundering closer. Joseph knew he should go home—Pam would be waiting—but not yet ... not until this glass was empty— and maybe one more after that. For now, he would sit back, put his feet up and watch the rain from the comfort of his office. Just a few more drinks and that shadow that loomed over him might feel a little less heavy. Just a few more drinks and he could convince himself he was happy.

'I did this,' Joe whispered as he lay his head back and closed his eyes. He said this often, to no one in particular. He liked to remind himself who was responsible for his success, his *rise*. He earned this, he deserved it. This power, this control, this security ... he wouldn't give it up for anything in the world.

Chapter
One

Steel and Concrete

On the closest thing to a good day, it would be a resilient beam of morning sunshine that woke Joe. Blistering, golden light would slice through even the densest mid-morning cloud and creep its way to the snoring, farting mass of limbs named Joseph, still tangled in his sheets. On this particular Friday, however, it was his radio alarm—or, more specifically, the opening brass band notes of *Jingle Jangle Jingle* by Kay Kyser—that did the job.

Yippi yay, there'll be no wedding bells for today

'Fuck me,' Joe groaned.

He flailed an arm to silence the ear-splitting, merry tune, failing spectacularly and knocking over a whiskey bottle instead; the now empty bottle that had helped him get to sleep the night before. It fell to the floor with an almighty, hollow *THUNK*.

Joe stretched out the side of his face with a stiff, clammy hand and let his mouth open wide in an aggressive yawn, as if to curse the sun for rising. He had turned forty-two the week before and every day since had been a taunting, spiteful reminder of how easily his body would give in under the slightest physical strain. Apparently now, simply waking up was asking a little too much. He gave one more strenuous groan and threw himself out from the bedsheets, nearly landing on the bottle he had just backhanded. The vile mix in his stomach rolled in place, launching a bitter, battery-fluid taste of acid reflux into the back of his throat.

'Goddamn,' he said with a scowl. He ran a hand through the thinning, pale hair of his temple and stepped up to the floor-to-ceiling window, stretching his arms out at unnatural angles.

It was a shitty day to say the least; the congested city street below was bathed in a miserable sheet of mist and stark blue shadow, cast down from the impenetrable, gray clouds high above. They were tumbling over each other like the froth of a swelling evening tide and barely a candle's glow of sunlight could be seen through the black. Joseph imagined the heavens were mocking him, daring him to hope for a good day.

Go ahead, asshole, I dare ya. I see half a smile and I'll be shitting hail.

All the pedestrians and cars eleven storys below were dulled in detail and volume, sealed away behind that magnificent two-inch glass. Joe liked the view from up here. It was the *distance* he enjoyed, the distance between himself and the swarm of always stinking, always staring nobodies. He regarded the impending storm once more before making his way across the small studio apartment into the conjoined kitchen. He made sure to nudge the bottle with his heel so that it rolled under the king-sized bed with a prolonged rumble. The final notes of the swing jazz monstrosity had finally burst through in distorted squawks and now the day's news was being read by the world's least entertaining DJ. His voice was a droning bass and he sounded about as pleased with his job as Joe was about his breakfast—the brittle remnants of a long-expired box of cereal.

'We have a big one coming in, folks. We're looking at a category two for now but keep me close because we may have a three on our hands. You don't want to be strolling around the streets of Dawn Valley during this one, that's for sure.'

'No shit,' Joe snorted. He spat the last bite of his sticky wheat cereal back into the suspiciously thick milk of his bowl.

He grabbed one of the last few apples from the fridge and gripped it between his teeth before snatching the Oxford button-down from the back of his one and only dining chair. The shower would have to wait until after work; he had set the wrong time on the alarm *again* and the large, red numbers were blinking at him with merciless repetition.

10:34. Shit.

He didn't dress quickly enough, however, to avoid seeing his reflection in the darkened glass of the window across the room. There's nothing quite like spotting yourself in poor lighting, especially while bent over trying to fish a tie from a pile of dirty laundry. He was, by any definition, well-groomed; he kept his haircut tidy and his face clean-shaven, but below the neck he was hiding a chest of tangled white hair and the early warning signs of a beer gut.

After deciding two seconds of self-pity were two seconds too many, he finished his Windsor knot, slipped on his black suit jacket, and laced up his Derby shoes. One of the greatest pleasures for Joe in his day was the feeling of the finely woven wool of the suit pants against his knees, and the way the sleeves hugged his biceps. This suit—a pristine Valentino—was the last remaining survivor of his collection. The rest had been sold for a painfully slight margin of their original cost, just to secure his place in what, for the last ten months, was now his reluctant home.

In a matter of minutes, he looked as though he could have been escorting the United States president across the Whitehouse lawn. Of course, the reality was far from being that glamorous. He stepped up to the window, doing his best to erase the—admittedly, still slightly intoxicated—shirtless sad-sack from his memory and replace it with the new, well-dressed doppelgänger. It was while adjusting his tie a third time that something smacked the glass with such force that it rattled the frame. It happened so quickly that Joe might have thought he had imagined it, had the sound not thrown him back and left what looked like a crack the size of a thumbnail on the other side of the glass.

'What the *fuck*?' he snapped, stumbling to his feet again.

He stepped up to the window and pressed his slightly crooked nose against the cold glass. Through the gloom outside, he could see the lifeless body of a crow being carried down to the traffic in a strong wind. It left a trail of small, black feathers on the breeze until it vanished amongst the blur of motion below with one last macabre, yet strangely elegant, pinwheel. He had seen a few birds hit the building before, but they were usually small house sparrows or pigeons, never a crow.

Poor bastard.

Almost as quickly as it had happened it was forgotten, and Joe was pocketing his keys and wallet at the door. This was his least-favorite part of the day, opening the door and stepping into the hallway to leave for work. There were at least six hours and numerous social interactions between that door closing behind him and it opening in front of him once again. Six long hours before his home would be welcoming him back with a short glass of Glenfiddich and an episode of *Cheers*. Like plunging into icy waters, Joe took a deep breath and wrenched it open.

'Buenos días, Joseph, how do you do?'

Damnit.

It was as if the old man had been waiting for him.

'Morning, Javier, how's it going?'

Joe made to walk past the elderly man, hoping this would convey a sense of urgency. It, of course, had no effect on Javier. Despite holding two large bags of groceries, he grabbed Joe's arm and stopped the much larger man in his tracks.

Son of a bitch.

Joe hated that. If it weren't for the guy's age, he probably would have given his neighbor a good shove. Javier was a friendly man, but therein lay the problem. He had an enduring toothy grin, exacerbated by the ocean of creases that curved around the corners of his mouth and across his olive-tanned forehead. Seeing this man beaming up at him almost daily did nothing but remind Joe of the dim-witted joy he was a stranger to.

'You make sure you stock up today, hermano. I'll be a fool if this storm doesn't keep us home for a few days at least.'

'Will do,' Joe replied stiffly, faking a smile and gently yanking his elbow from the old man's astonishingly firm grip. 'You have yourself a good day, buddy.'

Joe didn't know what *hermano* meant, but it was only one of the many strange things Javier had called him since his first day in the building. All he knew about Javier in return was that the old man had come over from Madrid more than thirty years ago, after doing a few tours in the Spanish infantry.

Was it Madrid? Maybe Malaga? Ah, who cares.

'Oh, I *will*. My grandson has sent me the *El Chavo del Ocho* box set. You should treat yourself to a viewing, Joseph. *Fantastic* show.' Javier chuckled to himself and stared off whimsically into the distance, dismissing the younger man with a weak slap on the shoulder. Joe couldn't help but wonder how Javier had made it out of the front door in this wind without being blown down the street like a dry leaf.

The elevator ride was delightfully silent, and Joe soaked up every second of it. He leaned his head against the glass-paneled wall and silently prayed that the drowsiness and hunger would drain from his body before the dreaded *ding* signaled his arrival at the ground floor. The generous helping of whiskey from the night before had left its familiar mark on him in the form of a pulsing ache in his temples. Each throb warped the mechanical whir of the elevator as it descended. He felt a little guilty for giving Javier so much attitude, but only a little. In retrospect he imagined that the old man hadn't even noticed.

DING!

Joe dragged his feet from the starchy, red carpet of the elevator to the reflective tiles of the building's lobby and sidestepped to pass a short

Indian woman in nurse's scrubs. She looked twice as tired as he did—a truly high, booze-soaked bar. She must have just finished a long shift, and this only earned her a hushed deference from Joe. Her blank, turquoise eyes stared past him and into the back wall of the metal chamber that would take her up to bed. Bed and the erotic audiobook she had been thinking about for the last fifteen hours, or so Joe imagined.

Joseph marched across the spacious lobby, feeling more awake with each step. Every fall of his feet against the marble floor sent the blood charging through his legs and into his groin. Despite the shabby state of his own apartment, the rest of the Royal Dawn was quite impressive. The walls and floor were a polished, eggshell white and the roof arched into a net of pale stone with gold trim. It all culminated in a tremendous, winding branch of gold chains that held a crystal chandelier high above; the gems threw spikes of prism light across the floor in a halo.

'Morning, Mr. Ridley. Just wake up, did you?'

Joe blinked dumbly at the young man behind the reception counter and replied with a dismissive grunt.

'Jesus Christ,' snorted the teenager, before exhaling dramatically, 'you look like shit, Joseph.'

'Piss off, kid, I'm nursing a migraine.'

'Yeah, *migraine*. Sure,' he replied, rolling his eyes. The young man stepped over to Joseph and thrust a large, paper coffee cup into his hands.

'Take this. The dipshits at Café Olay put in too much sugar and you *clearly* need it more than me.'

'I don't need your charity, Daewon,' Joe growled. He regarded the teenager through a squint but sipped the lukewarm coffee all the same.

He clearly remembered the moment that he had first met Daewon. It was two months into living at the Royal Dawn and he had woken at some ungodly hour to the roaring of his drunk, dead-shit neighbor. The miserable bastard was howling about how badly he wanted to beat the fear of God into the *fruity, new, black concierge* because he would not let him smoke in the stairwell. The fat asshole's choice of words might have been a bit more archaic than that. Once Joe had made peace with the fact he would not be getting back to sleep, he made his way downstairs in the hope of fetching a donut from the 7/11. He had found the young man talking to Rick, the disgustingly tall security guard, at quite an intimate distance. Once Rick had marched off,

with the floor quaking beneath his feet—
although that might have just been Joe's
hangover—Daewon turned from watching the
giant's rolling glutes to Joe. The teen's lips had
curled into a cheeky smile. 'Well, good evening,
sir.'

*This coffee really is terrible, the kid wasn't lying.
They may as well have served it in an ice-cream cone.*

'Giving you my trash coffee isn't charity, you
ungrateful prick. My date last night was charity.
He was about as interesting as sink water. Kind
of tasted like it too.'

Joe closed his eyes with a reactionary cringe
and swallowed the last of his coffee in a hard
gulp.

'What? Too much information?' Daewon
smirked, clearly very pleased with himself at the
obvious discomfort he'd caused. It was apparent
by now that the teen only said these things to get
a rise out of the man.

'I don't give a shit what you put in your
mouth, kid. Doesn't mean I want to think about
it.'

Daewon shrugged and meandered back to
his desk, calling back over his shoulder, 'The car
isn't here yet.'

'Good,' Joe said, striding past the desk and wrenching open the grand glass door. 'They don't let me smoke in the car.'

He heard Daewon mumble something before the strong wind and traffic drowned out all sound inside the building—something like, *'Talk about something you shouldn't put in your mouth.'*

The breeze was strong, and with it came a brisk chill that belonged in the last days of a January winter. Certainly not mid-July. Lighting the cigarette was a challenge, but after a few minutes of aggressive flicking—and a tirade of colorful language—the orange and blue flame finally snaked its way between his cupped palms. The fire licked the end of the silk cut, igniting it with a spine-chillingly pleasurable hiss, and Joseph felt an involuntary moan escape his lips. He had to hold the cigarette to his mouth so that it wouldn't be snatched away by the wind, but the hot tendrils of blue smoke exploding from his nostrils were enough to finally put a smile on his face, something so rare nowadays. The joy of his smoky breakfast gave Joe the confidence to bring his eyes to street level and observe the people rushing past him. Most were rosy red in the cheeks, huffing as they lugged bags of canned

17

food and water to their destinations. Some carried a year's supply of toilet paper under their arms.

Fucking panic buyers.

One particular young woman with *that* disapproving scowl—you know the one—made a show of coughing forcefully as she dodged a thin wisp of cigarette smoke, before it was whipped out of existence.

'Good morning,' Joe said with a toothy smirk. He took a theatrically large drag from his tailor and pointed the blazing red cherry her way like a dart. He laughed as she picked up her pace and disappeared into the throng.

'My God, Joseph, brush your hair, will you?'

A stocky woman in a finely woven, blue pantsuit with tightly plaited red hair snapped to Joe's side as if she had been brought in on the gale. Her nose glowed bright red, contrasting against the splash of freckles across her cheeks that were quickly turning blue in the cold.

'Are you fuckin kidding me, Kris?' Joe snarled. 'Have you seen the damn weather?'

He dropped the butt of his cigarette to stamp it out, but no sooner had it left his nicotine-stained fingers than it vanished from sight. The familiar sense of mortal regret sunk in as he exhaled the last warmth of the smoke. The sudden awareness of the tightness in his chest reminded him how much he hated the cursed things, or rather, how much he hated loving them.

'I'm sorry, Joe, we just have a big client today. *Please* don't fuck it up.'

'Who?'

'You know the drill—the book is on the dashboard.'

'Kris, did you give any more thought–'

'Like I said yesterday, and every other shitting day this year, Joe, I can't make it happen.'

'That's bullshit, Kris. I've been driving with you guys for over three years now. There's fucking taxi drivers that make more than me.'

'It *is* bullshit, but it's not my call. Raises come down to Vin and you know that scumbag likes you as far as he can throw you.' She threw a pointed glance down to Joseph's gut as she said this.

'Jesus Christ, it was nearly two years ago.'

'You fucked his wife. I'm not sure what you think the expiry date is on that fact, but you're lucky you still have a job at all.'

'Ex-wife.'

'Joseph.'

'Yeah, yeah, all right.'

'Wait until the old bastard gets himself another gold-digging bimbo and, if you're lucky, it'll put him in a good mood.'

With that, Kris slapped a shiny, black, plastic key into Joseph's open palm. She gave him one last, severe glare before turning on the spot and diving into the passenger side of a black Audi sedan. Parked directly behind that two-hundred-thousand-dollar vehicle was an immaculate, black-bodied Rolls Royce Phantom, one of the newer 2018 models. It was barely older than a newborn and twice as precious. Joe felt the blood that was refusing to enter his frozen cheeks rush to his loins. The sleek, polished steel of a luxury vehicle was one of the few things that still made his cock stiffen against his pants. He watched Kris' car pull away and strode to the driver's side of the Phantom like he owned it, looking around to make sure all the passers-by could see him get in. It was not his first time driving the vehicle, but hearing the sharp chirp of the central locking, and feeling the smooth leather of the driver's seat still made him feel like a king; a king that excreted sex from every pore of his body. That feeling always lasted until he arrived at the pickup location for his first client of the day; from then on, he was just the driver.

The car hummed to life with an electric purr and the dashboard ignited with an array of luminescent blue. Joe adjusted his dark hair in the rear-view mirror, deciding to simply push it back. Aside from some slight thinning at the temples and a few thin streaks of white in his fringe, he had quite a good head of hair on him. Had it not been for the crow's feet and shallow creases in his forehead, he could have passed for a much younger man. He locked eyes with the sharp, hazel ones in the mirror and looked away quickly.

Workin' on our night moves

Tryin' to make some front page drive-in news

'Now we're talkin.' Joe turned the sleek dial by the air-conditioning vents and Bob Seger's voice and bluesy guitar riff flooded into the car's interior space from every corner of the vehicle.

The drive was a slow one. It seemed that everyone within fifty miles of the city center had made their way in to stock up on supplies, as if the devil himself were on the way. Joe knew he had to pick up some cereal and pasta on the way home, but as he weaved through the chaos at a snail's pace, it did nothing but make him hot in the face.

'Get out of the damn way!' he barked. He was yelling at a young man on a moped in front of him but knew full well that no one but himself could hear his cursing. Only he could feel the rising heat in his cheeks.

He drove for at least another twenty minutes and kept a twitching eye on the digital clock by the steering wheel. Only ten more minutes and he would be late, an unforgivable sin in his line of work, even on a day like this. *Especially* on a day like this. Joe slammed the brakes as he found himself at yet another pedestrian crossing. His heart beat at his chest as he resisted the urge to headbutt the dashboard. City-goers hustled from left to right, right to left in front of his car, some of them taking a moment to eye the luxury vehicle on their way past.

'Come on, please. *Please.*'

Joseph knew that if he were to get even one complaint for being late, that douchebag boss of his would never sign off on a raise, a raise he was finding himself in more and more desperate need of with each passing day. He had more money in his pocket than he did his bank account at the moment, and most of that was coins. Hopefully, there was enough there to grab a slice of pie for lunch, but likely not.

He raised his face from a sweaty hand and looked out at the straggler shuffling across the road at an agonizingly slow speed. It was a young woman, probably twenty-something—dark hair, ample figure squeezed into a slim, white button-down, the whole deal. She looked like she was on her way to some corporate job, but there was something odd about her walk. Her feet shot forward in jilted, precise steps and her arms stayed straight by her sides. She wasn't looking down at a phone or avoiding eye contact with passers-by like everyone else; she was just staring straight ahead.

'What the hell is this girl on?' Joe wondered aloud.

She stopped in the middle of the street, directly in front of the Rolls Royce Phantom, and turned. A chill ran down Joseph's spine and goosebumps rose on his skin as he found himself staring into this girl's face. She stared back.

'Hey,' Joe said, under his breath. He could not look away.

There was something unnatural about the way she stood there, completely motionless. The stranger looked like your average, white-collar young woman, but something felt off. Something felt off the way it would if you came home from work and found the door already unlocked. Her hair did not move in the wind and her mouth hung open as if she had been mid-sentence and forgotten what she was going to say. Her large green eyes stared vacantly, burning through the car windshield—and through Joseph. What made his fingers tighten around the steering wheel, though, was the other pedestrians. The way they passed the girl by like she didn't even exist.

Joe finally pulled to a stop. The car gave a gentle, mechanical sigh. The GPS flashed, announcing his arrival just as Johnny Cash's voice croaked through the radio, joined by abrupt acoustic strokes.

The building was breathtaking in scale. The Dawn Valley Catholic Church. He hadn't come so close to a church in a very long time, not that he had ever been a man of faith. Despite his lack of spiritual belief—perhaps it could even be called an incredulous contempt for the religious—he had always nursed a quiet appreciation for the magnificence of the buildings, this one in particular. The three-story goliath of gray stone and oak towered from its perch atop an incline of grass that was greener than any AstroTurf he had ever seen. It was an odd sight, to see the—presumably brass—cross reaching to the sky, flanked by a horde of much taller but infinitely less impressive office towers.

The enormous wooden door at the top of the narrow, cement staircase swung open and a tall figure emerged from the orange glow inside. He must have been edging on seven feet and his black overcoat billowed around his shins. It gave the stranger the appearance of a certain bloodsucking nightcrawler. The man seemed to stare at Joseph through the tinted passenger-side window for a moment before marching down the slope two stairs at a time.

'Oh crap,' Joe hissed. He snapped out of his trance and burst from the Rolls Royce.

He bustled to the back-passenger door, closest to the approaching man, as quickly as possible without looking unnatural. With one not-so-subtle gasp for breath, he opened the door just as the man's foot landed on the last step. The stranger did not say a word before sliding into the warmth of the Rolls Royce; he only regarded Joe with a cold indifference.

Great, another prick. It was a thought Joseph was well used to hearing echo through his mind.

Once he was back behind the wheel and they had re-joined the almost immobile stream of traffic, he decided to steal one more look at his guest in the rear-view mirror. *Samuel Bub* was the name he had read in the client book just a short while earlier, along with a few other unimportant details of his newly created account with *Becker & Co Luxury Transfers.* He didn't look much like a Samuel, certainly not a *Bub.* His hair was cut almost to the skin—a faded stroke of dark hair across the top of his dome—and his pointed jaw wore a peppering of white stubble. The three-piece suit he was wearing was immaculate and the midnight blue contrasted against his olive skin with clear purpose. Joe knew the meticulous weave of the fabric and the character of the sleeve's stitching well; it was a Brioni Vanquish. He had felt the envious warmth of being in its presence once before, a long time ago; it was a forty-thousand-dollar suit. Most noticeable, though, was the sharp glare from the small, pale-gray eyes, looking right back at him through the mirror. Joe shifted his grip on the steering wheel and tried to make it look as though his attention was firmly fastened on the gridlock before them.

'Joseph Ridley, yes?' Samuel's voice matched his name as well as his appearance. It was a heavy bass, a deep rumble like approaching thunder.

Joe cleared his throat and looked back at the man in the mirror, as he had been taught to do.

'Yes, sir, and how are you today, Mr. Bub?'

'Splendid, thank you, Joseph. I enjoy nothing more than a good storm, don't you?'

'As a man who drives for a living, I'm not sure I can agree with you there, Mr. Bub.' This earned him the subtle curve of a smile from the man.

'I imagine some may feel humbled by a storm like this. So much raw, uncontrollable power sweeping over our fine city; what are *we* to something like that?'

Samuel never looked away; every time Joe looked back to the mirror he was met by those piercing eyes, housed in shadowed lines that made the man's brows droop. He was twenty years Joseph's senior, at least, and there was a blistering intensity in how he paused before each sentence.

'I must admit, I enjoy the way the rain and thunder drown out the other noise. I find it helps me to focus. You're not afraid of storms, are you, Mr. Ridley?'

'Not afraid, sir. Not much of a fan, though, either. They tend to get people acting crazy, y'know.' Joseph pointed a finger to the stream of panicked pedestrians rushing past outside.

'I see.'

Almost heaven, West Virginia, Blue Ridge Mountains, Shenandoah River

John Denver. God, Joe hated John *fucking* Denver.

'Ah, I do like this one,' Samuel said, tapping his knee in time to the plucking notes of the guitar. 'Would you mind?'

As much as it pained him, Joe turned the volume dial a little more and the music swelled as the chorus set in.

Country roads, take me home, to the place, I belong

The traffic was still moving in short, rolling bursts, but Samuel didn't seem to mind.

'Are you married, Joseph?'

'I was, sir.'

'What was your partner's name?'

Joe hesitated. 'Pamela … Pam.'

Samuel gave the courtesy of a long moment's silence before continuing his inquisition.

'You have a child?'

'A son—Marcus.'

Another pause, so uncomfortable that Joe couldn't help but find himself focusing on the music.

'It's a strange thing, to have a child,' Samuel mused, still staring. 'They bring the miracle of life, and yet it can feel that they also bring an end to the life we knew. They bring purpose, and yet it can feel that they also bring an abrupt end to all *other* purpose.'

What the hell is he talking about?

Joe wished it were Pam or Marcus riding with him, and not this strange, terrifying man.

'Do you have any children, sir?'

'I also have a son. Although he has long since left my *nest*.'

'College?'

'No.'

Silence.

'Do you believe in karmic retribution, Joseph?'

'I'm sorry, sir?'

'In church today, we discussed the Buddhist philosophy of karma. Receiving intent upon you, that you intend upon others. I would love to hear your thoughts.'

The question surprised Joe. He was used to small talk from his clients—if they took pity on his role of servitude—but it would hardly go past topics of work, family, and the weather, talking points that Samuel had used up in less than a few minutes.

'You were talking about Buddhism in Church?'

'Indeed we were. Your thoughts?'

Joseph felt his hands stiffen.

'I think if you do nice things, it comes back around.'

It was a bullshit statement, but just vague enough that Joe could avoid making any real point. Samuel smelled it, like a foxhound on the chase.

'Spare me the banalities, Joseph. I did not get to where I am by wasting time on nonsense like that.'

A thin layer of cold sweat crept from Joe's palms and glossed the matte leather of the steering wheel. The shift in Samuel's tone made the hairs on his neck stand up.

What's the deal with this fucking guy?

'I think,' Joe began again, 'life will shit on you from a very great height, no matter who you are. It's just a matter of when.'

Samuel smiled, showing a row of gleaming white teeth.

'Ah, there we go. That wasn't so difficult, was it? Honesty, no matter how troubling, is a sign of respect too commonly dismissed.'

The man shifted in his seat slightly and linked his hands over one of his knees, still searching for Joe's eyes in the mirror.

'It would seem to me that the more people you harm out of cruelty or indifference, the more people there are to wish ill will back upon you. Some may even try to exact some vengeance of their own. Now, you say that life *shits* on all, one way or another—do you feel that you deserve more than what you have?'

'I don't know, sir.'

'I believe you do know, Joseph.'

'Well, I guess I didn't picture myself driving rich assholes to work in my forties.'

The words escaped his lips before he could catch them; if Kris were here, she would have beat him to within an inch of his life for speaking that way to a client, especially such a high-profile one. However, Samuel smiled.

'I'm just doing the best I can,' Joe said, defeated and trying to save face.

Country roads, take me home

'The belief is that karma is little more than intent—intent thrust back upon the bearer. Those who intend good will receive good intent from those they help. Those who have intentions that benefit only themselves, well ...' Samuel caught Joe's eyes with his. 'I have learned a great deal in my line of work, Joseph, mostly patience. Sometimes people find themselves suffocating under the weight of their own failures. Some will weep, some will become consumed with spite, some will blame everyone but themselves and cry out *why me?* I have found it is the ones that hide from those failures that are the same people so often haunted by them.'

Samuel ran his fingers down the length of his dark tie, still tapping a foot to the final notes of John Denver's tune.

'What I'm saying, Joseph, is that sometimes, before we can rise to a place where life can't *shit on us from a great height*, hard as it may be, we first have to go all the way down. Down to where we bury things.'

A chill that had nothing to do with the weather rolled down Joe's spine like a mild seizure. Something in Samuel's voice, in his words, gave Joseph a grim and static feeling. He felt as though he were being detached from control of his own body. He willed his fingers to drum across the steering wheel, and to his relief they did.

The rest of the car ride was much less dramatic; in fact, Samuel fell silent after his preaching on *what goes around comes around.* He even looked away from the mirror and chose to instead direct his attention at the squall of pedestrians outside—something that Joe could not be more thankful for. Almost twenty-five minutes after they should have, the Rolls Royce crunched to a halt in front of an enormous, plain-looking office tower. Above the front entrance was a square sign, framed with gold-colored steel: *Valley South Acquisitions.*

Joe wasn't sure what he had expected to find at the end of the drive, but it had certainly been something a bit more exciting than this. Before he could exit the vehicle to open Samuel's door, the man leaned forward in his seat and spoke once more in his powerful, booming voice.

'I can let myself out, thank you, Joseph. It was truly a pleasure meeting you.' He reached out a hand and Joe swiveled in his seat to shake it.

'You too, Mr. Bub, take care.'

Samuel said one more thing before he opened the door and flooded the car with frigid wind, 'I heard an interesting thing today, Joseph. The condemned man is not he who does wrong, but he who cannot find the wrong in the doing.'

What a load of hippy bullshit.

The next seven clients were unremarkable. Only two of them tried to make conversation before realizing that Joseph would not be making any real attempt to engage with them. His last drop-off was Mr. Lundle, a portly man in a well-stretched suit who insisted on eating his powdered donuts over the carpeted floor. He then sprayed his sour cologne to mask the smell, insisting, 'It smells like street trash in here. This will spruce it up.'

The smell that Mr. Lundle had been referring to was a specially made Gucci car perfume called *Platinum Mahogany,* and it was one of the most complimented aspects of Joe's service. Now it was replaced with a bitter, citrus smell, like the odor of cheap, premix alcohol. Joseph might as well have been driving teenagers to the fucking prom.

Joe dropped off Mr. Lundle and then spent the entire drive to the Becker & Co car yard fantasizing. He imagined smashing that fat fuck's skull through the passenger window for leaving the interior in such a state. The satisfying crunch of bone and glass replayed in his mind, over and over. His blood boiled at the sight of the clouds of sugar coating the floor like snow, not only because he knew Kris would make him vacuum the interior before going home, but because such disrespect with fine things was a sin in his books. Had it been his car and not his boss's, he just might have tried to find the man's throat beneath the folds of blotched flesh, to choke him out. Once the anger subsided, he felt a familiar, uneasy vibration crawl down his spine and Samuel's voice jumped to the forefront again.

'Down to where we bury things.'

Long-hidden memories groaned from beyond the layers of drunken haze. Memories that beckoned and clawed, threatening to drag him down. Joseph reached down and unmuted the radio again.

Mr. Lundle had also asked for complete silence, clearly untroubled by his driver having to listen to his moist chewing and wet gulps as he finished his lunch.

Some old swing jazz was playing, nothing Joe was familiar with, but it was just chaotic enough to keep his mind off the thoughts he felt creeping up. It gave him a sick and guttural dread when he felt the shadow of his past drawing close. Some memories were a nostalgic and comforting guilty pleasure—his endless rows of expensive suits, the embracing rumble of his Maserati GranTurismo, Pam's perfectly smooth breasts illuminated by their skylight—but dwelling on the past was never worth the risk.

'Can you pay?'

Joseph stared up at the wiry bus driver, eyebrows raised.

'Pay? That's what this is for, isn't it?' He waved his transport card left to right, his cheeks becoming hot again.

'Machine's down, you have to pay.'

'The machine's down and it's my problem?'

The bus driver leaned across the armrest, staring up at Joseph with a severe, burning intensity. Truth be told, Joseph couldn't be sure whether he was speaking to a man or a woman. The skin hung loose on the driver's bones, creased with age from forehead to withered hands. Every part of this person looked too ancient to be operating heavy machinery, least of all a people container.

'If you want to travel, you pay.'

'Goddamnit, give me a break already,' Joe said.

He fished through his pockets, withdrawing what few remnants of silver and gold he could find. He slapped them down on the bus driver's tray and stormed off, his face carved in a scowl.

'This will do,' said the driver, the voice a gravelly croak.

Joe planted his forehead against the spastically gyrating window of the bus, perhaps a little harder than he intended, and closed his eyes. His palms still ached from being pressed into the corners of the Rolls Royce's interior, as he scrubbed the powder and crumbs from the carpet. It was a short trip, thankfully, and the weather had ensured that it would be a quiet ride home. There were only two other people on the bus—not including the driver—and they were seated together at least ten rows away, hissing at each other in quiet deliberation about how long the storm would actually last.

'My mom said that we could be shut in for a week.'

'Your mom's an idiot, Kevin.'

The bus was old; the seats were peeling their pleather skin and the handrails above were hiding freckles of rust beneath a thin coating of chrome paint. Worst of all, every strong current of wind rocked them on the suspension, threatening to topple them over and mix them all like a flesh salad. It almost felt like being in the belly of a large boat, caught in turbulent waters. Joseph didn't mind. He brushed the roof of his mouth with a dry tongue, imagining the amber liquid he would soon be pouring into a heavy-bottomed glass. It should have been enough to make him smile, but he didn't.

A sharp jolt flung Joe airborne, at least two inches from the surface of his seat. He rubbed his eyes and looked around in sharp turns, like a bear woken from hibernation. Had he fallen asleep? The teens were gone and now it was only him on the bus. Alarmed, he pressed his cheek to the foggy glass, praying he would recognize the street. There was little traffic, and almost no pedestrians, but the neon sign directly across from him read *Café Olay*.

Thank God.

Something else caught his attention. It was a man standing beside the café, staring back at Joe with his mouth hanging open. It was dark and the stranger was wearing a black cardigan, so Joe almost didn't see him, but as soon as he had, he could not look away. The man's shoulder-length hair twisted and roamed in the wind, violently snapping to each side like it was alive. His eyes were bulbous and almost luminescent in the city glow. The mouth, though—*Jesus,* that mouth. His cheeks and lips were stretched so wide that Joe could swear every tooth in the man's head was visible. He stared for a few seconds more before breaking away hastily and looking down at his feet. For the second time that day he felt a sickening terror tickle the pit of his stomach.

'What the hell is with people today?' Joe mumbled to himself. His gruff tone gave him a little relief. After a few seconds more he tried to steal another glance at the stranger in the corner of his vision.

'Shit,' he snapped, leaping back from the window and gripping the back of the chair with white-knuckled fingers.

The stranger had begun to sprint across the road toward the bus, his arms pumping at his side and his eyes still wild and bulging. His face suddenly became enveloped in a beam of bright streetlight and Joe finally got a good look at the man. The runner's mouth was hanging open so wide that his lips were tearing, sending thin webs of crimson blood into the spaces of his teeth. It was grotesque. Horrifying. Joe was frozen, watching the crazed man draw closer to the window. He ran with the unyielding form of an Olympic sprinter, causing his loose jaw to bounce violently.

'Hey!' Joe yelled, staggering away from the window but keeping the stranger in his sights. 'Hey, bus driver!'

The tiny, gray-haired figure at the wheel didn't respond. The driver didn't even blink, as if they were the only one on board, as if the only sound to be heard was the hum of the strong wind outside. The driver did, however, lurch the bus into motion. The engine roared to life and the bus cleared the path of the lunatic just in time. Joe crept cautiously to the back window and got one more look at the stranger before the fog and lucid, orange light consumed him. The figure was still staring, turning on the spot to watch the bus thunder down the road. His eyes never broke from Joe's. Then the stranger raised a disjointed, thin hand, and he waved.

'Welcome home,' mumbled Daewon. The young man didn't bother to look up from the screen of his phone as Joseph dragged his limp feet across the lobby.

'No place like it,' Joseph replied with a grunt. He yanked his tie with a hooked finger and let loose an exaggerated, self-pitying sigh.

Daewon shuffled the feet he had planted on the surface of the concierge desk, and only took one brief moment from swiping through his Twitter feed to give Joseph a raised eyebrow.

The elevator ride was infinitely longer when going up, and the groan of the pulleys felt especially strained today. Joe couldn't help but feel that the protesting sounds of the mechanics were only a reflection of the continuous whine he felt within himself—right up until the moment he had his ass firmly planted in his favorite, busted recliner.

DING

The doors slid open with a metallic sigh and Joe was welcomed by an impenetrable blackness. To call it darkness would be inaccurate, as it was not just the absence of light. Everything outside the weak, fluorescent glow of the elevator was just ... black. There was something else, an atmosphere that seemed to be creeping into the small lit space like a pungent gas; it was a jarring silence. Joe believed that if he were to put a hand into the dark, he would be surrendering a limb to the abyss. All of space and time outside of the elevator had been deleted. Before he even had time to hiss his well-used 'What the *fuck*?', the familiar, yellow corridor was there again. It had not flickered into existence; it was just there.

'I need a drink,' Joe muttered to himself, rubbing his forehead. He threw himself out of the elevator before the doors could seal him inside again.

He stumbled down the hallway, digging the small, steel key from inside his jacket pocket and trying to blink the strange events of the day from his mind. Just a short distance away, one of his neighbors was also looking for her key. She rummaged within the eternal depths of her comically large, and blatantly fake, Louis Vuitton handbag. She hissed quiet curses to herself and tried to brush her wavy, dark hair from her face with one hand, while the other burrowed ever deeper past lipsticks and chemist receipts.

Joe was pretty sure her name was Willow, or Wendy, or something like that, but to him she was always just the busty real estate woman a few doors down. The only two things he knew about her for sure were that he had seen her wrestling out of her Dawn Estate blazer more than enough times, and that she had tits that would make Dolly Parton tip her Stetson. He gave her a complimentary half-smile—which was more than he did for most—and she curled her mouth into a slightly pained smile in return, before returning to her archaeological dig of the bottomless handbag. He knew why she was less than friendly; she had caught him drunkenly *admiring the hardware* on his way downstairs a few weeks ago and now she presumably thought he was nothing but a pervert. It was true that she had joined him for many late-night (and early-morning) showers and sleep-ins, at least within the confines of his mind. Yet he still found it awfully conceited of her to assume he was interested enough to do anything more than smile, without further invitation on her part.

This subtle rejection did nothing but sour Joe's mood even further, and his feeble smile turned into a full-blown scowl as soon as he passed the woman. As if to taunt her, he unlocked his own door as loudly as possible and made a point of retrieving the key noisily before he even turned the handle and went inside. As soon as the door closed behind him, the low whistle of the elevator and the rattling of the busty real estate agent's search were sucked from the room, leaving only rigid silence. Off came the jacket and off came the shoes. Barely a minute passed before Joseph was leaning back in his armchair by the window with a glass of whiskey in his hand and a cigarette perched between his lips.

He bathed in the satisfying warmth of the alcohol and cigarette smoke, both inside and out, before his eyes drifted to the empty space on his bedside table. There used to be a photo of his wife and son there, but not anymore. Waking up in this godforsaken apartment and seeing their smiling faces before his body was even able to move lasted no longer than two days. He had put the photo delicately into the top drawer, but Pam's kind eyes and Marcus' innocent smile were seared into his brain. He could still see them there, in that little space beside the clock radio.

Marcus was so happy the day that photo was taken. He had no idea …

Christ, how Joe missed seeing that smile.

'My son. My beautiful boy,' Joe said softly, his chin drooping lower to his chest.

The smile, stretched from ear to ear, so much joy.

Lips torn, blood glazing his teeth. Still the boy smiled, why?

Pam's kind eyes, always so sincere. Now they were bulging, webs of broken blood cells speckling the white with dark, sickening crimson.

Why?

'*What did you do, Joseph?*'

What did I do? God, why?

'*I imagine some may feel humbled by a storm like this. So much raw, uncontrollable power sweeping over our fine city; what are we to something like that?*'

It was still dark, so incredibly dark when Joe felt his eyes open. The shadowed shapes of his apartment furniture swam into view, as if they floated in from a mirage. He couldn't be sure he had *woken up*, or if perhaps he had never been asleep to begin with. He was simply there, on his bed, on his back, staring at the pale figure in the corner.

The stranger said nothing. It stood with its inhumanly skeletal back to him, with its face resting against the door.

Joseph was afraid; the terror had pinned every molecule of his body in place, but there was no warning tingle of danger bristling the hair on his neck. What scared Joseph the most was that he felt if he were to look away, for even a moment, he would forget the figure had been there at all. The thin person made a slight groan from its place in the corner, a guttural, gurgled sound that grew in volume until it was a pained squeal.

'Why are you here?' the words left Joseph's tongue without so much as a thought.

He was surprised mostly by how calm he sounded. He had noticed now, by what faint light the window provided, that the figure was naked. It was bare from the back of its almost hairless skull to the practically translucent, claw-like feet. The skin over the figure's buttocks looked so thin and frail that under a warm enough light you could surely watch the veins and muscles do their work, in nauseating detail.

The figure simply moaned again, rolling its body slightly and showing the motion of every bone pressed against the skin. It was as if it was trying to face Joseph, but it was impossible to tell in the dark.

Something strange and unfamiliar inside Joe's fogged mind compelled him to … *help* the stranger.

With a wet crack the figure's head spun to look at Joe, much more quickly than its emaciated body should have allowed.

Now came the warning tingle. *Now* the hairs on Joe's neck bristled to attention.

The figure was a man, a sickly, horrifying man. Joseph knew this not by the stubble on the stranger's bloated and vascular throat, nor by the shriveled penis retracted in on itself, as if in a cold wind. He simply knew.

Crunch.

The figure lurched toward the bed, every joint in both of his legs grinding over each other.

Crunch.

The specter wailed, jaw hanging limp and thick ropes of mucus and drool hanging from its chin. Joseph could not move. Not because he felt paralyzed, but rather his fear was wrestling with his will to stay right there.

I can't move. I won't move.

Another anguished moan, desperate and pleading. The eyes, sweet fucking *Jesus,* his eyes were sewn shut with thick, rust-colored wire. The figure was at the foot of the bed now, face turned down to Joseph and body fully exposed to the cold, blue glow of night. The only thing worse than the moaning, the eyes, or even the pulsing in that bulbous throat was the silence that followed. The *long,* unrelenting silence.

Chapter
Two

Those Above

Joe woke as if he had been thrown through the windshield of a moving vehicle, launching himself from his bed and landing in a crumpled heap beside the window.

I'm Flying high but I've got a feeling I'm falling

His heart was slamming against his chest so hard that for one terrifying moment he believed he might be having a heart attack. After a full minute of gasping for breath, his senses settled and he found it was just him sweating against the carpet as Annette Hanshaw belted out her old, jazzy tune. He was still dressed in his work clothes and the white of his Oxford button-down was almost transparent with sweat. The more he tried to remember going to bed, the faster the memory evaporated. He wiped the cold beads from his eyes and looked around from his spot on the floor, desperately groping for his bearings on reality. The clock showed 10:30am, but the sky outside the window was as dark as night, the clouds barely visible through the haze of crimson and black.

Joe crawled to his feet with the pathetic frailty of a ninety-year-old and silenced the radio before Annette could start on her next verse. The apartment was much as he remembered leaving it the night before, but still he could not find the memory of stamping out the cigarette butt that was standing erect in the ashtray on his recliner. He certainly didn't remember washing the lone whiskey glass resting beside the sink.

'Another day in paradise,' he grumbled.

Dragging his feet, he made his way to the bathroom and flicked on the light switch. Nothing.

'Give me a break,' he said, defeated.

He hunched over the small, marble sink and turned the knob. He splashed his face three times with increasing force, but no amount of freezing water cleared the static in his head. Despite the dark, he found his face in the mirror. He looked like shit. His cheeks were worn and sagging; his eyes were home to large, shadowed bags that made him look far beyond his years. He turned away, nursing his stomach, but noticed something in his peripheral vision as he stepped into the kitchen. Something in the mirror, something out of place. All he found was the corner of his tired face looking back. His stomach groaned menacingly. It was either cursing his late-night drink session in somersaults of rebellious motion, or it was crying out for a meal in much the same way. Only when Joe snatched the last apple from the fridge did he remember that he'd forgotten to pick up some more food.

'Damnit. Come on, Joseph.'

He took a greedy bite from the fruit, stretching his mouth wide. Instead of a satisfying crunch, he felt his teeth sink into a soft and gelatinous mush. With a sharp jolt, Joe spat the apple onto the door of the fridge and slipped backwards, falling hard onto his ass. A stab of white-hot pain shot through his tailbone and into his spine like an electric shock. He looked down at the glistening, red orb in his hand and saw that, within the confines of the large bite mark, was a wet, gray paste.

'What the damn *hell*,' Joe roared, his temper finally reaching boiling point.

He flung the apple against the kitchen wall where it exploded with a sickening squelch, sending shards of rotten shrapnel onto every surface. The taste was the worst part; it was as if he had bitten down onto the tail end of flattened roadkill. His nostrils stung and his tongue recoiled against the rancid, chemical flavor glued to the walls of his mouth.

Joseph hoped that no one would leave their apartment as he made his way to the elevator. He knew full well how bad he smelled, and how rugged he would look. The thought of a hot shower, even one taken in the dark, was almost painfully tantalizing. Still, it could not come close to competing with the thought of a fresh bagel—or seven—from Café Olay. Despite all his loud, shuffling footsteps, no one came out into the hallway. In fact, it was unusually quiet. Even apartment 1105—the real estate agent's—which would normally be blasting Abba at this time of day, was silent. The corridor was lit more dimly than usual and there were no lights under any of the doors. The blackout must have gotten the entire building, or perhaps everyone had left town for the storm. While Joe watched the elevator digits slowly tick closer to eleven, he decided to see if Kris had tried to call. It was likely work was canceled today, but she could be a real mean bitch if he waited too long to get back to her. The phone screen ignited, hurting his eyes in the gloom. There were no notifications.

However, the small antenna icon at the top of the screen was sat beside the words, *SOS only*.

'Good enough for me,' Joe said. His mouth curled into a stony smirk.

He lurched into the elevator and punched the lobby button. Joseph could feel his saliva heat up and moisten his mouth the more he imagined stuffing the hot, cream-cheese-smeared bagel into his mouth. This went on for a few floors until a violent jolt shook the elevator, as if a hand had pulled on the wires. It kept moving downward, but it did so with a passive vibration that Joe didn't remember noticing before. Of all the scenarios he could imagine, being stuck in this elevator during a blackout was the current worst.

The doors rattling open to present him with the ground floor was a welcome relief and he allowed himself one humorous grunt.

'Better luck next time, pal,' he muttered, giving the metal surface a slap on the way out.

He knew he had better take the stairs back up for that one. The lobby was almost completely dark, lit only by the blue glow of the storm outside. Before he was even close enough to see, he could feel and hear the rain thundering down just outside the glass doors. It was much worse from down here; the sidewalk could barely be seen just a foot from the exit. Joseph had resolved on being fed even if the sky itself was falling, but as he passed the vacant concierge desk, he noticed that something large and square was sealing the doors closed. The shape cast a warped shadow onto the marble floor. It was a sign, attached to the glass and zip-tied to the handles.

All residents must remain inside the building until further notice.

By order of the city council.

We apologize for any inconvenience.

'Sucks, right?'

Joe jumped from fright and spun on the spot, instantly angered by the embarrassment flushing into his cheeks. Daewon was standing against one of the walls, his arms crossed and his features almost indecipherable in the dark.

'They made me stay overnight to tape the windows and shut off the basement, and now I'm stuck here too.'

'What do you care,' Joseph snapped, a little too hastily, 'you've got your own room here, don't you?'

'Yeah, I do,' the young man replied, gesturing with his head to the door behind him, 'but being stuck here with no lights or Wi-Fi isn't what I had in mind for my day, dickhead.'

'Yeah, well, at least you've got food,' Joe said. His voice was barely more than a grumble. He collapsed onto one of the benches and ran a hand through his knotted hair.

'You want to come in and have a bite?' Daewon said, in a softer tone. The young man stepped forward and waved at the door behind him.

Joseph almost felt a 'hell yeah,' roll from his lips, but then a vision flashed before his eyes. He saw himself leaving the room of a homosexual nineteen-year-old and being met with the judging glares of every one of his neighbors. He watched as they all scanned him from head to toe, their eyes lingering on his crotch to see if his belt was unbuckled. He heard them whisper to each other; he saw the men shake their heads and heard the women laugh.

'And what?' Joe spat, 'Eat cupcakes and chat about the Kardashans?'

Daewon recoiled and shot Joseph a disgusted, hurt look, visible even in the dim light.

'I'm gay, you absolute douche bag, not a fucking Disney character.'

He spun on the spot, pulling his over-sized woolen jumper closer into him and marched back to his apartment. 'And it's the *Kardashians*,' he yelled over his shoulder, before slamming the door closed.

Joseph sat in silence for a few moments, staring into the dull pot plant opposite him and grinding his teeth. He felt an odd turn in his stomach, guilt maybe? It was more likely to be that nagging hunger. Something caught his eye, just in the corner, as his reflection had earlier. It had looked like someone sprinting to the windows and coming to a stop just inches away, but when Joe turned to squint through the blur of rain, he could see only pavement and vapor. A tremendous flash of lightning illuminated every corner of the lobby in white light. Joe noticed a small figure standing by the door to the stairs, just as a deafening crash of thunder engulfed the room and drowned out most of his senses.

'Joseph, you are hungry, my friend?' the figure spoke, only just audible over the rain.

Joe recognized the curled Spanish accent. It was Javier, being the nosey, well-meaning, little bastard he was. Joe bit his lip and decided that rejecting another offer would be unwise, being that no one else in this building would be so kind.

'The storm came in a lot faster than they said it would,' he responded, with his best attempt at a grateful tone.

'Yes, it did. Lucky for you I have plenty of food. You saw me carry it in yesterday, remember?'

Joseph felt the hair on the back of his neck prickle. The old man had remained motionless at the other end of the room, still completely coated in shadow. His silhouette was hardly intimidating, but Joe decided to close the distance anyway and rose to his feet. He hoped the sweet building fragrance and smell of rain would mask his musk at least a bit.

'I'll just grab one meal if I can, then I'll be out of your hair,' Joe said as his steps echoed off the walls in loud knocks.

'I have little hair for you to be in,' Javier replied with a hollow chuckle. The silhouette finally moved to raise a hand and tap its dome.

Only once they both stepped into the fluorescent, buzzing light of the stairwell did Joe see the familiar, sun-beaten features of the man he tried so hard to avoid each morning. His stomach throbbed and groaned, and the taste of the rotten fruit had not yet left his mouth, so enduring the small talk as they ascended eleven flights of stairs was manageable. The polite company he would have to give this old man for the next few minutes would not have been an option under any other circumstance.

'It's pretty quiet today. I don't think I've seen any of the other tenants,' remarked Joe.

'Something tells me you like the quiet, my friend.'

'Yeah, I guess I do.'

'You don't like people?'

'I wouldn't say that.' Joseph turned to look at the elderly man, who was climbing the endless flight of stairs with surprising ease. 'Maybe I'm just one of those introverts.'

'Oh no, friend. I've known many men like you, not one of them were these … what you say, *introvert*.'

'With all due respect, Javier, you don't know me.'

'I'm an old man, I know enough. You get caught up in your pride, my friend, you can miss a whole life of possibility.'

'Is that so?' Joseph felt himself growing tired, but Javier had barely lost a breath.

Only three more floors to go.

'Yes, yes. When all is said and done, people see you for the things you *do*. Remember that, hermano.'

Sure sounds a lot like that karma crap.

'You know what I remember most about my late wife, Joseph?'

Joe met eyes with Javier and felt a small, faint wisp of sympathy rising in his chest.

'Waking up next to her, something like that?'

'She was a horrible cook, always burned the eggs.'

Javier's lips peeled back across his suspiciously white teeth and he laughed. An involuntary smile spread across Joseph's mouth and before he knew it, he was chuckling along with the old man.

'She would always tell me, *I know, love, I cook poorly. I do better tomorrow, my love, I do better tomorrow.* She did not shy away from her flaws, that woman.'

'Did they ever get better then? The eggs?'

'Oh no, I think they may have gotten worse.'

The stairwell echoed with laughter as the two men climbed higher.

'A man like you should not be alone, Joseph. You need to find yourself a woman.'

'I dunno about that, pal. Good women are in short supply these days.'

'Bullshit,' Javier waved a hand dismissively, still smiling. 'I get to be alone, I'm an old man. I still notice these women, good women. Some of them beautiful too. Too beautiful for me. But you? You would have a chance if you tried smiling, hermano.'

Joseph was about to change the topic of conversation with a half-hearted compliment, but something stopped him. He paused with his foot raised over the next step.

'C'mon, you're not too old f–'

It was a faint, stretched-out groan; it had come from the door they had just passed. The peeled blue paint glared out from the gray, cement walls and looked exactly as a door should.

'You hear that?'

'Hear what, my friend?' Javier continued ascending the stairs, barely slowing his pace.

'Something,' Joseph muttered. He could have sworn the doorknob jiggled. It was impossible to recall in the gentle flickering of the light.

'I thought you were hungry,' Javier teased from above.

How the hell did he get up there so fast?

Joseph chased the old man up the remaining stairs, feeling his joints burn and crack in protest. Finally, they both stepped onto the landing marked *Level 11*.

'I hope you like gnocchi,' Javier enquired in a sing-song voice.

Joe felt the walls of his mouth moisten instantly. He did like gnocchi; he liked it a lot. It had been one of the most common meals he, Marcus, and Pam would share. In fact, it was one of the first he had ever cooked for his wife.

Easy to make, sure, but delicious. It sure did make it look like I knew what I was doing anyway.

No, focus on the hunger. Not her.

As soon as the old man's door swung open, Joseph smelled it. The pesto, the cheese, the potato; it filled his nostrils in warm wafts and his stomach churned in anticipation. They stepped over the threshold of Javier's unremarkable home and the old man waved him toward one of two deep-cushioned armchairs in front of a small television.

'Sit, hermano. I'll fetch you a bowl, fresh from the stove.'

Joe had planned on grabbing some food and leaving to eat it in the comfort of his own room, but he knew better than to jeopardize a meal,

61

especially when he was so close. Truth be told, he might have even been starting to enjoy the old man's company; the Spaniard was actually pretty funny. Joseph surveyed his surroundings as his rear sunk low into the floral-patterned flannel and found himself slightly disgusted. Everything looked cheap and fragile, as if Javier had only decorated with purchases from the dollar store. Most eye-watering of all was a towering, bamboo flamingo. It was perched on one thin leg and its neck arched over a small table holding an ancient-looking clock radio. It was a monument to tacky and reminded Joseph of the mom and dad operations he would sell his service to back in his heyday. Ambitious, inexperienced, and sitting on a shiny new business loan. He had already been spectacular at his job but selling advertising packages to these people was especially easy. Hanging on the wall above the flamingo was a framed certificate, celebrating ten years of teaching at *Romero Public School*. Why did that sound so familiar?

'Here you go, my friend,' Javier announced, jostling back into the room with the hot bowl held delicately between his fingers.

Joe snatched the food—a little too quickly—before the elderly man could drop it and wasted no time in spooning a generous helping of the little, fluffy dumplings into his mouth. Every molecule of his being exploded with satisfaction, and a loud moan escaped his throat.

'Ah, it's good, yes?'

'It's perfect,' Joe mumbled through puffed cheeks, his eyes still closed as he shoveled spoonful after spoonful into his mouth. He meant it. 'I owe you.'

'You do not owe me, my friend,' Javier said. The old man shuffled away to somewhere behind Joe, his voice trailing off with him. 'You should always ask for help if you need it.'

Joe's eyes met the certificate again as he scraped up the last remnants of the meal. Romero Public School. It was etched into his mind; he could hear the words being spoken to him, but the voice didn't belong to anyone.

'You were a teacher?' Joe called out, gulping down the last bit of food.

'I was,' Javier replied in the distance. 'It wasn't as pretty as those private schools, but I enjoyed my time there.'

Then, like the lightning outside had reached in and struck Joe, he remembered. As soon as the memory resurfaced, the clock radio across from him ignited in a green glow and a voice filled the quiet.

'Why can't he go there? He wants to stay with his friends.' The voice belonged to Joseph's wife; it was Pam. She sounded angry and desperate.

'Because my son isn't going to a fucking public school, Pamela.' That was Joseph's voice this time, coming from the radio in crystal clear lucidity, as if it had been from his own mouth.

'He's my son too, in case you've forgotten.'

Joe gripped the corners of the armchair he was sinking into so tightly his knuckles went white. He remembered this conversation, so long ago.

'Javier?' he said, choking on the knot in his throat.

'Marcus isn't going to Romero Public School. It's a cesspool. We're better than that. End of story.'

The radio went silent, but the green light stayed on. Joe stared at it, his vision wavering and his breath caught in his throat. Then the radio spoke once more, with Pam's voice.

'It's your fault, Joseph, it's all your damn fault … you're a virus.'

'Javier?' Joseph yelled this time.

'Split the skin, dig it *out*,' the voice came in a gurgle from behind Joe. He spun in his chair, just in time to see Javier standing over him, carving knife held high.

The old man's eyes were bulging and spotted with red. His mouth was hanging loosely from nose to liver-spotted chin, so wide that his lips cracked and sent blood pooling behind his teeth. With a hysterical and maniacal wheeze, the old man swung the knife down and Joseph leapt backwards, shielding his face with the back of his hand. He felt the steel slice a white-hot path through his palm and a thick line of blood sprayed across his face.

'What the fuck!' Joe cried out, falling to the floor and kicking himself backwards through a pile of *El Chavo del Ocho* DVDs. 'Have you lost your damn mind!'

Javier snapped his head backwards in a swift and sickening motion. He laughed so wildly that it drowned out the dull thuds of rain against the window. Blood was falling from his mouth in elastic strands and his hands were gripping the knife to his chest like a newborn.

'Dig it out, Joseph, I can help, let me cut it out,' the old man growled. He rolled his head lazily to meet Joe's eyes. Javier was dragging the point of the knife over his own exposed chest, leaving a deep gash in its wake.

'Jesus *Christ*,' Joe said. A strangled sob rose in his throat.

He scurried to his feet, clutching his wounded hand to his stomach. No sooner was he up than Javier had thrown himself over the armchair, slashing the glistening, red blade wildly. Joe made a break for the door but felt the blistering sting of cut flesh on his lower back. The shock sent him sprawling into the bamboo flamingo. It cracked and bent under his weight and sent him to the floor again.

'How much will all of it matter when your intestines are spilling into your hands, Joseph?' taunted Pamela's voice from the radio. 'The private school, the *image*. You will die and none of it will matter.'

Javier mounted Joseph, pinning him to the floor between his powerful thighs. The maniac cackled in hoarse and twisted bursts. He dragged the edge of the knife from his neck to his already skewered chest and let the blood flow down onto Joseph's writhing body.

'That's a fine jacket, sir,' Javier sang, raising the knife high again with two hands, 'oh so nice, I'll wear it when I cut you out.'

Joseph shielded himself again with his mutilated hand. He groped blindly for something, anything, with the other.

'Please, *please* don't!'

Joe gripped a broken piece of bamboo just as Javier brought the blade down. He managed to swivel, catching the edge of the knife with only the skin of his shoulder. He thrust the bamboo upwards, hoping to knock the madman back but instead driving its point through the underside of the old man's jaw.

Javier fell backwards still wheezing, although much more muffled now through a fountain of blood. Joe wasted no time in dragging himself toward the door and launching himself at it. Instinctively, he tried to open it with his right hand, but recoiled when he felt the agonizing sting of cold steel against his open cut.

'Too good for my company, are you?'

Joe shot a look over his shoulder and gasped in horror. Javier had pulled the bamboo from his jaw and was crawling on all fours, slowly, with the knife still clasped in his hand. The man's jaw swung loose as blood gushed from his mouth; his eyes had become a sickening shade, all of the white smudged with crimson. The radio blasted to life with a chorus of trumpets.

How lucky can one guy be? I kissed her and she kissed me

Joe turned back to the door and grasped desperately for the knob, but it spun in his palm, lubricated too thoroughly with his own blood.

Like a fella once said: 'Ain't that a kick in the head?'

Javier rose to his feet, only an arm's length away. His body jerked with the mechanical twists of a demented scarecrow. Joe snatched a fleece sweater from the hook beside the door and used it to turn the doorknob, wrenching it open just as the old man lunged forward. Joe exploded from the room so quickly that he slid into the opposite wall, leaving bloody skid marks in his wake and bashing his jaw. Javier and the notes of Dean Martin's merry tune followed Joe out and he wasted no time in breaking for his apartment.

'Help me, he's insane!' Joe screamed, not embarrassed in the least at the pitch his voice reached. 'Someone fucking *help* me.'

Not a single neighbor's door opened as Joe ran through the hallway. He could hear the frantic, excited breaths of the old man just behind.

'No, come back! I won't hurt the suit. I said get the fuck back here!'

With a desperate burst of adrenaline, Joseph barged into his apartment and slammed the door behind him. Fumbling for the chain latch, he thanked whatever god sat above that he hadn't locked the door when he left.

'Come on, come on, fuck, fuck, fuck!'

He finally got the lock to slide home and stumbled backwards, his hand leaving bloody streaks on the wall with each step. He would not turn his back on the door. Javier was barred by just two inches of wood and the old man's manic muttering hissed through the silence.

At least an hour passed as Joe stood panting, his breath cracked and frantic. After tremendous internal debate, he finally stepped back to the door, as quietly as he could manage. He pressed one watery eye to the peephole.

Javier was still there; he was standing in the corridor, about ten feet away beside his own door. Blood was pooling at the old man's feet in dark torrents. It poured from numerous cuts on his body, washing his skin in glistening red. The knife was still hanging limply from his fingers and his mouth was dangling sloppily. Javier's tongue licked at his busted lips, and his bulbous, bloodshot eyes shifted ever so slightly to meet Joe's. Joseph's heart leapt into his throat and he flipped to the side. He pressed his back to the wall and dug into his pocket with his good hand. He withdrew his phone and pressed the home button as rapidly as he could manage, feeling a strained moan catch in his throat. The 'SOS only' was still displayed on the screen but Joe felt if ever an emergency was justified, this was it. He dialed 911 and pressed it to his ear, cursing at every unanswered ring.

'Hello, what is your emergency?'

'Oh thank God, I need police and an ambulance right now. He's trying to kill me.'

'Okay, sir, take a breath. I need you to tell me exactly what is happening so I can get help to you.'

'I'm locked in my apartment and there's a bloody madman in the hall with a knife. He's cut me bad; I think I'm losing too much blood.'

'Are you secure right now? Is he able to get to you?'

'I've locked the door and he's an old son of a bitch, so I don't think so.'

'Hmm, that's a shame.'

'Excuse me?'

'My apologies, sir. Is there anything there that you could use as a weapon? Have you tried breaking his skull open?'

Joe's breath caught in his throat so aggressively that he had to choke the next words out. 'What did you just say?'

'Please listen carefully, sir,' the woman at the other end of the line replied, in a sweet and earnest tone. 'What I said was that you should find a weapon, open the door, and bust his fucking skull to pieces. Or you could let him cut you open. I think you'll find either way to work a treat.'

There was an earth-shaking boom of thunder outside the window and Joseph felt the phone starting to slide from his fingers.

'You could cut yourself free, Joseph. Wouldn't that be better? Oh, you could use the window. You could jump and leave all of this behind. What do you have left anyway?'

The phone fell to the floor and Joe felt his vision darkening. His legs were becoming weak, too weak to stand.

Oh God, I'm going to bleed out.

'What's going on?' he said weakly.

Joseph staggered into the kitchen and yanked a drawer from its tracks. He watched as it fell with a crash that was dull to his ears and allowed himself to collapse onto the floor beside it. His hand throbbed with each wave of blood that it sent onto the tiles. His white Oxford shirt was patched and smeared with red now. With the last of his strength, he grabbed a knife and a roll of duct tape from the crippled drawer. He pulled a strip of tape free with his teeth and wrapped it tightly around the cut on his hand; it was far from what he needed, but it would have to do. He tried to pull his tie free but failed. The dark was truly setting in now; Joseph couldn't be sure if the room was losing light in the storm, or if he was simply losing consciousness. His eyes were heavy, much too heavy. He slid himself into a corner of the kitchen with the knife gripped slackly in his hand.

'*I don't want Pam to see me like this,*' was Joseph's final thought as the dark swallowed the light.

Chapter
Three

By My Hand

The clock radio burst into life.

I'm flying high but I've got a feeling I'm falling

The song startled Joseph so violently that he spun onto his knees and nearly impaled himself with the knife he was holding.

'What the hell?' he groaned.

He dropped the blade with a flat whack and clutched at the searing pain in his right palm. His hands were coated in dry, flaking blood and the makeshift, duct-tape bandage he had given himself was cemented in place like papier-mâché. The memory of the day before struck Joe with the force of a punch.

'Oh shit.'

He scrambled across the tiles and onto the carpet where he had dropped his phone. The screen was dark and no matter how much he punched the home button with a shaky thumb, it remained dead. The storm outside sounded much worse than it had before; the rain was belting the glass with rapid and heavy thuds. Each few seconds was met with a flash of lightning that ignited the shadows of the otherwise pitch-black room, and the ensuing boom of thunder almost drowned out the brass band notes of Annette Hanshaw's tune. Something was odd about the song, just barely noticeable. It was as if it had been warped or slowed, ever so slightly. Joe decided against questioning how the radio could even be operational during the blackout. His mind was flooded and aching with much more frantic concerns. He dragged himself unsteadily to his feet to get a better look at the clock.

7:28 am

He had been out almost a full day, which was no surprise. He looked at the door, which stood as plainly as it normally did. The lock was still fastened in its slide. With gentle and shaky footsteps, Joe stepped up to the door and delicately placed his hands on either side of the peephole to steady himself. With a quivering breath he leaned in and searched the dull light of the corridor for his attacker. Javier was not there. Where there had been a pool of blood on the diamond-checkered carpet, there was now only woven blue. A disorienting thought crept into Joseph's mind.

Did I dream that?

The hallway looked too untouched, too calm. Joe actually felt relief sinking in before the pain in his hand and back flared. One look at the streaks of red that snaked down his wrists and into the cuffs of his shirt was enough to know it had been no dream. He had been cut open by the maniac down the hall. The phone call, Pam's voice, maybe *those* were from the shock. The memory of Javier's bulging eyes filled Joseph's mind like dense fog. His hands trembled as he remembered the way it had felt when the bamboo spike popped through the old man's jaw. No, that part at least was real.

'I'm getting the fuck out of here,' Joseph snarled. He clawed deep within his gut for courage, at least enough to get him out of this room.

He turned on the spot. He could feel the anger surging through his blood; it gave life to a new wave of energy. Flexing his knuckles, Joseph snatched a thick piece of 2x4 from the pile of unbuilt IKEA furniture beside his television. It was strong, strong enough at least to pop someone's head open like a coconut.

Don't leave me now
For I've got a feeling I'm falling
Falling for nobody else but you

The song finished and the monotone radio DJ followed up immediately. Joe was only half-listening as he made his way to the bathroom; there was something comforting about another voice in the room. A voice that wasn't edged with the gurgles and splutters of blood.

'Well, what did I tell you, ladies and gentlemen? The storm has arrived, the storm is here. I gotta tell you folks, I'm watching the rain and the lightning from my window here at Studio P12 and it looks like the wrath of God himself is upon us.'

Joe shoved his face under the cold stream from the faucet and lapped up the water like a dog chained in the heat; each gulp was life-giving and the spray against his face was cool and refreshing.

'So if you didn't make it out in time, I hope you've got food and water to last—we could be here a while, folks.'

Joe shoved his tie between his teeth and exhaled in fast and wild huffs. He shook himself violently and thrust his cut hand under the stream of cold water. A crash of thunder shook the building at that moment, enveloping his screams as the blood spiraled the sink drain in black and pink tendrils.

'And for my pal, Joseph Ridley, you'd better lock yourself up tight, my friend.' Joe heard this bit; it made him straighten immediately.

'Lock yourself up reeeal tight, because they know you're here now.' The voice became drawn out and dulled, as if the radio had been dropped into water.

'They're going to hang you up by your toes and rip open your ribs like a Thanksgiving turkey.'

Joseph marched from the room in a panic and snatched up the piece of timber he had leaning against the bathroom door. He swung the plank with his strong hand, shattering the radio in place. He struck it again, and again and did not stop until the static buzz had either died or been swallowed by the rain.

'I'm losing my damn mind,' Joe groaned, rubbing at his forehead. He felt the sticky moisture of blood, blood from his cut hand or new blood from gripping the wood so tightly. He couldn't be sure.

Joseph didn't have any means to stitch and bind his wound, but necessity breeds creativity. After a few minutes with one of his old, gray socks and a lot more duct tape, he had managed to stop the bleeding—at least for now. He knew what he needed to do: leave the building and get to a hospital or a police station; it didn't matter which. No old man or zip-tied warning sign was going to stop him. He gave one last cautious glance to the storm outside the window before reaching for the door. The glass was coated in a nearly impenetrable layer of rain and fog, but he could just make out the dark gray clouds clashing and swirling far off. The only light was a faint, red glow behind them, as if the sun itself were being suffocated.

Joseph launched himself into the corridor. He held the plank high, ready to spin the jaw of anyone who dared get in his way. It was silent, so quiet that he might as well have been floating through outer space. Much like the day before, there was no noise and not a single light from under any of his neighbors' doors. Javier was Joseph's direct neighbor, so with clenched teeth and a quickly thickening layer of sweat, he crept by the old man's door. He shuffled step by trembling step, his back glued to the opposite wall. Javier did not show; judging by the dense coat of dust on the door handle to 1106, no one had been home for a long time. Except that wasn't possible. Less than twenty-four hours earlier that polished steel had been dripping blood. Once Joe had cleared a comfortable distance between himself and Javier's apartment, he turned and ran. His legs burned and sang with protest but he moved forward, charged with adrenaline. He slid to a stop in front of the elevator doors and bashed the down arrow button at least twelve times. There was no electric response. He hit the button a few times more before noticing that the little screen above his head was an empty black. Where it would normally display the floor the chamber was at, it was now as blank as his phone had been. He could see his own tired reflection looking back down at him.

'Screw you,' Joe hissed. He hurled himself at the door to the stairs and rattled the handle aggressively. It was locked. He didn't even know this door *could* lock.

'Come on, please,' Joe groaned weakly. 'Please.'

He dropped the plank and threw his full weight down on the handle over and over, praying for it to come loose. It was like the door had been built from brick; it would not budge. He staggered backwards, winding himself up for the mightiest kick he could muster. He had taken two lurching steps forward when he heard a familiar *DING*. The little screen above the elevator was buzzing once more, showing 11, this floor. The smallest curve of a smile made its way onto Joe's face and he staggered toward the elevator again, more than ready to leave this yellow and blue death trap behind. There was a long, uncomfortable pause before the doors made their advisory buzz and each second *burned*. Finally, they opened and before he could jump over the chamber's threshold, someone was exiting, pushing an empty wheelchair. It was the small, Indian nurse, dressed in her tidy scrubs and looking as drained as ever.

She jumped a little at the sight of the bloodied man in front of her and her eyes widened in fright.

'Oh thank God,' Joe gasped, leaning forward.

She pulled back. Her grip tightened with a gentle squeak on the plastic handles of the wheelchair she was pushing. Joe immediately realized how he must look and put his hands up as calmly as he could manage.

'I'm not trying to hurt you,' he said softly. 'I just really need your help. The old fucker down the hall went crazy and sliced me up. He got my hand real bad. My back too. I think I need stitches.'

She was still silent, but her eyes traveled from Joseph's poor attempt at a bandage, to the lines of blood that decorated his shirt.

'Sit down,' she said cautiously, nodding at the chair in front of her. Joe looked anxiously at Javier's apartment door, just twenty feet away.

'Can we go inside first?'

'You're not coming into my home,' she snapped. Joseph could still see fear in her tired eyes.

'Okay, fine,' he replied hesitantly before collapsing onto the uncomfortable, plastic sling.

The woman crouched beside Joseph and began digging through a bulbous canvas pack with the obligatory red medical cross stitched into its side. It might have been the loss of blood, but Joe felt a momentary wave of calm pass over him as he watched the woman search for her tools. She was actually quite beautiful, despite the dark circles under her eyes and the stress lines engraved into her forehead. He could even see small creases at the corners of her mouth, etched into her skin from a lifetime of smiling. She withdrew an empty syringe tube from the pack, as well as a long plastic sheet with an intimidatingly thick needle inside.

'That's one hell of a needle,' Joe grumbled, barely attempting to follow up with a chuckle.

'For the pain,' she replied, still emotionless and firm.

Joseph wondered if all her patients were privy to this warm demeanor or if she just held particular contempt for him. He couldn't imagine why it would be the latter. He watched in silence as she put together the syringe with the clinical precision of a hitman assembling a firearm. She put the needle into a small bottle of clear liquid that smelled like turpentine.

'You said the old man did this?' she said coldly, still not looking away from the needle. She crouched further over her pack once more.

'Yeah,' Joe groaned, flexing his fingers, 'the old Spanish guy. He just went batshit crazy, attacked me with a kitchen knife.'

'Did he seem angry?'

'I don't know about angry—mental is the more appropriate word. He was cutting himself too. Now you mention it. Do you have a phone? We should really call the police. He could still be here.'

'People do strange things when they're angry, don't they?'

Joseph felt this was an unusual thing to say when given such urgent and alarming information, but this woman was going to be stitching his wound, so he decided to indulge her.

'Well, no shit, but I didn't *do* anything to the guy. He invited me in for food, and then out of nowhere he starts stabbing me.' He decided to leave out the part about hearing his wife on the radio; the last thing he needed was the nurse thinking he had really lost it. He couldn't even be sure that memory was real.

It was shock, that's all it was.

'What makes you so special, Joseph?' The nurse had stopped digging through the pack now and was hunched over the syringe, turning it in her fingers. A familiar, uneasy chill ran through Joe's spine; somehow, he knew he was in imminent danger, like a cat with its tail bristled.

'The hell are you talkin about?' he asked softly, slowly lifting his ass from the chair.

'People get angry,' she whispered, so quietly he barely caught the words. 'They lash out, do silly things. I'm sure he didn't mean it. People get angry, they lash out.'

'Fuck this,' Joe hissed. The warning tingle in his neck had reached the point of electrocuting him in place.

He lunged forward but the nurse was just as quick. She sprang from her knees and plunged the full four inches of needle into his thigh. She had pounced and injected him like a snake would its prey. The effect was utterly crippling and instantaneous; Joseph slumped back in the wheelchair, paralyzed entirely. He could only move his eyes and they shook in horror as the nurse leaned in to meet his stare with hers. Her jaw was hanging limp in that same grotesque gaze he had seen Javier wearing the day before. Her eyes were positively bursting from her skull. She seemed a sickening mirror reflection of the man in front of her, blood dripping from her chin as drool dripped from Joseph's.

'Welcome *us*, Joseph. It's your time.'

Every atom in Joseph's body screamed and willed for the ability to move, but he was powerless. He felt the weight of his arms and legs against the cold plastic, but the small, electric signals from his mind met no response. The nurse circled him, her arms snaking around his shoulders seductively.

'Look at you, look at yooou.'

She mounted Joseph's lap and gripped his jaw in her twisted fingers. She stared into his eyes with an inhumanly fierce hunger. Her eyes burned through him, searching his entire being. Her groaning sounded human, but she was not. She could not be.

'If blinded you were, blinded you will be,' she said.

Suddenly her blood-glazed tongue rolled in her mouth and a cloud of excruciatingly hot, black mist shot from her throat into Joseph's face. Like the needle, the effect was immediate. His eyes twitched in searing agony and his vision faded to a blur: a red-tinted pinhole. It happened as quickly as shutting his eyes.

He could not scream, he could not speak, but he heard his voice all the same.

'Get the fuck *off* me.' His booming yell filled his mind clearly, cutting through the dull fog of terror that dazed him.

Through his impaired vision, he could see the nurse's brows curl into angry daggers, somehow making her even more horrifying. She slid from his lap and stepped behind the chair, well out of view. She walked with rigid, disjointed movements. Joe's eyes followed her as much as they would allow, but once she vanished from sight he could only listen as intently as possible. He tried to block out the heavy thuds of his own heart against his chest and hear something, anything. The chair suddenly rattled to life and he felt himself being driven down the corridor. He was being carried far from the bright light of the elevator bay and the fragile safety of his own apartment.

'We're going to hang your skin from the fucking window, Joseph,' the nurse hissed. She snickered gleefully into his ear as the chair picked up pace. It began to shake and sing with clicks of steel on steel.

'Everyone will know how empty you are. They'll see. We'll peel you back layer by layer and they'll see.'

Joseph could feel the blistering heat of her breath against his ear, but found he was much more focused on the shapes at the very edge of his tainted vision. He could see they were passing doors at an increasingly blurred speed. There were too many, far too many for this hall, and each one seemed to open just as they passed out of sight. Once or twice he could have sworn he saw figures blocking the squares of auburn light from the storm. Figures that stood tall, unnaturally thin apparitions, bare and pale. His heart raced in time with the clicking of the wheels.

No, please no. I can't see; Christ, I can't see.

The chair had reached the speed of a full sprint and he felt bursts of excited breath on the back of his neck. He urged his arms, his legs, and even his fingers to wake and give him back control.

'Down we go, Joe, down, down, down.'

The nurse began to laugh hysterically. She howled and cackled as they drew closer and closer to the closed door at the end of the hall. With every second, Joe's sight seemed to fade even more. The speed they had reached now was inhuman. Even in his current state, Joseph was sober enough to know that impact with a few inches of compact wood would easily annihilate his skull. He would have screamed had he been able to, but all his mouth released was more drool and a weak moan. The door drew closer with terrific speed.

Closer.

Help me.

Closer.

Please stop, please don't.

Closer.

Someone help me!

The wheelchair flipped forward. The numberless door flew open and Joseph found himself rocketing into darkness. A darkness so intense that it seemed to vacuum light from the hall in with him, before extinguishing it entirely.

It was impossible to say how much time had passed as Joseph stirred to life on the thinly woven carpet of God knows where. It was the dark of night, but not quite the endless black he remembered falling into. His movements felt slow and groggy but being able to move his arms below him was a more-than-welcome surprise. Even more pleasing was that, despite the gloom, the burning in his eyes had dimmed and his sight was almost entirely back, except for some red blotches in his peripheral vision.

Crack

A strike of lightning engulfed the small bedroom in light. It was only for a moment, but it was long enough for Joe to find he was no longer in the presence of the psychotic woman. With no small amount of effort, he pushed himself to his knees and rolled his back against the dresser beside him. The drawers wobbled with a chorus of brittle creaks. Something felt different about the storm outside the window; it was much calmer than it had been that morning. The rain was persistent, but no strong winds were pressing the glass.

'Damnit.' Joe stumbled a little as his left leg loosened under his weight. He could feel an ache from where the needle had bitten into his flesh, agonizingly apparent and settling home next to the pain of his other cuts and bruises.

Another flash of lightning made something else quite clear; this was not the apartment building he called home—the layout was much too foreign. The walls were close and sloped and the window was small and squared into quarters. The surroundings were much more reminiscent of a homely, town flat. It was only in a brief second of quiet that Joseph heard a shallow breath and realized he was not alone. He crouched—with much difficulty—into the shadowed corner by the window and used the soft blue light from the moon to inspect his surroundings. It was a lightly furnished room, and directly across from him was a large, wooden-framed bed. In it was an unknown person, apparently sleeping with their back to him. Most unusual, though, was that beside the bed was a wheelchair. It was different to the plastic hospital chair Joe had found himself glued to just before. This one was cushioned and looked new, more indicative of the personal models that people would use for the long haul. The sleeping stranger made Joe uncomfortable, but there was no warning taste of dread in his throat—that was a feeling that seemed to accompany whatever it was hunting him. Something else caught his eye, something that made his heart pulse with a victorious thump. The window was unlatched and open, by just a finger's width. Without a word, or any attempt not to awaken the sleeping stranger, Joe pounced on the window and yanked it skyward. It caught on its rusted tracks for a moment, sending his stomach into his throat, but then it shot home and the sound of rain on asphalt filled the room, bringing with it a rigid breeze.

'You beauty,' Joe cackled.

He reveled in his small victory and poked his head out into the cold. The rain was light, but it was heavenly against his skin, which until now had felt stiff and dry. Even more exciting was that just below the opening was a small fire escape and accompanying ladder. It descended two floors to an alley. Joseph wasted no time in crouching through the window and surrendering his whole body to the wet and the cold. His cuts flashed with pain against the icy moisture, but only for what felt like a second. He could not help but laugh as he let his head fall back and catch every drop of rain the dark blue sky provided.

Joe stepped forward to lower himself onto the ladder and was startled by the window slamming shut behind him.

Fuck it, no way in hell am I going back in there anyway.

He started toward the ladder again but was stopped by a flash of motion below. With as much caution as the last twenty-four hours had taught him to use, Joe peeked over the edge of the cast-iron railing and saw that a large SUV had parked below him. It was hard to make out in the dark and the rain, but a convenient flash of lightning showed a figure digging around in the back of a bright-red Range Rover. The sight of the car, *that car*, sent a jarring shockwave through his body. He knew that car. He knew that car, parked in that spot on this rainy, cold night. Another flash of white illuminated the alleyway and another figure caught Joe's attention. It was very clearly a broad-shouldered man, drunkenly stumbling toward the SUV. He was hunched forward and his steps were slow and quiet, masked by the pitter-patter of rain against the cement. The drunk stranger was sneaking. It was terrifyingly apparent—and the closer he crept, the more a thin, hooked shape extended from his closed fist.

'*No,*' Joe gasped. It couldn't be, it simply couldn't.

The SUV figure still hadn't noticed the intoxicated man. He kept searching the trunk of his car for something that was important enough to keep him standing in the rain. The drunk was only a few feet away now and the object in his hand was now at full length. It was a long, dark rod, hooked at the end and wedged; it was a crowbar. Joseph's breath became rapid and panic paralyzed him as truly as the nurse's syringe had. His fingers were wrapped around the railing so tightly that he could feel his knuckles straining against his skin.

The drunk man was too close now, directly behind the SUV person. Another flash of lightning engulfed them both and Joseph's fears were confirmed. He recognized the man with the red Range Rover, and he remembered what was to come. The drunk seemed to falter for a moment in quiet contemplation, but when the SUV man reached up to close the trunk, all hesitation washed away with the rain. He raised the crowbar above his head and Joseph lurched forward high above, almost falling into the open air.

'Don't!' he yelled.

Both figures far below froze, as though puppets paused in a sick matinee. With a few seconds that felt like an eternity, Joe watched through wide eyes, his glare locked on the crowbar still held high, willing it not to strike. Then the men turned their heads toward him and their eyes met his through the rain and mist.

'Please don't,' Joe pleaded once more on a silent breath.

He knew the men below; he knew one of them better than most. The crowbar-wielding man was Joseph, albeit a drunken, disheveled version of himself. Then both men smiled, wide and true with gleeful malice.

The Joseph above knew what was coming next. He felt it coming like the rumbling of an oncoming train. The Joseph below brought the crowbar down into the small of the other man's back with a sickening crunch. SUV man collapsed instantly. Neither of the smiling men looked away from the Joseph trembling against the iron rail. The crowbar fell again and then again, each time finding its way to the victim's spine. This continued relentlessly for about half a minute. It was a lifetime to Joseph. It had been then, and it was now. It was in this moment that something snapped inside of him, a deep boiling rage exploding to the surface like a primeval shark.

'You son of a bitch, I said stop!'

This time the Joseph below did stop; he dropped the crowbar with a deafening metallic clang and backed away from his work in sheer horror. The smile was gone now, replaced with a gaping mouth and trembling lip.

'He deserved it, he did. *You* deserved this,' the drunken Joseph panted.

He pulled at his soaked hair, not able to look away from the crippled man. The SUV man lay with his face against the wet concrete. He spasmed and wheezed in the dim light of the Range Rover's trunk. His hands reached out for help that wouldn't come. Joseph above watched as his suddenly sober double ran from the alley and out of sight, looking more panicked by the second.

'Beware the smite of Joseph Ridley,' an ominous voice spoke. It rendered the sound of rain and thunder mute. Joe looked back at the injured man and found his smile too was gone now. It had been replaced with a sickeningly wide, silent scream.

'Your choices. They *burn* us.'

The man moved. He flipped onto his bloody palms and let his head roll back at an unnatural angle to get a better look above. His bulging eyes caught the rain, but did not blink, not even once.

'They burn us!' the broken man screamed, rocking Joseph's body out of its frozen state.

With those words the crippled man sprang onto the ladder and rocketed upward two rungs at a time. His legs dangled behind him and slapped against the metal like those of a lifeless doll. The rain streaked the blood from his crazily dislodged jaw across his face as he climbed, giving him the appearance of a murderous circus clown.

'Christ,' Joseph spat.

He threw himself at the window he had only just escaped through. He pulled at it with savage determination. It gave way only an inch at a time. All sound seemed to have been plucked from the world, all but the maleficent screams of the possessed man and his twisted body hitting metal.

'Come on,' yelled Joseph.

Every vein in his arms pressed against his skin as the window edged open portion by minuscule portion. Joe's eyes moved upward as he strained and what he saw made his teeth clench tight. The figure in the bed was sitting at attention in the dark and watching him. The stranger's face was the same as the man who climbed toward Joseph now. All he was missing was the slack, bloody jaw and bulging eyes. Deciding he could only take his chances, Joe gave another almighty pull and the window came loose, sliding home into its bracket. He jumped and tumbled into the room's depths. Wasting no time, Joe burst to his feet and bounced toward the door, throwing a cautious glance over his shoulder. The bed was empty, the sheets thrown aside as if they had been removed in a hurry. Joe wrenched open the door and was met with the inside of his apartment. He was looking in on the bed and armchair he knew so well, as if he had just opened his own front door.

'Who are you?' a trembling, panicked voice spoke.

Joseph spun on the spot and gripped the doorway with icy, blue fingers, ready to throw himself inside if need be. Sitting across from him, beside the closed window, was a small, thin man in a pale blue pajama set. He was coiled like a frightened animal and holding onto the rails of his wheelchair's tires for dear life. The man was far from intimidating, even in the dark. His large head, thick, graying hair and small youthful frame made him seem like a teenager in a rapidly aging body.

'W-what are you doing in my home?' he stammered, moving backwards slightly.

Good God, this man was terrified.

Waves of visceral dread and nauseating guilt flooded through Joseph's body as he watched this small, paralyzed man cower in his chair.

'How- how could I have known?' was all he could say as he backed into his apartment and slammed the door.

There was a current traveling through the dark space that drained the energy from Joseph's body as he stumbled across the room. The storm was back to its full might now and the red glow lit his furniture in a featureless haze. The rain and wind had begun to sound more like running feet and desperate screams than any kind of weather anomaly. Each earth-shaking crash of thunder felt like the planet itself was splitting in half. Despite all of this, Joseph heard the low humming buzz when the TV flickered to life. It lit the room in a wash of shimmering white noise that was as turbulent as the storm. The glow pulled his gaze and he watched, numb and fatigued, as Pamela's face came into view. Her cheeks were freckled by the dancing white and black static. She seemed to be looking directly at him through the screen and, although he felt tears brimming his eyes, Joseph spoke words that he did not think to speak.

'What?' he said in an agitated tone.

'Was it you? Tell me it wasn't you.'

Pamela spoke at him through the television as if they were having a conversation face to face. Except, they had done this before, in person. Joseph remembered it vaguely through the daze of whiskey. The memory quickly surrounded him and locked his body in place, here and now, to relive it.

'What does it matter?' Joseph replied after a hesitant pause.

'Oh *fuck*, Joe, fuck!'

'Pam, please calm down, will you? Jesus. No one saw me. It was weeks ago. I'd have been arrested by now, or at least been interviewed if they had any evidence.'

Pamela put her hand over her mouth in disbelief; her eyes glistened with tears. Although Joseph was reliving the conversation moment by moment, he remembered how it would end. He remembered this as the moment that ultimately ended his marriage. He felt hot tears blurring his vision, but still they spoke.

'You saw the police report, Joseph. It wasn't *him*.'

'It doesn't matter.'

'You paralyzed an innocent man.'

'It was a mistake, goddamnit!' The sound of a lamp shattering against a wall filled the small apartment. 'What the hell was I meant to do? What were the chances?'

'Because they drove the same fucking car? Are you *insane*?'

'It doesn't matter, Pamela, all that matters is us.'

'This isn't you, Joseph. You're cracked.'

'Shut up!' Joe found himself yelling, so loudly his throat felt instantly hoarse. Still the tears fell, trailing through what remained of the dry blood on his cheeks.

'I'm sorry, Pam, I am. I didn't– I fucked up. You don't deserve any of this … but we have to stay quiet about it. It's the only way we can get back to what we had. It's our only chance.' Each word caught in his throat; Joseph had to fight to set them free. 'I'll find a way to make this right, I promise.'

'I'll keep quiet, Joseph,' Pamela spluttered through sobs, 'but we will never be able to forget what happened. Especially not now, not after what you've done to that poor man. I feel like I don't know who you are anymore.'

'I'm still me, Pam.' Joseph reached out a hand and Pamela recoiled. She was scared of him; he could see it in her eyes. Joseph's heart fell in his chest and more tears blurred his vision. She had never looked at him that way, even in the worst times.

The TV went black so suddenly that it might have not been on to begin with. In a wave of electricity Joseph felt himself fall backwards onto the bed. It was not like falling asleep; there was nothing peaceful about it. A more accurate description would be that someone, something, had gripped him and pulled him deeper into the pit of an empty black void.

Chapter
Four

Island of Gray

The sound of Joseph's apartment door exploding inward could have been heard from the street below. In one moment it had been dead silent, and in the next there was chaos; the deafening cracks of splintering wood and furious yells filled the room. Joseph woke violently, his heart beating so hard he was sure it had lifted him into a sitting position. He blinked through the fog of sleep and found he was being flooded with light—six, seven, maybe ten beams of white waved side to side before landing on his face, blinding him.

'Put your fucking hands up!' screamed a deep, male voice.

'Hands in the air, motherfucker, now!' roared another.

'Show us your hands or we'll shoot!' shouted a third.

'What the fuck?' was all Joseph could say.

'Last warning, put your hands in the air. Now!'

Joseph flinched against the dazzling light that continued to streak across his vision but managed to lift his tired arms all the same.

'What's going on?'

'Shut the fuck up,' one of the strangers replied.

Joseph felt a pair of strong hands grab him by the back of the neck and force him onto his stomach. They pushed his face into the mattress so hard that he could barely draw a breath.

'Joseph Ridley, you're under arrest for the murder of Javier Torres.'

What the fuck?

As the officer began reading him his Miranda rights, 'You have the right to remain silent …,' Joseph felt cold steel slide across his wrists and lock into place with a metallic click. The cuffs were tight, too tight, but Joseph didn't care. He wasn't even listening as the police officer kneeling on his back continued reading him his rights. He was staring through the window across the room, through the glistening opalescent cracks made by the ill-fated crow. The sky was dark, but rays of golden sunlight had sliced through the clouds and were illuminating the building across the street. The storm was gone, the sound of thunder and rain replaced with car engines and street musicians.

Police radios chattered and crackled as Joseph was pushed from his apartment, nestled between an escort of at least six large officers in protective vests. Some still had their hands at their sides, ready to pull their pistols and glue Joe to the wall with lead. Perhaps some were hoping they could. His mind raced and sweat moistened the cracks on his lips.

Murder? Javier?

Joseph looked up as they passed the old man's room. Police tape barred the doorway, but there was enough light from the window inside to see the shape of a small man on the floor, covered in a blood-soaked sheet. Joseph knew what lay beneath: old Javier, sliced from chin to stomach. He had watched it happen. The blood was still on Joe's shirt and sprayed across his arms.

The blood is on me ... oh fuck, the blood is on me.

Curious faces were peering from behind their door frames as Joseph was dragged toward the elevator. He could see the busty real estate agent, the nurse, even a child from one of the far rooms. Their stares bore into him. They wouldn't even blink, as if they believed they couldn't be seen.

'I didn't– he attacked me,' Joe protested as the metal doors banged closed.

'Shut up,' was the only reply.

The fluorescent light swam and spun; the floor beneath Joseph's feet tipped this way and that. No sooner had the doors closed than they opened again and he found himself being pushed across the lobby, awash in blinding midday glare.

'Mr. Ridley?'

Joe's head rolled upward and found Daewon standing just a few feet away, his face a portrait of confusion and concern.

'What's going on? What happened?'

'Out of the way, kid,' barked one of the officers. Daewon ignored the command and stepped closer.

'Joseph, what happened?'

'I don't understand,' Joseph groaned. His legs collapsed and the police officers yanked him upright again. Daewon looked from the blood-soaked man to the giants carrying him, and his jaw clenched.

'Is there anyone I can call for you, Joseph? Who should I get for you?' The young man got as close to Joseph as the police would allow, walking backwards and trying to meet the man's delirious gaze. Joseph looked at Daewon and continued to mutter under his breath.

Murder? I didn't kill anyone. The storm ... Doesn't make any sense ...

At least two hours had passed since Joseph was made to sit in a small, gray room at the back of the police station. He couldn't even remember the trip; one moment he had been pushed from the lobby of the Royal Dawn, and the next he was here. He was leaning forward in his chair and staring at his glass of water; there was perhaps a mouthful left. He had drunk the rest as soon as the sour-faced detective had given it to him, but it didn't quench his thirst. His tongue was still as dry as sand and every swallow tasted like copper and snot. What would that last sip of water do? Would he taste it? Would there be more? The room was too quiet; his thoughts were loud. He could feel himself clawing for air from the inside. A small part of himself was swimming up desperately, like a man in a lake with cement boots. His head would surface above the water just long enough to realize he was not making any sense.

How did I get here? Think, Joseph, you stupid piece of shit. Think.

Then he would sink again.

I'm so thirsty, why can't I taste it?

The door snapped open and a man in a mustard-colored shirt entered.

'Good afternoon, Joseph,' he said.

Joseph put down the empty glass and looked up. The detective smoothed down his tie and sat next to Joe, so close that their knees touched.

'We tried to call the number you gave us, Joseph. No luck.'

This got Joe's attention.

'However,' the detective continued, 'we did do a bit of searching ourselves and found a number that did go through.'

'Pam?'

'That's right.'

'What did she say? Is she coming here?'

'Not exactly.'

'What do you mean?'

'Here's the thing, Mr. Ridley. We didn't find any Pamela Ridleys in the area, but we did find a Pamela Byrnes.'

She changed her name back?

'Are you sure that's her name? Just as you spelled it?'

'Am I sure of my wife's name?'

The detective's lip curled into a snarl. He clearly didn't appreciate the attitude.

'I spoke to Pamela Byrnes, but there's a problem.'

Joseph's heart began to beat a little faster.

'She says she doesn't have a husband.'

'We're separated.'

'Yeah, you mentioned that. Far as she's concerned, you don't exist.'

Damnit, Pam.

'Take it the split was messy?' The detective leaned forward, so close that Joseph could smell the coffee on his breath.

Joseph put his face in his hands and shut his eyes so tightly that constellations of color burst across his vision.

'You wanna talk about it?'

Silence.

'I'm divorced,' confided the detective. 'Must be, what … eight years ago now?'

I don't care.

'Can't say I'm too torn up about it, though. She's a right miserable bitch. Hell, she may be the devil.'

I don't care—why does he think I care?

'I suppose that's not all true. I mean I was hurtin for a bit; the part about her being the devil is spot-on, though. Maybe I wasn't always the best to her, I guess. I loved her, God knows I did, but she had a way of making me feel small. Things she'd say, her attitude, made me feel like a stupid kid, y'know? Anyway, we never had kids or anything but the nail in the coffin was probably when I found her gettin' cozy with some fucker from her office. I coulda blasted the both of them, let me tell you that.' The detective slapped the side of his waist where his gun would normally rest. 'Yeah, I wanted to, but in my line of work I knew better than most how that would end. Is that what happened with you and this Pamela Byrnes, Joseph?'

Joseph looked up, his eyes sunken and dark. 'What?'

'She fuck around? You bust her bumpin' uglies with someone else?'

'No,' Joe growled. Heat rushed to his cheeks, his fingers curling into trembling fists.

'Did *you* do the fuckin' around?'

'Shut up.'

The detective didn't look away; he stared through Joseph like he were made of stone.

'I'm sure you know why you're here, Mr. Ridley. Can you tell me?'

Silence.

'Why do you think you're here, Joseph?'

This isn't right.

'Okay, well, you don't have to talk, but you're going to listen.' The detective shuffled even closer. He stunk like cheap cologne and the deep lines on his face gave him the appearance of a bulldog. 'You're here because last night you killed your neighbor, Javier Torres.'

Last night?

'I'll be honest with you, Joseph, that much isn't really up for debate here. We have your prints on the knife, your bloody footsteps in the hallway, and you've got his blood on you as we speak. Put simply, you're fucked. What we want to know is why.'

'Why?'

'That's right. Why? Why did you do it?'

'I didn't—'

'C'mon now, Joe, let's not waste time with that. Did the old man do something to piss you off? God knows people that age can get on your last nerve—trust me, I know. You should see the way my father-in-law talks to me sometimes. Christ, I'd be lying if I said I haven't thought about cutting the fucker's stomach open from time to time.'

'What?'

'All I'm saying is, people can be annoying. Sometimes you have to teach them a lesson—is that what happened? Is that why you're here? Talk to me.'

'B-but he had the knife, I never—'

'Did you kill him because he's a foreigner?'

'What? No, I never–'

'Okay, so then why?'

'I didn't do it. It wasn't my fault.'

'Too noisy of a neighbor maybe? Kept interrupting your beauty sleep?'

'I didn't–'

'Don't worry, I get it. You're just trying to get to work and they want to flap their fuckin gums about God knows what–'

'I didn't fucking kill him!'

The detective's placid, calm demeanor shifted like the sun passing behind a cloud. His brows furrowed over and the bulldog bared his teeth.

'We found that old bastard with his guts in his hands, and all his neighbors pointed us to your door. Need I remind you that you were caught red-handed?' The detective picked up one of Joseph's bloody hands to illustrate his point, before throwing it back onto the table.

Joseph saw Javier reaching out and grabbing his arm as he passed in the hallway every morning, just to say hello. It would make Joe so mad, so mad that he wanted to choke the old timer against the wall. That was then … now, it just made his stomach turn like a rolling stone. The ancient, wide smile seemed so far from the face he had seen in the dark that night, eyes that bulged red, a jaw that hung so low it tore the lips. There had been no trace of Javier left, only fury.

'I never wanted to actually hurt the guy,' Joseph croaked.

'But he got under your skin. Do people get under your skin often, Joseph?'

'I get angry sometimes, I don't know why.'

'And you want to hurt the people who make you angry.'

'I want to hurt them.'

'You want to ram a knife into their gut.'

'I want to ram– No! I want to hurt them, but I don't.'

'Why?'

'I don't know.'

'Sure you do. These people get under your skin and you want to lash out. You say you don't, but why? Is it because you don't *really* want to hurt them, or is it because you don't want to end up here?'

'I don't know.'

'You do lash out, though, don't you, Joseph?'

CLANG!

Something made a loud noise outside the interrogation room, but the detective didn't so much as blink. The ringing of metal on concrete reverberated in Joseph's head. Heavy steel, slick with rain, echoing off the alley walls.

I lashed out.

'This is your last chance, Joseph Ridley.' The detective's face smoothed out and became calm once more, perhaps even a little morose. 'Believe it or not, I'm trying to help you. This is your last chance—tell me why you're here.'

Joseph opened his mouth to protest again but the detective cut him off.

'Really think about it.'

Joseph stared back at the empty glass. He could see the shape of a face reflected back and he found his mind wandering to Pam and Marcus. He felt something warm flicker inside his chest ... relief? Thank God Pamela couldn't see him like this. The warmth turned to ice. It's not that she couldn't see him; she didn't want to.

Far as she's concerned, you don't exist.

There was no one for Joe to call, no one that would come. There was no one in his life left that would believe he didn't do this. Pamela would turn on the news, she would see that headline— *man kills elderly neighbor in gruesome homicide*—and the footage of Joseph being taken away in handcuffs. How much further could he fall from her grace? How much less could she think of him? A sharp pain stabbed through Joe's chest as he saw her. He could see Pam watching the television, her hand over her mouth and her eyes watering. His heart ached more as he saw a different version of Pam turning on the TV. She sees him, she sees the headline, and she walks away to make dinner, utterly unperturbed. He searched his mind for a memory where he existed to her and didn't cause her pain. His brain refused with a painful throb.

How did I get here?

'I don't know what you want me to say,' Joseph croaked. The detective closed his eyes and sighed.

'Okay then.' He got to his feet, nursing his large stomach. He snatched the document folder from the table and gave Joseph one last disapproving glare. 'Best of luck, Mr. Ridley.'

Joseph watched as the man turned a knob on the wall and exited the room. He disappeared around the corner as soft music flowed in from a speaker mounted high on the wall. The door was still wide open and the faint chatter of a busy office crept in. Minute after minute passed as Joe looked out into the motionless hallway, expecting someone else to come marching in. The minutes became an hour, and the hour became two. The song faded out in a piano riff and left a quiet, electric hiss.

Joseph hadn't ever been in an interrogation room before, although he was no stranger to police stations. He and Pamela had been frequent visitors for a brief, terrible time. Joseph remembered the last welcome had been much warmer, painfully so. He had sat across the desk from a detective that never broke eye contact. The way the man's lips turned down at the edges, the way his hands nervously shifted papers back and forth to the same spots, Joseph had hated him for it. It was always pity. Burning, poisonous, pity for the weak. Pam never seemed to notice … she was usually miles away when they sat there, surrounded by ringing phones and chatting officers.

I should call her myself … if I can just speak to her for a minute.

Joseph rose to his feet, staggering a little and lurched toward the doorway. The air was frigid, his skin prickled with goosebumps. He leaned out of the room and looked left to right. There was no movement, although he could hear voices behind some of the doors. More music broke the quiet, vintage-sounding jazz.

I'm flying high but I've got a feeling I'm falling

Joseph froze, gripping the door frame so tightly that his fingernails bent.

Oh shit.

He fumbled for the volume knob the detective had used. It snapped off in his hand with a pathetic crack.

Show me the ring and I'll jump right through

One of the conversations in a nearby room sounded as if it were becoming heated. The voices were dulled behind the walls, but Joseph caught a few words.

'You have ... motherfucker ... sick.'

There was a loud thump from the room and the yelling turned to inaudibly muffled gags.

'Hello?' Joseph called.

As soon as he spoke, the lively chatter stopped. The voices behind every door were silenced like the flick of a switch and all that remained was the music.

'Hello?' Joseph said again, softer now.

A scream shattered the quiet, bouncing from every wall, impossible to pinpoint. Joseph's nails dug into the wall and he felt his throat tighten. He turned to look at the other end of the hall again and saw that the lights had dimmed to almost complete darkness, creating an infinite, cascading tunnel of black. It vibrated through the air, through Joseph, he could feel—*sense* it advancing closer.

'Hello? Someone?' The yells wouldn't even echo; they vanished into nothing. The lights from the other direction faded too now, the illumination from under the doors providing only a flickering glow. Joseph's small, gray room was an island in an endless, empty ocean. The silence was so heavy that it felt like his skull might pop.

'Somebody help me!'

Chapter
Five

What Is Yours

Annette's voice was warped and slow, like she had recorded the song blind drunk. It was still enough. Enough to pull Joseph from the bed in a quick spin, like a broken marionette. He exploded from the sheets in one swift, arched leap and landed with both feet on the floor. He refused to collapse under the pain.

His head throbbed with the force of a battle drum and his vision was tainted red—no, wait ... The cherry glow was from outside. It was not red like the rising of the sun, which would bring warmth; it was dark and unsettling. It reminded Joseph of the cold, eerily silent rooms that the photography kids at school used to develop their film. The clouds were bruised with pulses of crimson, as if they had been burned and wounded.

No more. Please God, no more.

The storm was back. The room was back. Joseph was not sure he had ever left. His apartment door stood tall and bare, not a single scratch to show a SWAT team had only just burst through. Joseph pressed his shaking hands to his ears, not looking away from the radio, the radio that should have been in pieces under his feet right now. The music was the least of his concerns. He foolishly hoped that blocking his ears and closing his eyes was all he needed to do. If he did this, maybe he could calm the deafening roar of the storm's wind. If he was lucky, he would even have some relief from the vibration in his head. It had grown louder and more debilitating with each passing day since this nightmare began.

Joseph stood like that for what could have been a few minutes or an hour. He stared into the dizzying dark of his eyelids and chanted the mantra, *'This isn't real, none of this is real.'*

I'm having a breakdown. Stress ... too much stress.

He turned groggily to the window and fell against it, hoping to at least feel the cool glass against his cheeks. He felt the cold, but it brought no satisfaction. He cast a glance through the blinding rain and fog and felt himself sober immediately. He straightened up and pressed his nose to the glass, a little too quickly.

What was that sound? Was that a crack? No ...

Somehow, he could see down to the street. Large sections of the road were visible through the storm, though it had doubled in intensity since the day before. Through the darkness and downpour, standing far below were hundreds of people, maybe more. They were all crowded on the street, utterly unperturbed by the weather and looking directly up. Directly at Joseph. Their faces were blank, emotionless. Not one of them blinked. It was like they were waiting for something.

And you know it too, you caught my eye

The radio sang on, fading in and out of earshot abruptly. Joe wished he was home, his *real* home. He wanted it so desperately that it weighed on his limbs and anchored him to the floor.

I hope the weather is better there.

Pam liked the rain; she would open the window, close her eyes, and take a deep breath. Her nose would scrunch up and blend the freckles together, then she'd smile. She loved the way it smelled; she loved the cool breeze it rode in on. Something told Joe that Pam wouldn't enjoy *this*. If only he could trade places with a Joseph four years younger. He would be home. He could kiss his wife; he could hold his son. Joseph wanted to be that man; he willed it with all his strength as he stared into the hurricane. That man had not known what he had, or the horrors in his future. Backing away from the window, Joe was faced with a moment of quiet. It was not a peaceful quiet. It was a raging, rumbling stillness that brought with it an understanding. True dread infected every corner of his mind as he finally realized how scared and alone he truly was.

'I don't want to die,' he whispered.

The movement of his mouth to form the words stung his pale, cracked lips. He turned and walked with slow steps to the kitchen sink, sticking his face under the faucet and blasting it into action. The cold water was a painful—but sweet—treat. He lapped at the stream and sighed as it provided much-needed moisture to his lips, eyes, and bruised cheeks. Just as he opened his mouth for another gulp, the water began to spit and choke. The stream of clear liquid vanished with one final, loud burst, and was suddenly replaced by steaming, black bile.

'Argh *shit*!'

Joseph swung backwards and collided with his fold-out table. It spun across the floor and hit the opposite wall, splitting in two with a mighty snap. His face was searing with white-hot pain and he could feel the inside of his mouth sizzle. His tongue was already beginning to coat itself in a defensive pool of hot saliva. The taste was somehow worse than the burning. It was as if he had been made to drink from the belly of a two-week-old corpse. He panted against the back of his forearm, staring fiercely into the peeling kitchen wallpaper. It looked all wrong.

That– that wasn't like that yesterday.

Looking around, Joseph realized something about his small flat was different than the day before. Even in the nearly blinding dark he could see that it looked much older, more worn. The benches sagged ever so slightly, and patches of wall were bubbled or peeling. He stepped backwards into the bedroom and noticed the carpet felt spongier under his weight. He was sure it was filled with moisture; he could see the fabric had an unnatural shine. It was hard to take full stock of the changes through the intermittent booms and flashes of the storm, but he could smell it. Something rancid; something that shouldn't be there.

Rot.

Joseph hesitantly rocked toward the door, daring to peek through the peephole again. He breathed a sigh of relief when he found it was not only vacant and blood-free out there, but once again well lit. It was bright enough at least to spot the numberless door at the opposite end of the hall, an abnormal distance away. The image of the crippled man's silhouette flashed before Joe's eyes again and he forcefully bashed his forehead against the door.

BANG! Ow. Again BANG!

Joseph wasn't sure he could even feel guilt anymore. *Proper* guilt anyway. Sometimes he would snap a little too quickly and wish he hadn't, but most of the time he simply felt nothing at all. Maybe sometimes it wasn't just regret, maybe it *was* guilt … or shame. Either way, it gave him the same feeling it always had, disgust. Absolute revulsion.

Joseph turned to go lie down again and was met with the other side of his door, only a breath from his nose. He staggered backwards, looking around wildly and gaping. Somehow, he found himself standing in the hallway, surrounded by the claustrophobic confinement of yellow walls and stiff, blue carpet.

How the hell? I don't even remember opening the fucking door. Did I– I didn't … I didn't.

Joseph threw himself at the small, dark gap of his open door, hand outstretched. In an instant he felt the wood brush his fingers as it slammed shut, sealing him out with a thunderous crash.

'No!' he roared. He shook the door handle ferociously and beat the wood with his injured fist. 'Let me in, damnit, let me in!'

Suddenly, Joe was met with a prickling wave of tension. It was an unusual and ominous feeling; his body felt stiff, his neck refused to turn his head. It was the feeling of watching someone step out from behind a dark corner two blocks away, as you walk home alone. Joseph was not sure how, but he knew someone was looking out at him through his own peephole. He leaned back and steadied himself against the wall, too unnerved to look away. Out of the corner of his eye, he realized something else that only added to the terror—Javier's door was wide open. Flashes of white stabbed through the blood-red glow of the storm that seeped out of the old man's apartment. Javier's door was *open*, and as soon as Joe became aware of this, he heard the music playing inside. It was soft, crackling, and giving off light pops as if it were being played on vinyl.

I'm sorry that I made you cry
Oh my, I didn't want to hurt you
I'm just a jealous guy

Abandoning any attempt at being inconspicuous, Joseph spun on the spot and limped toward the emergency stairs again. He would not dare to do so much as cast a glance over his shoulder. He got to the elevator and swiped at the button on his way past. The last thing he wanted right now was to be stuck in an elevator, but it would sure beat the alternative. Going round two with the psychotic, retired war veteran—especially in his current state—would not go in Joe's favor.

Almost immediately, there was a sound from within the elevator shaft, not at all dulled by the steel doors. It was not an electric ding. It was not a mechanical whir of the chamber sliding into place; it was a snap. It was the loud, unmistakable snap of steel cable, followed by the crack of it smacking the wall of the shaft. Joseph froze in horror as he heard the increasing rumble of the elevator rocketing downward from high, much too high, above. Worst of all were the screams. They grew louder and louder as the chamber fell from the heavens. He stood helpless as they passed, shaking the walls and piercing his brain for one brief, nauseating moment. The pitch of the squeals reached its climax and fell away again just as quickly.

Then, for one single second ... silence.

CRASH!

There would be no elevator travel today. If those doors were to slide open and a warm light spill out, he wouldn't get close. Even if an elevator drifted into existence, packed wall to wall with naked, big-breasted women holding plates of chicken and pitchers of cold beer, it would not be enough to tempt him. Joseph would not be stepping foot into one of those goddamned suspended metal baskets. Perhaps he never would again. The screams were real, or they were more illusions; it didn't matter. He could still hear them, falling and passing.

Voom

The sound was like a large machine powering down; it came from every direction. Just like that, the lights were sucked from existence. It was not dark; it was the void, the absolute absence of everything.

'This life isn't yours. Weep for the time lost, stolen. It is lost to them and wasted by you.'

The voice was disembodied and hissed from every direction, but for once it did not startle Joseph. He felt confused, disoriented, but numb. The voice was something in the nothing. He was still here. He still had thought. Was he still able to be scared? Had this demonic fever-dream severed the nerve ending that provided that

bastard response? No, no ... the fear was most
certainly still there.

Light filled Joseph's vision, soft, gloomy,
yellow light. It was being cast down by a crooked
roof lamp that hung on two rust-colored chains.
He stepped forward, leaning against a small desk
for support, and inspected the room he was now
standing in. It was a classroom, that much was
clear. The walls were plastered with lopsided
paintings and mathematical posters.

Is this ...

Joseph found he was standing in the back of
a room filled with children. All of them were
facing away from him. They were still, too still;
they sat just a little too straight. The children were
watching a man at the front of the class, their
teacher. He was also facing away, dragging a
piece of chalk across the board in rigid, spastic
movements. Joseph thought he recognized the
bald spot on the back of the man's head, and the
offensively yellow sweater.

'So, Alexandre Dumas says, *It's necessary to
have wished* ... ' The teacher had begun to speak,
and then stopped abruptly.

The man's thin face turned to the side in a
quick snap. His hooked nose turned up and

sniffed the air. The children moved too, just minuscule shuffles and twitches. Joseph didn't notice. He could see the world outside the window; it was dim, almost colorless, as if shadowed by an eclipse. The black bean tree waved gently; even nature dared not disturb the quiet.

'Joseph Ridley, pay attention.'

This caught Joe's attention. He turned back to the teacher, his heart freezing in his chest. The man was facing him now, tall and slender. He didn't look quite right; his limbs went on for a little too long. He looked as though he had been stretched by the wrists and ankles. The teacher's face was slightly shadowed by his protruding brow ridge, but Joseph could see he was glaring. The small, beady eyes did not meet his; they were locked onto the black-haired boy just a few steps away. The child was sitting as straight as the others, but his hands were linked behind his back. Something white was clutched in his small fist.

'Are you listening, Joseph?' The man was still speaking to the boy, but it sent a chill down Joe's spine all the same. The tone was not that of a teacher scolding his student; it was pointed, almost *intimate*.

The child nodded, and flicked the hand still tucked behind his back. The thing he had been holding spiraled through the air and landed at Joseph's feet. It was a scrunched-up ball of paper. Without hesitation, Joe crouched down and plucked the paper into his hand with two fingers. As he unfolded it, he saw it was a note and something sparked in his mind, something buried deep. He remembered this. He knew the familiar, purple gel ink.

U n Mr. Fowley hav the same nose
Just kidding! lets go to the big table at lunch ok?

There was a drawing under it, a smiley face with its tongue sticking out. Pam signed off almost all her notes that way. He must have seen a hundred of these notes, and he was sure Mr. Fowley had seen them pass more than half. They never got in trouble, as long as they kept their giggling under control. Joseph looked up to where he remembered Pam would sit, diagonally across from him. It was empty, the chair pushed back.

'I fucking told you to pay attention!'

The teacher was talking to *him* now. Those beady, gray eyes were firmly locked on Joseph. All the children were staring, turned in their seats. They wore blank stares and their mouths opened and closed in silent chatter. Mr. Fowley was stepping forward in great strides. His eyebrows were curved so sharply that they touched in the center and the corners of his mouth shook with rage. He looked to be getting bigger the closer he came, his limbs becoming further and further out of proportion. The black-haired boy was gone now too; there was only one Joseph left in the room. There was a door, a possible escape, but it was on the other side of the teacher.

'Why don't you listen? Why don't you *ever* pay attention, Ridley?'

Mr. Fowley was close now, his eyes bulging from their sockets and becoming dotted with webs of broken red.

'Get away from me!' Joseph stepped backwards, groping in the dark around him for a weapon.

'Selfish, miserable little cunt. Come here, Joseph, come here so I can *make* you listen.'

'Get back!'

'I said *come to me!*'

Mr. Fowley was so tall his head brushed the ceiling, his arms swung and groped at the air. His hands were enormous and pressed with veins. Joseph clutched at a thick, hardcover copy of *The Count of Monte Cristo* and brought it smashing into the side of the thin man's head. Fowley staggered sideways, just enough for Joseph to squeeze past and break for the door. The children muttered faster. Their whispered voices rose to a loud hiss. It was deafening.

'Don't run from me. Come back!'

Joseph could hear wet snaps behind him, but he refused to slow his pace. He slid through the aisle of desks and lunged for the door. Relief washed over him like a warm tide as he felt it fling open. He threw himself into the dark and chanced one last look over his shoulder.

Mr. Fowley was standing in the space at the back of the room, illuminated dully by the overhead light. His arms were outstretched and disjointed, resembling a twisted arachnid. His hands were firmly clasped onto the skulls of two placid children. They stared across the room at Joseph, as lifeless as ventriloquist dummies. Even in the dreary light Joseph knew who they were: Pamela Byrnes and little Joseph Ridley.

'Look, child, look at what you've become,' Mr. Fowley said.

The teacher's fingers pressed deeper into their skin, his nails piercing the flesh. Joseph heard the crazed man speaking until the door slammed closed behind him.

'Poisoning the time that was not yours to spend. Wicked, vile, miserable cu–'

The door crashed shut with such force that the wind pushed Joseph forward a step. He was surrounded by rows of pale green lockers and windowed, timber doors. He had walked these halls decades ago, though they had been better lit back then. He stepped forward and his feet made a delicate splash. The ground was covered in a shallow layer of water, barely reaching the tops of his soles.

'Hello?' Joseph called out.

He needed to get out. These visions, these *nightmares*, had a way of getting worse before they got better. Joseph knew he had to escape quickly, while he was still alone.

The lights flickered as he ran from corner to corner. The turns looked familiar, but the memory was too old, too faded. The water felt deeper now; he needed to pull a little harder to free his feet from the surface. Perhaps he was just becoming more tired. It was wonderous and terrible to feel so fired up and yet so utterly exhausted. Water was seeping into his shoes, drenching his socks in unbearably cold moisture. Suddenly, there was another splash, not too close but not at all far-off. Joseph turned wildly, slipping and falling into the door of a locker. He blinked through the sweat and dizzy fog and searched the shadows. There was nothing. Then there was another splash, so Joe spun again. He saw it this time, a man dashing past one of the corridors. A tall, pale, naked man.

'Where's the damn exit?' Joe said through clenched teeth.

He set off again, in the opposite direction of the stranger. He passed at least twenty more doors and a hundred more lockers before he heard a sound. He slid to a stop and tried to steady his breathing, pushing back a lock of sweaty, black hair. There it was again. It was a cry, or perhaps a muffled scream. Joseph stumbled forward, slowly and quietly. The water was above his ankles now, so he withdrew his foot from the pool as gently as he could.

Splash.

He was being watched; he could feel it. A moan broke the silence again and Joseph turned his head. It was from the door to his right.

'Oh fuck!' Someone yelled, muffled by the wooden barrier. Joseph knew that voice.

'Pam?' He flung himself at the door. It shook against the hit, but the handle refused to turn.

'Shit!'

'Pam?'

Joseph stepped back, no longer concerned with how much noise he made or the figure stalking him in the dark. He barreled forwards and felt the door crack inward. It folded slightly upon impact and swung open, slamming hard against the other side of the wall. Joseph tumbled inside, landing on his hands and knees. He looked up to see he was in a dark bedroom; the only light was the luminous white from behind him. His eyes met four others, wide and staring.

'Joseph?' the two figures said in unison.

Joe looked up at the bare ass of a teenage boy with dark brown hair. He was crouched between the legs of a girl about the same age. Her tanned skin blended with the sheets she was tangled in and her freckled cheeks were quickly turning red.

'Pam?' Joseph gasped.

'Dude!' said the boy. 'Not a good time, man.'

Joseph frowned, tears swelling in his eyes. Pam was there, she was so close. But he knew it was not *really* her. This was Pamela Byrnes, student at West Park High; it was not his wife. They stared down at Joe in disbelief, the boy trying to cover Pam's breasts with a pillow.

'Seriously,' the boy yelled again. He got to his feet quickly and modestly pulled his underwear over his privates.

'It's me,' Joseph said breathlessly. He was kneeling, reaching out for the girl who was shielding her body with the sheets. Noise pulsed his head; loud, thumping music and drunken chatter.

The teenage boy pulled Joseph to his feet by the arm and pushed him back toward the door.

'Not cool, bro,' he said, shaking his head with a disappointed frown. Then a sinister shade swept over the teenager's face and he leaned in close.

'Lost to me, wasted by you. Wasted by you.'

The door slammed in Joseph's face and all that followed was quiet.

Joseph stood with his forehead pressed against the door for what felt like a lifetime. Tears snaked down his cheeks and fell to join the water at his knees. It was cold, impossibly cold. His feet were so numb that he couldn't be sure they would carry him another step.

Pam had been so close that he could almost have reached out and touched her. More than that, she had looked so young, so unburdened. Embarrassed and startled, sure, but her face did not wear the crippling stress of a broken marriage and a ...

My Pam ...

'There you are.'

Joseph turned and saw a young man digging through the locker across from him. He had black hair and broad shoulders, with a cheap, busted backpack slung over one. The teenage boy turned and looked over his shoulder. His hazel eyes met Joseph's for just a moment, before passing by and catching another pair. It was Pamela again. She skipped forward and leaned against the locker next to young Joseph's. The water was at her thighs, soaking the bottom of her blue dress and turning it black. Neither she nor Joe's junior doppelgänger seemed to notice the flood. She gave the older Joseph a blank look up and down as well, before turning to the other.

'I've been looking for you everywhere. I need your help.'

'What could you possibly need my help with? You're the smart one, aren't you?' The boy laughed and Pam gave him a playful punch on the arm.

'Stop, Joe, I'm serious. I'm kinda stuck and you're good in these situations.'

Joseph, the real Joseph, was at least ten feet away, but he could feel it. He felt the warmth rising in his chest, the nervous butterflies in his stomach. He could smell her: vanilla and jasmine.

'Yeah, all right. What's up?'

'Awesome, you're the best.'

He could feel her breath, so close. God above, how he wanted to hold her cheek in his hand, how he wanted to push her against the locker and press his lips to hers. His face was getting hot, his crotch twitched in his pants. The two teenagers were staring at each other, a little too long. She stepped from one foot to the other, the cold water rippling around her legs. Young Joseph scratched the back of his head with a sweaty hand.

'So uh, what's up, Pam?'

'Right,' she said, tucking a length of wavy hair behind one ear. 'So Valentine's is obviously coming up, and I'm out of ideas as far as gifts go.'

'Yo!' A third figure stepped out of the dark now, splashing through the water and pulling Pam into an embrace from behind. 'My main girl and my main man, that's what I like to see.'

It was the young man from the room, the one that had been thrusting himself between

Pamela's legs. He leaned over her shoulder and caught the other boy's hand in a tight shake.

'What's up, dude?'

'Not much, Rod. Hear anything back yet?'

'Yeah, what did they say?' Pam turned around and wrapped her arms around the boy's waist, before standing on her toes and kissing his neck.

A vile twist spun Joseph's gut, *both* Josephs.

'Nothing yet, guys, I'm keeping the phone close, though.'

'You've got it, bro,' said young Joe, closing his locker and slapping Rod's shoulder.

'Hell yeah,' added Pam.

Rod beamed, a row of glistening white teeth winking out at them in the gloom.

'God, I love you guys.'

'Eh, you're *okay*,' replied Joe, before breaking into a laugh. 'Love you too, man. I mean someone has to.'

'Get in line,' Pam said, pulling Rod's face down and meeting his mouth with hers.

Nearly two years of this, and that sinking in Joe's stomach never stopped. Anguish beat his brain so hard that it ached. He wasn't angry, not anymore; all that was left was the miserable, cold, plummeting weight in his gut. His body became

140

as heavy as lead, just the same as it had the day his two best friends—his *only* two friends—had told him they were dating.

I was going to finally tell her. It was time.

Young Joseph believed that, but the worn and beaten reflection of himself standing just across the hall knew that was bullshit. The older Joseph watched frozen, almost literally as the water crept higher around him. It touched the tips of his fingers; it might as well have been ice. The teenagers spoke for a while more, about other students they disliked and how much they planned on drinking that weekend. Eventually, Pam gave her boyfriend a final kiss and walked away with her textbooks pressed tightly to her chest. She was smiling as she left. Joseph hadn't seen that smile in years. It was a warmth in this chill, however small. He trembled; his hands were blue.

I have– I have to– move. I have to– to move. Escape.

'Wait up a sec, will you, Joe?'

Rod grabbed young Joseph by the arm, and older Joseph also found himself stopped dead in his tracks.

'Listen, I need to tell you something, but I need you to promise me, okay? Promise you won't tell Pam.'

An excited flutter prickled through Joe's chest.

'Uh, okay?' Teenage Joseph laughed nervously. 'You sleep with the cafeteria lady or something?'

Rod laughed.

'Asshole. Shut up, though, this is serious.'

They went quiet for a moment, and Rod took a deep breath, as if about to dive into shark-infested waters.

'So, we got an offer.'

'What? Are you for real, dude?'

'Yeah, I got the call just before.'

'That's amazing! Why didn't you say something?'

'Because it's not in the city like we thought. They want us to go over to Australia …'

'Oh.'

'Yeah.'

'What did you say?'

'I said I would think about it. I don't know.'

Joseph remembered this conversation, but the words escaped his memory, like a dream that fades as soon as you wake. Rod's dad had created something, something ground-breaking. What was it?

Something for your car ... something to do with fuel? No, it was something to do with putting computers in a car.

Rod's family were being flooded with offers, and his father had been attempting to negotiate for himself to have some involvement in the production.

The teenagers stood in silence for another long minute.

Splash

The naked, skeletal figure was watching at another corner of the hallway, closer now. Then it dashed away again.

'Do you think your folks would let you stay?'

'You know them, Joe, of course they would. My nan will still be here at the house, but ... I know they want me to go with them. This is really important to Dad, y'know.'

'You have to go,' young Joseph said. It was quick, without hesitation. Both Rod and even Joe himself seemed surprised by this.

'Well, shit, push me onto the plane now, why don't you?' Rod said jokingly, but visibly taken aback.

'I didn't— I didn't mean it like that. Sorry. It's just such an amazing opportunity, you know.'

'Yeah, I know, but leaving feels weird. Also … y'know.'

'Pam.'

'Pam.'

'She would tell you to go too.'

'Yeah, I know, but it doesn't make it any easier.'

They stood, all three of them, in the wet and the dark, two of them burdened with the weight of what *could* happen, the older Joseph encumbered by the weight of what he knew *would* happen.

'I have to do this, don't I?'

'Yeah, man, I think you do.'

'Do you think Pam would stay with me? Maybe we could do a long-distance thing?'

'I don't– do you think that's fair on her? It's the other side of the world.'

'Yeah, but I could fly out every few weeks maybe. I could pay for her to come see me?'

'Rod.'

'I don't want to lose her, man.'

'I know, brother, but you have to think about what's right … for her.'

'Fuck, dude.' Rod's voice shook and he sunk his face into his hands. Joe wrapped an arm around his friend's shoulders and gave him a reassuring squeeze.

'I'm going to miss you,' he said.

Rod turned and pulled Joe into a hug.

'You better come see me.'

'I can barely afford new shoes,' Joe replied with an earnest chuckle. 'Around-the-world flights may be a bit out of reach for a while.'

'Not for me. Didn't you hear? My dad just made a fortune.'

The boys burst into genuine, bittersweet laughter. Their eyes were glazed with tears, and the longer they laughed, the less time there was to crack. Boys don't cry in front of each other, not in the middle of school anyway.

'Hey, listen, Joe,' Rod said, his face suddenly looking more serious. He put a hand on young Joseph's shoulder and gave it a gentle squeeze. 'If you need to stay at my place anytime, you still can. My nan will be there. To be honest, I think she loves you more than me anyway. If you need to get away from—'

'It's cool, thanks.'

'No sweat, dude.'

The cold water was at the older, more fatigued Joseph's chest now. It froze the air from his lungs and what little breath he could muster came out in small, white clouds. The boys were gone, maybe they had been for a while. The lights had fizzled to a faint, flickering glow. Joseph felt the same sorrow in his chest, the same shame, that he had that day of high school. He had been truly sad to hear his friend tell him about the move and encouraging him to go was the right thing to do. Of course it was, but that was not why Joe did it. From the moment he heard that Rod might have to move overseas, the only thought that filled his mind—the only thought that formed his words—was *'Get him away, get him far away from Pam.'* Rod would not have had the strength otherwise; he loved her too much. The boy practically worshipped the ground that anyone he cared for walked on, including Joe. Joe had to push him, as much as it stung. He nudged Rod on the right path, the path to Australia, the path away from Pam. That was all that mattered. Joseph knew she was meant to be with him anyway. She was never Rod's.

Tell your parents you'll go.

Tell Pam you love her, but this is for the best.

This is the way, Rod. You're going to have an amazing life.

'I did it right,' Joe sobbed. The water rose over his chin.

146

No, you fucking didn't. You stole his life, and you wasted it. We wasted it.

Rapid splashes drew closer and the lights fizzled out one by one with static pops. Joseph could see the towering, thin figure getting closer; they were running, arms outstretched above the liquid surface. Joe sank beneath the water, powerless and paralyzed. He felt himself pulled into its frozen depths. He sunk lower than the floor, lower than the foundations of the school. Joseph sank like a stone in the black, suffocating, empty ocean.

'What life do you think I could have had, if you hadn't ruined mine?' Pamela's voice floated through the crushing abyss—adult Pamela, his wife.

'What life can I have?' That voice was different; it was a child's.

Joseph opened his mouth to speak, letting a flow of water past his lips and down into his throat. His mouth could not find the word, but he heard it echo through his mind, nonetheless.

Marcus.

Joseph faded in and out of consciousness violently, with every few rigid, unbalanced steps of the person that carried him over his shoulder.

The grip the person had on his waist and knee was vice-like and unforgiving, pressing in on the already battered muscle.

'Let mmmguh,' he heard himself mumble before fading to black once more.

He came to as he felt the inertia of his body falling through open air. His eyes flicked open before the soft, but still much too firm, impact of the mattress against his back. He was too exhausted to even cry out in pain, and the cold wet fabric of his suit still weighed down his aching body. Standing by his feet he saw the pale man. The emaciated man. The man with blotched skin, pressed thin against his bones. He was still naked and his throat was still swollen and pulsing, but his eyes were now open. The steel string hung bloody from the lids. Then the stranger spoke.

'Deeper yet, higher we go,' he croaked. He stepped backwards and grabbed the back of Joseph's favorite blue armchair. Without breaking eye contact with the man laid out before him, the thin man planted his bare ass in the chair's cushioned depths.

Chapter
Six

The Passing Heat

The opening notes of the song were barely recognizable anymore. The band instrument's notes were warped and distorted. Annette Hanshaw's voice sounded like she had filled her mouth with nails and was trying to recite the alphabet. It didn't matter. Joseph knew the words, and he knew it meant he was still stuck in this nightmare.

And I've got a feeling I'm falling

He could not be sure how he was still breathing; he couldn't even be sure he cared to know.

'I have to get home,' he found himself saying. For the first time in a while, the words were his own. They weren't being forced from his mouth through some twisted reimagining of a long-buried memory.

'I'm going home,' he said again through clenched teeth.

Joseph rolled himself to a sitting position with every ounce of willpower he could muster. He lurched forward and ripped the drawer from the bedside table, sending the radio clattering to the floor in a shower of plastic and static. Again.

Annette managed a final verse before crackling out with a hiss:

Don't know if I should, but gee, it feels good

Joe found what he was looking for, a photo frame housing a picture from a lifetime ago. Pamela, with her hair blowing around her head in a halo of curled, brunette locks, and little Marcus. The boy's attention was locked on the German Shephard that had been running past at the time with its master's lunch clenched firmly in its jaws. Joe's family were smiling in the photo, genuinely happy. A lifetime ago.

'This was real,' he wheezed.

He had not had a moment to catch his breath these last few ... *days*? Let alone a moment to try to rationalize this labyrinth of punishment.

Am I going mad?

It was a good question. He had felt the seductive influence of unconventional and twisted thoughts before, albeit nothing more than perhaps a pill-fueled ride out of existence. He had boiled it down to the vortex of shit that his life had been thrust into—that and the life of seclusion. The monotonous, repetitive cycle of driving for assholes and eating stale cereal could send anyone a little crazy. Right?

He closed his eyes with a shaky breath and tried to find an island of calm within the chaos in his mind. His thoughts were a storm only slightly more tumultuous than the one outside, the storm on the other side of the glass threatening to tear down the building with every deafening crash of thunder. He could see Pam staring into his padded cell through the one-way mirror, a look of utter contempt on her freckled face. She was shielding Marcus' eyes, sparing him from the dribbling, restrained mess that had once been his father. Behind them, staring through the glass with bulbous, bloodshot eyes and slack jaw, was the pale man. Every blue vein was visible through the skin and strings of blood, spit, and bile were dripping from his teeth. He glared furiously at Joseph, and then he was looking down at Pam, down at Marcus.

'Stop,' Joseph spat, coming to with a jolt.

He was still sitting on the bed, drenched in cold sweat. The photo frame was gripped so tightly in his hands that his fingers had turned white between the spots of blood and purple bruising.

So hot.

The haze in his head washed away in a swift and vicious wave. His senses sharpened once more, fueled by adrenaline. He became immediately aware that the room was much too warm. Even through the dark, he could see the ghostly waves of pure heat pressing mist onto the windows of the apartment. It did little to dim the red glow, and every thunderous drop of rain still shook the glass, but it was debilitating all the same. Sweat was pooling above his thick eyebrows and glazing his upper lip in heavy, salty beads.

'All right, c'mon, Joe,' he grunted through gritted teeth, staggering to his feet and loosening his tie with a hooked finger. 'No more of this bullshit.'

He felt a familiar and comforting emotion boiling up inside of him. It charged him upright with an electric snap. He was angry. Extremely *fucking* angry.

'No more!' Joe roared.

He swung an already bloody fist into the wall beside him. His hand broke through with little effort; he was too weak in this state for that to be normal. The wall was brittle and soft, as if it were the survivor of a one-thousand-year winter. The room itself looked decayed and beaten, an ironic reflection of its sole resident. He looked around at the sagging ceiling and blackened walls and couldn't help but let out a solitary, '*ha*.' The remnants of the moldy apple he had bitten into a few days ago was now a mass of oozing, black tendrils that stretched across the kitchen bench and wrapped the sink faucet in its grip. Most unusual of all was that the room itself seemed smaller, by just a little, but enough to notice. Every bit of fading furniture was just a few inches closer to each other; he was sure of it.

I don't want to go out there; I won't. The twisted manipulations of his past had been tormenting enough, but Joseph knew there was much worse he could be tortured with. There were other memories, much *worse* memories.

The heat was now at an unbearable temperature, threatening to set the carpet below his feet alight.

'You want me out, don't you?' he called to the corners of the room, forcing a chuckle for flavor.

'What's next, huh? Who else have you got?'

A sharp twinge of mortal regret stabbed his stomach. Taunting this place could not be wise. But the words were already said, and Joseph rarely held back once the floodgates were open.

'Fuck you! Whatever this is, whoever you are, *fuck* you. If I see another one of you freaks, I don't care who you look like, I'm splitting your fucking head open.'

He snatched up another thick piece of IKEA timber to illustrate his point. He even gave it a practice swing and almost toppled himself in the process. He kicked a stack of DVDs into the wall and shoved a set of shelves to the floor with a tremendous crash.

'No more games!'

He marched across the room and wrenched open the door, immediately welcomed by a powerful surge of soothing, cool wind. As soon as his feet were pressed into the crisp, blue carpet of the hallway, the door slammed shut behind him, leaving a final kiss of blistering warmth on the back of his neck. Every door in the hall was shut. The handles were all coated in a layer of dust as deep as fresh snow. The only sound was the low, static buzz of the lamps mounted on the wall, giving out an appreciated, though lackluster, light. Joseph limped forward, sure that this time he would be going through that fire escape, rain, hail, or blood-red sunshine.

He made it quite close too, before he heard an unexpected sound. A scared, fragile voice.

'Hey,' he heard it hiss. 'Are you one of those *things*?'

Joe turned groggily and spotted half of a woman's face looking out at him from behind a door frame. The busty real estate lady's door frame. Her eyes were wide, terrified, and set above long streaks of mascara that twisted down her smooth cheeks. Joe cocked a sincerely confused eyebrow and steadied himself against the wall.

'You mean the psychos with their mouths hanging open, right?'

She nodded frantically, 'Of course that's who the shit I'm talking about.'

'Do I look like my eyes are popping out of my damn head, lady? Is my chin on the floor?'

'You look like shit, and they change … they always change.'

Admittedly, Joe was just thinking the same thing.

'Well, I'm not one of them, although they have kicked the shit out of me. I need a hospital.'

She eyed him up and down for what felt like the hundredth time, and then she reached out a hand for his. Joe stared down at it; it was clean of all the mess he was coated in but quivering severely. He felt his anger extinguished like a cheap candle and once again he was scared. He felt the bristle on his neck, the warning of impending danger, but if he was truly not alone here … well, that could be his ticket out. He took her hand in his and immediately he was pulled into her apartment with surprising strength. The woman slammed the door shut and shakily slid the lock home before turning and giving Joe an uncertain look.

'My n-name is W-Wendy,' she said.

She was still afraid of him and, truth be told, he was scared shitless of her too. Joseph swung backwards, looking for a chair and accidentally knocked a stack of paperback books into the wall. Each one sailed to the floor with a *WHACK* like a fat, dead pigeon. The woman jumped a little and backed into the door, as far as her figure would allow.

'I'm … sorry,' Joe mumbled, rubbing his forehead and collapsing onto a stool.

Lightning flashed outside, followed by an earth-cracking boom of thunder and all too suddenly he realized how lightheaded he had become.

Shit, the blood loss is finally getting me. Focus, Joe, get it together.

'I need– God, I need a doctor,' Joe gasped, not at all embarrassed by the pitch of the whine that followed. His head was throbbing, and his vision was swimming. It melted all the shadows of the room into one. He could taste something on his tongue too, acidic and powerful.

Whiskey?

'If we can get downstairs, I think we can get out. The d-door to the stairs is open, I saw it.' Wendy's words drifted in and out of earshot, echoing through Joseph's skull. '*Down*, Joseph, that's the way out.'

'What are you talking about?'

'You want to get out, don't you?'

'I have to get to a hospital. I need help.'

'Then you need to move.'

'I need help,' Joseph said again. He could barely hear the words he spoke, his mind drifting in delirious circles.

'You need to move from the path.'

'The path?'

'Let's go, Joseph.'

'I need to move,' Joe said, his vision fading to black.

He spun on the stool and felt his eyes become flooded by warm, orange light, reflecting off a wall of bottles. His nostrils were engulfed with the smell of cigarettes and booze. The sound of thunder and heavy breathing was drowned out by lively chatter and clinking glass.

Looking around with the grace of a half-broken bobblehead, Joe realized he was in a bar. A familiar bar at that, although one he had only visited once. He felt something snaking around his waist and he looked down to see a hand sliding over the wool of his slacks. Fingers with painted, magenta nails crawled over his thighs to the increasing bulge at his crotch. The bones in the hand were popping out of place and rolling back again in sickening, circular motions, but still his cock grew harder in anticipation.

'Hey,' someone had dropped onto the stool beside Joe, somehow oblivious to what was going on below.

'Yeah?' Joe replied. He was once again a passenger in a conversation from long ago. A conversation he had replayed in his mind a thousand times already.

Zzzp!

The hands below had loosened his belt and now opened his pants, exposing the base of his pulsing shaft. A face had also come into view now, eyes bulging and freckled with broken blood cells. Her jaw was hanging lazily—like a snake that had unhinged its jaw for a meal—and her enormous, perfectly round breasts were completely exposed. Joe looked down at Wendy through the fog of intoxicated arousal and willed her to continue. He soaked in every inch of her bare chest that rose and fell with each frantic breath. Somewhere inside his mind, somewhere deep, Joseph was screaming. The creature that clamped its tongue around his cock was inhuman and he knew it meant harm, but still he talked.

'What's your name?' said the young woman beside Joe, her eyes not shifting for a single second to the bobbing, blonde head just inches from her knee.

'Joseph R. Ridley,' he grunted, successfully managing a glance at the girl before returning to his whiskey.

He bit his lip, gripping the glass tighter with every stroke Wendy gave. The girl beside him could have been no younger than eighteen and no older than twenty-two, presumably a student at the college down the street. Her hair was an unnatural shade of black, framing a pointed but delicate face. Everything about her—from her generously exposed cleavage to her full, supple lips and freckle-less cheeks—was as far from his wife as he could imagine. This girl was the fucking anti-Pam, and it made his member as hard then as it was now.

'My name is Molly,' the girl said sweetly, grabbing one of Joe's bruised hands in hers without hesitation.

'Pleasure to meet you, Molly.'

They talked for a long time about nothing in particular, about five glasses worth of time. Still the manic pumping from Wendy, or what was once Wendy, continued. Joseph did not feel close to climax, but as time went on the erotic bliss turned to perpetual waves of indignant anticipation. Every time he looked down he saw those wild, bloodshot eyes staring back at him. His crotch was now soaked in a disgusting broth of spit, precum, and Wendy's blood. He could hear his own screams in his mind; he could feel himself fighting for control. Still she sucked, like a starved leech. Was this pleasure? *Could* this be pleasure? His body and his mind were out of sync. It was all wrong.

'So,' Molly said slowly, leaning forward with her cheek on her hand, 'does your wife know you're out at a college bar?' She cast a glance down at Joe's wedding band and raised an eyebrow.

He snorted, throwing back the last of his amber medicine.

'It's none of her fucking business where I am.'

'I was hoping you would say that,' Molly said softly, leaning in close to Joe.

Her small but perky breasts pressed into his arm and her breath kissed his ear.

'The thing is, I like older guys. Especially ones that I shouldn't.'

She slid a hand down Joe's chest and teased the skin below his belt with one twisting finger. Joe followed the hand down and caught Wendy's eyes again. He would have jumped, had he been able to. She was no longer buried between his legs; she was just staring up at him with the elastic mess leaking from her open mouth. She looked dead, head slack against the underside of the bar. But he knew she was not; she was still gripping his knees in her powerful, gaunt hands.

Suddenly Joseph felt his stool being wrenched backwards and he fell, for what felt like a lifetime, through the floor and every layer of earth beneath it.

BANG!

Joseph was pushed into the metal hood of his Maserati in hard, circular thrusts. He looked up to see the bouncing, B-cup breasts of Molly squeezed tight between his fists. She moaned with each roll of her hips and Joe felt himself pushing back into her.

'I bet your wife doesn't fuck you like this anymore,' Molly whispered through a moan, taking one of Joe's thumbs and wrapping her thick lips around it. She flicked the tip of his thumb with her tongue and bit down playfully.

Joe felt no control over his body; all the strings that tied his consciousness to his limbs were severed. In spite of that, he felt the sensations as true as he had that day outside the college bar. Perhaps even more now. Looking up at this girl, this young anti-Pam, Joe realized something that brought a dagger of shame through the middle of his chest.

He had never told Pam about this night, or this part of it at least, and he had always found it easy to forgive himself. All he needed were a few simple considerations.

I was drunk, way too drunk, can you blame me for having a drink or ten?

It didn't mean anything, it's the only time I've ever cheated.

I wasn't thinking of Pam, I wasn't thinking of anything.

But he knew now this wasn't true. He was thinking of Pam the entire time he fucked this college student; he was thinking of Pam as Molly rode him and he was thinking of Pam when he bent Molly over the cold, polished steel. He was not imagining he was having sex with Pam; he was only thinking about how she had *made* him do this.

Maybe if she stopped giving me that fucking look, I could be doing this to her instead of some random skank.

I know what she thinks of me, I know what she tells people.

I deserve this, after everything ... I deserve to be happy. I deserve to fuck someone who wants me.

Locked within the confines of his mind and forced to watch as a mere passenger, Joe was faced with one of the many truths he had kept trying to outrun. Pam needed him, and he was off using some poor kid as a sexual punching bag.

Molly and Joe finished in unison, although the sensation of orgasmic climax was saved on Joseph. He knew that was no accident. This pleasure was not deserved the once, let alone twice. His head rolled to the side, dotted by the few drops of rain that would be a precursor to an almighty storm. Through the alley window just a few feet away, Joe saw two women staring back. One was Wendy, still bare-chested and drooling, and the other was Pamela, tears streaking her tanned cheeks.

'Pam,' Joe wheezed, flailing a hand pathetically for his wife.

'Ugh, it's Molly, you douche.' The college student giggled, slapping Joseph's knee playfully and pulling her denim skirt back up her thighs.

Wendy was circling around Pamela now, pulling her into an embrace. Pam let loose a single, inaudible sob and the demonic creature holding her moved. It sunk its face to her neck and stroked the freckled skin with a disgustingly long tongue.

Joe felt his body roll off the hood of the car, once again like he was a living marionette. He turned to face Molly as she adjusted her top.

'I have to go,' he panted.

'Of course you do,' she said, smiling and rolling her eyes. '*Work* called you, right?'

The spit of rain turned into a light shower and Molly jumped back beneath the cover of an overhanging fire escape.

'I need to make something right,' Joe answered, not caring if the girl heard him or not. He cared even less if she understood.

He crouched down and picked up an old, rusted, crowbar. He turned it over in his hand and tried to blink away the drunken blur.

'Whatever, man,' he heard Molly say. Her words were followed promptly by the rapid, clop-clopping of her boots as she made her way out of the alley, presumably back to her friends at the bar.

Joe staggered after her, but not in pursuit. He knew where he was going; he'd done some searching earlier that day. He knew exactly where to find the man with the bright-red Range Rover.

Joseph woke with a start and immediately threw his battered arms in front of his face to shield himself from the heat. He was lying on his back in the middle of Wendy's apartment, with the stool collapsed beneath his legs. Orange light was illuminating the room in vicious snaps. Through the spaces between his fingers, he could see that just a few feet in front of him was Wendy, kneeling and staring. She was engulfed in an enormous, and blisteringly hot, flame that licked the ceiling and spread across the linoleum floor in blue rings. She did not scream or fight to put out the blaze; she just knelt there and watched as Joe crawled away in horror. The skin of the breasts that had so often sent Joe into a dick-tugging frenzy were now bubbling and peeling away in sick blotches of red that immediately curled over. Her skin had turned black, resembling the crust of volcanic magma, and her blonde hair was plucked away in a stinking waft of dense smoke. Every part of Wendy was being burned away, except for those unyielding, piercing eyes.

'I'm sorry,' Joseph gagged, burying his mouth into the skin of his elbow. 'I'm so sorry, I shouldn't– I shouldn't have come here.'

As soon as he spoke the words, Wendy imploded into a nauseating heap of burned flesh and charred bone. The fire spiraled upward as if in a rage. No longer feeling the intoxication or debilitating arousal, Joe sprinted for the door. He yanked on the handle desperately and felt the searing pain of glowing steel against his skin.

'Fuck!'

He looked around feverishly for something, anything, that could guard his hand from the blazing red knob. There was nothing, the room had become absolutely bare, save for the all-consuming fire that was creating a wall around him. The heat was so fierce now that he actually felt the impact of each wave against his skin, as hard as a punch.

'Okay,' Joe sobbed.

Tears fought to escape his eyes. He knew what he had to do, what the building *wanted* him to do. He reached down with his cut hand and gripped the handle with every finger. Despite all he had endured so far, in that moment, he was sure this hurt the most. He could feel his palm melting against the metal, and as he turned the handle he knew his skin was giving way.

'Aaargh!'

Joe screamed at the top of his lungs and swung his shoulder. He turned the knob and barged the door open in one sweeping, agonizing move. In an instant so quick that Joe thought he might have passed out, the flame and the heat were gone, snuffed from existence. He could hear a scream fading away behind him; he thought it sounded like Wendy.

I shouldn't have involved her. I shouldn't have gone in there.

The fire was gone, but something much worse followed Joseph into the hall.

'Where are you going, young man? We aren't finished, are we?'

Joe was sure that every drop of blood in his body had frozen. He felt glued to the carpet, paused in time. His heart felt so heavy that he feared it might drop through his stomach at any moment. That voice, those words … they were a blade that cut deeper than any other.

Don't, not this. Please.

Joseph launched himself away from Wendy's room and increased his pace, staggering toward his apartment door as quickly as his broken body would carry him. He heard the heavy thuds of boots, slow but close behind.

'Do not turn your back on me,' the voice called, each syllable curled with an increasing rage.

Joe stumbled forward, throwing his full weight forward with every dragging step.

No, no, no, no, no.

Of all the tortures, this one was truly unacceptable. He would *not* let this one take him.

'I said *get the fuck back here*,' the voice growled.

The boot falls were getting faster, to match Joe's pace. He heard something else, a sound that had haunted him for far too long—a belt being loosened, the slap of a heavy metal buckle against denim.

'Get back here!'

Joe broke into a run, ignoring every wailing fragment of his being that protested. The boot falls grew heavier and faster also. His pursuer was so close that he could feel their fingertips on the hair of his neck. As if to provide aid, his apartment door swung open and Joseph felt himself being plucked through the air and into its depths. As soon as he collided with the wall of his apartment's entry, the door slammed shut again, between him and his would-be attacker.

'Let me the fuck in there, you little shit,' he heard the voice yell. There was a pounding of a belt against the door and shaking of the handle.

'You don't lock these doors, you hear me!' The voice became low and demonic, each vowel echoed in a chorus of sub-human bass.

Joseph had felt powerless many times in his life, most notably these last few days, but nothing made him feel as helpless as that moment. The sound of the heavy, steel belt buckle rung through his mind, suffocating his thoughts.

Joe woke again in a gentle, but unnerving wash of static vibration. His eyes peeled apart, resisting against the coating of blood and toasted eyelash. The absolute silence of the room was almost as jarring as the storm had been, making him painfully aware of the pulsing in his head and the unnaturally heavy thumping of his heart against his chest.

'I've been here before,' the thin man hissed in his raspy voice. He towered over the bed and cast a tree-like silhouette onto Joseph's crumpled body. 'I remember everything.'

The stranger reached down and clasped one of Joseph's ankles in his disjointed, bony fingers.

'Don't touch me,' Joe groaned, kicking out pathetically with his other foot.

The pale man ignored him and turned to walk toward the window, dragging his victim behind him in slow, grinding steps. Something was different about the terrifying stranger; his flesh was ever so slightly plumped with muscle and fat; the bones were a little less detailed against the now pale, pink skin. The man's chest was a little fuller and his penis was now flaccid and swaying with each stride.

THUMP!

Joe fell onto the floor back first, his leg and ass still raised high. He slid across the floor, pulled behind the figure like a lifeless doll.

'It's nearly time.'

When they finally reached the fogged, moonlit window, the man dropped Joe's leg and gave him one last, blank stare. Then he turned and smacked his face into the glass with a sickening crunch.

'This way,' he gurgled through a mouthful of blood.

He swung his head back, enough to catch Joseph's horrified gaze with his, and brought it hammering back into the glass with another smash of bone and teeth. There was another sound that followed, only just audible over the wheezing breaths of the men in the room, a single crackle of glass splintering.

Joseph watched the naked man rearing back for another swing, elastic threads of blood trailing from the dark glass to his shattered nose. It was not watching this man, this creature, beat himself to a bloody pulp that made Joe's limbs freeze solid. What horrified him was the birthmark, just above the right buttock. It was shaped like a blotchy bird with its wings spread wide. He knew that mark better than anyone. He knew that mark because he had seen it in the mirror his entire life; this monstrous abomination that had stopped to tilt back in Joseph's direction … was Joseph.

Chapter
Seven

Always More

Joe woke a second before the—now completely incoherent—song started up for the day, hyper-aware of the moment the first note would play. All he could do was stare at the throbbing, slickly oozed ceiling above and exhale one long, jagged breath.

'I should be dead.'

It was the first thought that had come to mind, and now he reflected on it as casually as one would about where that last slice of pizza went. He didn't want to die, of course—the thought still elevated his pulse in an anxious flood of stress—but he knew he *should* be dead. He did not believe he deserved to be dead, but rather the injuries he had sustained, the pain and the hunger and the thirst, they should not be within the threshold of human ability. If he were not dead, something was keeping him alive, and somehow that scared him more.

Joe rolled onto his side, patiently awaiting whatever force would expel him from the fragile safety of his apartment and into the open, bleeding arms of whatever was next.

'Let me in!' the memory stung with the intensity of a cattle brand and Joseph hurtled into a sitting position. He immediately looked down at the scorched leather of his shoes.

Something caught his eye; a fresh, pristine packet of Silk Cut cigarettes were resting peacefully on the sagging birchwood of his bedside table. They were standing upright, beside the upturned photo of his wife and son.

'Hm,' he mused wearily with a weak shrug, 'don't mind if I do.'

He slid one of the slender, orange-tipped smokes from its sheath and studied it in an open palm. He had half-expected it to turn into a worm or a severed finger, but perhaps he had to put it in his mouth first.

'Screw it,' Joe snorted. He gave it a theatrical twirl before pinching it between his aching teeth.

'Would you mind?' he mumbled politely, raising an eyebrow and regarding the ceiling above him. On cue the end of the cigarette burst into a brilliant but small blue flame, before fading to a glowing red cherry.

No worm, no finger. Just pure orgasmic bliss as the familiar warmth crept down his throat and exploded from his nostrils in blue, wispy tendrils.

'Thanks.'

It felt weird to thank whatever it was that had given him the courtesy of a cigarette and a moment to sit. Perhaps it was the same force that was keeping him trapped in this godforsaken building, but it felt right, nonetheless.

I should be dead.

He wondered if the man he had crippled that stormy night thought the same thing. Beating him bloody while his back was turned had been easy enough when Joe was blinded by booze— and what he'd thought was after-fuck clarity. It hadn't been so easy seeing the man in the pajamas, cowering in his wheelchair.

I wish I was dead.

It was not his voice that echoed in his mind this time, it was Pam's. Deep inhale this time, so deep the smoke curled in his throat, begging to escape. Exhale, deep exhale. A tremendous crash of thunder and lightning ignited the darkness, highlighting the floating wisps before painting the room once again in blood-red shadow. The song finished in a fading slur of white noise and the monotone radio presenter erupted through at full volume.

'Day 5 in the storm, ladies and gents, and the big guy here is telling me that we're on the home stretch.'

Five days? Somehow it felt like it had been both much more and much less time than that.

'Don't get too comfy, though, because like my main man Keb' Mo' would say, the worst is yet to come.'

Joseph got to his feet delicately and shuffled toward the window, catching only one quick view of his reflection before another strike of lightning disappeared. His face was sagging and luminescent, only the skin beneath his eyes showing a shade above paper white. Strangely enough, he still looked better than he felt, for what little that was worth. He pressed his face to the glass, only now noticing a small web of thin cracks that wound outwards by a palm's width. Where before it had *felt* like the storm was tearing the building apart, Joe was now quite sure it was … in the most literal sense. Through the blur of wind-whipped rain he could see pieces of concrete and scaffolding rolling and pouncing across the street below, only narrowly missing the many stationary figures that stood there. A hundred people at least could be seen lingering just outside the building, each of them looking directly up at Joseph, unblinking and impassive. They were utterly unperturbed by the storm, and the debris. Why should they be bothered? Not a single piece of rubble or gust of wind touched a hair on their heads. Joseph stared back and pressed one of his bruised, bloody fingers to the glass, hoping the figures would be able to see him flipping them off. As if to illustrate his contempt, he flicked the now lifeless cigarette butt at the glass, leaving only a minuscule smear of ash in the cracks.

'I don't suppose you'd zap me a burger too?' Joe said, stuffing the rest of the smokes into his pocket.

Nothing. *Fuck it, was worth a try.*

He considered taking another go at drinking from the kitchen or bathroom sink, but the abomination that had once been apple remnants now covered most of that area in its black, slimy vines and oozing bile. The smell was suffocating enough from this distance and getting even a drop of that mysterious liquid on his skin seemed to run a very real risk of harm. Of course, there was only one way forward and Joe knew if he did not go toward it now, the storm would make him.

'The door is open, I saw it. Down, Joseph, that's the only way out.'

Joseph remembered Wendy's words, as clearly as if she were there beside him again. The building was keeping him here, in this nightmare.

Of course, he had tried to leave already, but every time he came close to escape, he was intercepted by a distraction or a threat.

'That's it, isn't it?' Joe said.

I have to get down, to the ground.

The building, the storm, or whatever it was that fed on his misery, desperately did not want him to reach the ground floor. That could only mean one thing; that was where freedom waited for him. If he could only get to that door, Joseph was sure he could leave to go find Pam. He could tell her everything, convince her he was sorry. They could be a family again. Pam would understand; she would know how sorry he was. She would know that this, *all* of this, could not be his fault. Joseph knew he had been weak, that he had failed his wife and his son, but what man or woman hadn't fallen before? Who could truly say they were never weak? If he could just tell her he was sorry …

Pam will know, we can be a family again.

'I know the way out.'

Thick, gelatinous sludge immediately exploded from Joseph's throat. It sprayed the moth-eaten, gray sheets of his bed in slime and what looked to be … *fur*. Before he could yell one of his favorite curses, another wave belched forward, wrenching his entire body and threatening to push his eyes from their sockets. He fell to his knees and solid objects collided with his tongue and teeth on the way out; casting a watery gaze downward, he saw small feet and sharp-looking bones. Something else was resting on top of the slush, writhing and squealing. What could not be mistaken as anything other than a half-digested yet living rat.

'Nuuh–' Joe managed to moan before another torrent surged forward, more painful than the last. He threw himself toward the apartment door and crawled.

Blargh. More bile, more squirming rodent meat. He could feel the hair bristle the inside of his throat and stick to the roof of his mouth.

Closer he crawled, swinging one shiny, glazed hand in front of the other.

URGBLUH *splash*. Squeal.

Using the coat rack as a crutch, Joseph dragged himself to his feet and painted the door in a final, torrential fountain of vomit. He wrenched it open and collapsed into the yellow wall of the hallway.

As soon as the door had slammed shut behind him, he felt the grip on his stomach loosen. All that was left was the nauseating flavor of decay and blood in the back of his throat. Before he had barely a moment to collect himself, he heard a scream. His fingers gripped weakly at the wall and his back went rigid. It was a woman's scream, sheer and dreadful, and much too close. The fire escape door was open; he could see a single shaft of fluorescent, white light stretched across the other end of the hall. That's where the scream had echoed from and Joseph began to limp toward it, clenching his teeth so tight that he worried they might shatter.

That's it, that's the way out.

'Help me!'

The scream seemed just slightly further off now, still reverberating out of the stairwell and into the hallway. It could be a trap, it likely was, but Joe's pace only quickened. He wasn't sure if he was moving toward the screams for help or the open door; either way he knew he was going toward *something*.

BANG!

The door in front of Joseph burst open—or perhaps it would be more accurate to say it burst *apart*—and sprayed the opposite wall in a shrapnel explosion of splintered wood. Joseph didn't stop lunging forward; he only slowed a mere fraction. Someone came stepping out into the hall just a few steps in front of him, three heads taller and four times as large around. Joseph had only seen this man twice before, but it was the type of person you don't forget. He knew him much better as the voice through the wall, yelling drunken, racist idioms about the concierge, the nurse, and anyone else who got in his way. He was vile then, but he was truly monstrous now. Every inch of skin was stretched and bulging over handfuls of fat; the man's complexion was greasy, unwashed and blotched with patches of dark blood bruises. What little hair was on the man's head was slicked down with sweat, and blood oozed from between his toes as he stepped further out onto the shards of timber. He was too tall, too big; no human could fill the hallway so completely. The large man bent forward and then snapped to the side in a grotesque, clicking jerk, staring at Joseph with challenging menace.

This neighbor had disgusted Joseph before; both times they had met he had been shirtless and clutching a bottle in his chubby, oily fingers, but now he was positively revolting. Dense chunks of paste were dripping from his swollen, blue lips and falling in clumps from his limp, hanging chin. His eyes were watery, red, and positively bursting from their sockets.

Joseph gave a yell as he weaved away from an outstretched hand and barged the round man with his shoulder. The gigantic figure toppled back into the depths of his stinking, storm-lit apartment. Joe managed to put a good amount of distance between them before he heard the neighbor rise again. With a furious roar the man began to chase Joseph with thunderous, quaking footsteps.

'Argh!' Joe screamed, falling to his knees.

Something had sent a blinding stab of pain through his foot; it arced through his leg and into the bottom of his back. Falling forwards with his hands outstretched, Joseph gasped.

The glass sliced into the already skewered palms of his hands as easily as a blade through water. He pulled back reflexively and tried not to look over his shoulder as the big man's booming strides drew closer. The floor between Joseph and the fire escape—which he could swear was further away now than it had been a moment ago—was buried beneath a thick layer of broken, blue glass. He looked down at his feet, leaking thick, almost black currents of blood into the curved base of a broken bottle.

Where the fuck are my shoes? I didn't take my shoes off … did I take my shoes off? No. Where the fuck–

His train of thought was cut short as he felt himself being lifted by the ankle. The big man had reached him.

'Mmm,' the neighbor moaned, hungrily eyeing the glaze of blood dripping over Joseph's heels.

Joe tried to pull himself free but every time he reached for a hold he was met with only more jagged glass. Before he could open his mouth to protest, the neighbor closed his demented jaw around Joseph's foot and began to drink the ooze with a frantic, lapping tongue.

It was disgusting to see, but more than that it felt like he was being sucked dry. Joseph could feel his energy, his life, being drained from the wound. His leg became numb in just seconds and he could feel a wave of cold creeping into his sternum.

'MmmMm,' the big man growled. He sounded like a dog with a bone, pushing the foot further into his mouth with curled, strong fingers.

'Stop!'

Joe grabbed a handful of glass and swung it with as much strength as he could muster directly into the man's thigh. There was a sickening spray of blood, both of their blood. The big man only flinched slightly, but enough for Joe to swing his other foot up and spin the neighbor's flaccid jaw with a wet *WHACK*. If the man had looked frightening before, he was horrific now. The jaw was still hanging limp, but now torn almost completely free of the skull; the lips were torn apart into bloody strings and the tongue rolled out over the yellowed teeth like a skinned eel.

Wasting no time, Joe crawled on hands and dragging feet. He refused to acknowledge the pain and would not look away from the square of light ahead. He would not let it move out of reach. He was making it to that fucking escape. Joe crawled frantically until his legs returned control in mechanical jerks, then he launched himself to his feet and ran. He heard the woman's scream again, further still but close enough to galvanize him into a full sprint. His knees threatened to buckle and surrender him to the blackened fingers at his neck, but he urged himself onward, blinking through the burning sweat in his eyes. He felt the girthy fingers snake into his collar and tighten their grip, but he was there now. With one almighty twist, he threw himself into the mercilessly cold, blue light of the stairwell and sent his attacker reeling with one well-placed swing of his elbow.

He tumbled violently down the steps and his head collided with the concrete landing of the next floor. He could only watch numbly as explosions of flashing white geometry blinded him, wave after crippling wave. As the ringing in his skull faded out, the incessant buzzing of the fluorescent lights above came in.

'Please God,' Joe found himself saying through cracked lips, 'please help me.'

Joseph was not a man of faith, even in his youth, but who else but God could help him now? He had prayed once as a child; he had prayed for the hand bathed in light to descend from the heavens and pluck him up. He prayed for it to take him somewhere safe, anywhere he would not feel so powerless. His prayer was never answered, so Joseph found his time was better spent saving himself.

'God does not cast a light on this peak.' The booming voice came from the top of the stairs that Joe had only just came crashing down. His sight returned just in time to see a slender silhouette slam the fire-escape door shut.

Standing was difficult, likely due to the myriad injuries he was miraculously tolerating, but also due to the returning sensation of hunger and thirst. He felt weaker than he had ever been. His stomach thrashed and screamed in violent protest. His throat felt constricted and dry, so dry he could exhale dust. He leaned against the stairwell's cold, blue handrail and cast a cautious glance over the edge. Concrete stairs spiraled down as far as the eye could see, fading into a black void and holding little promise of salvation. Little promise was more than enough.

I made it. I just have to get down there. Just go down, easy.

Joe began his descent, holding the rail firmly and throwing one foot after the other. He leaned forward and let gravity power him forward. Two rows of steps to each floor, ten floors to the bottom. He counted the steps out as he went, 'onetwothreefourfive,' moving as fast as his bleeding heels would allow.

Damnit, I'm thirsty.

Floor eight. Was it eight or was it seven? The peeling blue paint on the wall that had once been a number gave no clue and keeping count had become increasingly difficult. His stomach cramped in furious turns, making each step harder than the last.

I need water, some food. Fuck, what I would give for a box of wings. Damnit.

Onetwothreefourfive … six. No, four. Fourfivesix.

What floor am I on now? Eight, right? No, I was just on eight, which means … seven.

Step after step. Every footfall leaving in its wake a small pool of sticky, dark blood.

If I survive this I'm going to clean out the entire liquor store. Oh God, I could use a glass of whiskey right now.

Joe's desperation felt almost powerful enough to will the amber-filled glass into existence; he even thought for a moment he heard the clink of ice.

Down.

Down.

Each step indistinguishable from the last.

Down.

'Fivesixseven … fivesix … fuck.'

Down.

He had been climbing down for an hour now. No, he had been climbing down for twenty minutes. Perhaps thirty minutes. He had been descending for too long.

Joe feared that if he spoke his tongue might crumble to ash; he could feel the dry coarseness of each tastebud glued to the roof of his mouth.

'I have to be close now, I must be.' He bounced off of the wall as he turned to find more stairs, leaving a long, bloody handprint behind him.

Down.

Down.

I'm coming, I'm on my way.

Joseph staggered into the door of the next landing, paralyzed momentarily as he hyperventilated against the wood.

'A door?' He didn't remember passing any other doors.

That can't be right.

'I have to be close.'

Joe reached down and turned the handle.

I'll just check which floor I'm at, I won't go in.

The steel rattled as he pushed on it, refusing to open. He slammed his fist into the wood and reeled back in pain.

'Come on!' He turned and charged, lowering his shoulder and bracing.

THUD!

Joseph rebounded off the stone. The stone … He stared at the featureless, canvas of gray in disbelief. He had never seen a surface so solid and flat. There was no door. There was no door on the last landing either, or the one before. Joseph was sure of it.

He collapsed into the staircase handrail and pushed back a strand of filthy, damp hair. He pulled himself forward, rested his chin on the cold iron and looked down. His heart plummeted in his chest and he felt himself fall to the floor in a pathetic, weak mess. Should he have been surprised by what he saw? Perhaps not, but what little hope he had left for escape had tumbled into the dark below; Far, far below into the bottomless spiral of concrete and shadow.

Joseph had been descending the stairs for hours now, or days, he could not be sure. He had lost count of how many times he passed that same streak of a bloody handprint. The hair on his face felt thicker; the bones in his hands looked more visible against the skin. His hunger and his thirst had reached a relentless peak that he was sure could not get worse. It brought him onto the floor, shaking, and then back onto his feet just as slowly. Down and down he staggered, mind lost in that limbo between inebriated consciousness and restless absence.

Down.

Hungry.

Down.

Thirsty.

Down.

Joseph thought he saw another door but when he reached out, his fingers pressed into more flat stone. Sometimes he thought he heard the creak of hinges behind him; he thought he heard panicked breaths. There were no doors; there was only steps and walls. He considered making his way back up but only for a moment.

Down.

Down is the only way, the only way.

Had it been weeks now? The cut on his brow from falling into the stairwell was still fresh and wet.

I must be close.

There is no close.

Joseph thought perhaps he would turn the next corner and find himself standing at the center of the earth. He would enjoy the warmth before his body was snuffed out in blinding fire.

That would be wonderful.

Down.

Hungry.

Down.

Thirsty.

Down.

Joseph staggered into the door of the next landing, paralyzed momentarily as he hyperventilated against the wood.

'A door?' He didn't remember passing any other doors.

That can't be right.

'I have to be close.'

Joe reached down and turned the handle.

I'll just check which floor I'm at, I won't go in.

The steel rattled as he pushed on it, refusing to open. He slammed his fist into the wood and reeled back in pain. He lowered his shoulder to charge and stopped.

This— I did this. This happened already.

Down.

Down.

How long has it been now?

Shut up.

Why am I even still doing this?

Shut the fuck up.

Maybe if I lie right here, it'll let me die. Whatever it is will just let me die.

Shut the fuck up!

'Help! Help me *please!*'

Joseph came to a wobbly stop and turned to find another unremarkable door. He had heard the scream; he was sure of it. The scream he had heard just before—or a lifetime ago—in the level eleven hallway.

He peeled his lips apart and attempted a 'hello' but all that came out was a strained moan.

The scream pierced the silence again, echoing above, below, and from every gray, flat side. It had come from behind the door, as if the screamer's mouth had been pressed against the wood.

Joseph gave one last cautious glance at the steps layered below and then turned back to the door.

I should keep going, I must be nearly there.

What's the harm in taking a look?

I should keep going down ... or should I take a look?

Why not?

He leaned forward and grabbed the handle in a firm grip. The knob turned and pulled away from him as if someone had opened it from the other side. There was no one waiting there; there was only a pale white glow and the smell of long-forgotten dust. Joe wandered curiously into the dark, brushing the frame of the entrance with his fingertips. The only light was a soft luminescence cast down from an old, pull-chain light bulb, barely an inch from Joe's head. Everything outside the light was impossibly dark; he could feel the absence of space like one standing on a ledge. The door crept closed behind him, and he let it. He knew the rules now; he knew he would go where the building wanted him to. There was no other way; there was no way down.

As soon as the door clicked shut, Joseph felt the air stiffen and he knew the walls had come into their homes around him. He turned on the spot and felt papers shift beneath his feet. They crumpled and hissed on the wood. A foot from his face were the stacked, thin gaps of a closet door, layered from floor to low ceiling. He pushed on the door with a gentle shove and it did no more than groan in protest.

'That seems about right.'

Suddenly a light clacked on from the other side of the door and Joseph found himself a voyeur, looking in on a fancifully decorated room. He pressed his face against the wood, eyes darting from left to right. He became immediately aware that he recognized the ornate copper bowl on the hall table just a few feet away.

He remembered the hand-woven rug just below that trailed to a tall, glass-paneled door.

This is—

The door flew open and a man in an expensive, creased suit came stumbling in. His thick, black hair hung limply over his forehead, heavy with rain. His eyes wore a red glaze that only a full bottle of whiskey could deliver.

Another figure came into view, passing only a breath from the closet door and advancing on the drunk.

Joseph felt a familiar aroma fill his nostrils as they passed. It was a smell that filled his eyes with moisture and brought a sharp pain through the center of his chest. His wife had always used the same inexpensive perfume; it had been one of the few—more modest—luxuries that Joseph hadn't insisted they upgrade. He loved that smell: vanilla and jasmine.

'Pam,' Joe croaked, thrusting himself forward at the door and bouncing back twice as hard.

'What the *hell*, Joe?' she said. She was not talking to Joseph in the cupboard; she was talking to the Joseph that was steadying himself against a coat rack, fighting the urge to hiccup.

'Joseph,' she said again. She pulled her nightgown closer and flicked aside her long brown hair. You could see she had just brushed it, probably preparing for bed. Joe had always found that a strange thing to do before sleep; it had annoyed him even.

'Pam,' Joseph croaked again.

'Pam,' Drunk Joe groaned, 'don't start, please. I'm too fucking tired.'

'No shit,' she hissed, 'you're always tired. You're always like *this* now.'

'Pam, come on.'

'No, Joseph.' Her voice cracked; she was fighting back tears. Joseph didn't remember that part of this conversation. He did not remember much of this conversation at all; all their conversations had started to melt together.

'No. You said you wouldn't do this again, you promised.'

Drunk Joseph slammed a fist against the wall beside him, making both Pam and the man watching from the closet jump.

'Give me a fucking break, Pamela! I didn't really think—when I made that promise, I didn't think–' He bowed his head and banged his fist again, just a little softer this time. 'Just lay off.'

Pam seemed to think on this for a moment, and Joseph watched eagerly through the closet slats as she fidgeted with the knuckles of her right hand. He wanted to see her face so badly; he wanted to see her eyes find him.

'This isn't hard just for you, Joseph,' Pam finally said, firmly but with a measure of sympathy. 'You're needed now more than ever.'

'I don't care, Pamela,' Joe replied, shuddering under the weight of a violent hiccup. He stumbled forward and slid the rain-soaked jacket from his shoulders, throwing it lazily to the floor. 'I just don't care.'

'That's just great, Joseph,' Pam replied, her voice wavering again. 'I will see you tomorrow, or not.' She and Joseph both stepped away from each other, before Pam turned toward him again.

'Oh, by the way—'

'God fucking damnit, *what*?'

'I just thought you would be interested to know, the police called. It wasn't the gym teacher. They just had the same car.'

Drunk Joseph froze. He swayed just a little before steadying himself against the doorway to the next room. Joseph in the closet pushed his face further against the wood so as not to lose sight of either living memory.

'What?' Drunk Joe could barely be heard, his voice a breathless gasp.

'The teacher they were investigating, turns out he was with a football team when it happened. It wasn't him. So they're back to square one.'

'Oh God,' Drunk Joe groaned. 'Oh *God.*'

'What?' Pam said, concern infused in every syllable.

'Oh Jesus,' Joe said, before dashing forward and out of view. Pam flinched as if she might follow but stopped. She instead looked down at her trembling fists, still tightly clutching her gown.

Joseph, watching from between the wooden panels, blinked angrily at his tears and tried again to force the door open.

'Pam,' he yelled hoarsely.

His wife did not hear the rattling or the cries. She simply bent to pick up the wet jacket and stepped forward to hang it on the coat rack.

Joseph shook the door again before something new caught his eye. A monstrously large figure came creeping past the door, and Joe's eyes met the bulging, blood-speckled eyes of his obese neighbor. They only exchanged looks for a second before the large man stepped noisily toward the entry hall. Pamela was there, looking through the fogged glass, out into the rain. She somehow did not hear as the monstrous man approached.

'Oh no, oh *shit*.' Joe felt his chest seize up and his joints turn to steel.

'Pam,' he croaked breathlessly.

This didn't happen, this isn't what's meant to happen.

'Pam!' This time louder, much louder, every syllable a blade in his throat.

He's here for me, not her.

Joe unfroze and slammed his fists into the door. He kicked and punched and charged.

'Pam! Goddamnit, Pam—look out, Pam!'

The neighbor was close now, only a few steps away.

Joe looked around for something, anything, but was met with only more darkness. He reached out. He flailed and begged God, begged Jesus, begged the devil for help. He felt something. Cool, heavy glass. He lifted the bottle of wine and wasted not a single breath more before swinging backwards and bringing it crashing down against the door. The brittle wood blasted to pieces in an explosion of froth and splinters. Joe lurched forward into the hall and

199

saw Pam swing around in fright, her hands clutched to her chest.

'Joe?' She gasped, confused. Then she noticed the giant to her side and leapt backwards with a blood-curdling scream. Joe lunged forward but all the light was plucked from his sight. Once again, he felt the chilling silence of the void all around him; he felt the absence of space.

'Pam?' Joe stepped forward but found that his foot had landed in the same place he had lifted it from.

'Pam?' It was a sob now, a dry, hopeless, utterly despairing sob.

'Don't worry, dear.' Another voice, soft and ethereal, pierced the impossible quiet. It chilled Joseph to his core.

No, please.

'Shush, my dear.' The voice echoed from his left, his right, below him, above. 'Don't worry, young man, let me take care of you.'

Clink. The sound of a metal clasp snapping open and slapping against denim.

'Fuck this,' Joe grunted, flinging himself into the void and feeling his shoulder collide with a tall, hard surface.

The door instantly gave way and he found himself toppling into the faint, but welcoming, glow of a familiar apartment corridor. He dragged his face from the stiff blue carpet and looked up to find those cursed yellow walls. Even though his vision was swimming, he knew they were closer to each other now. The ceiling and the walls were pressing in on him, constraining the air and making the breath in his lungs feel used, and rancid. He could hear the faint hum of wind and hail tearing the outside world apart, but he could *feel* its power. He felt the threat of its furious rage coursing through every fiber of the nylon flooring that pressed into his cheek. He didn't move; he did not care to. He saw his apartment door at the end of the hall. He knew it was waiting for him to come home.

Joseph lay on that patch of carpet for what might have been a day, just as it might have been a minute. Time had a way of operating in a different realm for those who no longer counted their seconds, past or future.

A presence filled the space behind Joseph's head; he could feel it. His senses sparked the hairs on his neck erect. Still, he did not move.

'We aren't quite there yet,' said the voice. It was low, hushed. 'The great fall is soon, so very soon.'

A scream scattered the fog in Joseph's mind, the same scream he had been hearing all day.

Days?

He watched as a woman came lunging out of one of the rooms and crashed into the opposite wall, barely ten feet from his nose.

'Help, oh God, help,' she cried frantically, barely a solid breath behind one word. She had not yet seen the man lying motionless and watching through weary, tear-filled eyes.

She spotted Joseph's door ajar at the end of the hall and began limping for it, dragging a twisted, blood-soaked foot in her wake.

'Hey,' Joseph muttered weakly. He rolled onto his elbows and rocked himself forward. 'Hey!'

The woman stopped for just a second, enough time to turn and see the large man barreling clumsily into the wall behind her. Her eyes were panicked and bloodshot, and her hair reached out in almost every direction, creating a mane of bright red.

'Stay the fuck away from me,' she squealed, increasing her pace.

'Damnit, I'm not trying to hurt you.' Joseph followed. He was stumbling and weak but gained ground easily on the woman with the crushed foot.

She did not hear a word he said above the *thud fffft* of her run and the painfully violent beats of her heart against its cage. She would not have listened if she had.

She finally reached Joseph's door and swung herself through, using the door frame for momentum. Before she could rally herself to block his entry, Joseph had followed her in and pushed the door aside with such force that it shook the decaying, blackened walls.

She screamed again and swung at Joe, catching his right cheek with a sharp, splintered fingernail.

'*Shit!*' Joseph swung his hand and knocked her aside. The stranger squealed and tumbled onto his pile of unfinished IKEA furniture. He watched as she howled and pulled her convulsing, deformed foot to her lap.

'Please don't kill me, please,' she whimpered, tears carving filthy trails down her blood-spattered cheeks.

Her lips were peeled back over red gums and there were gaps where teeth should have been.

Her eyes twitched as she blinked through the shock. This was not the fear that you would see in a movie; such a desperate will to live could not be learned or made pretend. This was not the fear you would see on a patient hearing a terminal diagnosis, quiet and dizzying. This woman believed she was about to die, right now, and every cell in her body was screaming to the universe for help.

'I'm not going to hurt you, damnit,' Joe said, clutching his ribs and falling back against the wall.

The woman's expression didn't change; he could not be sure she even heard him.

'Please don't kill me,' she said again, softer now.

'I'm not–' Joe snapped, his frustration tipping over. The woman had not broken his stare, not even for a second, and he could see his pain reflected in hers. He knew this woman on a level most could not know anyone, and they had never met.

'I'm not trying to hurt you,' he said with an exhausted sigh. He slid down the wall onto his bruised ass and watched as the door moved, ever so slightly, in its frame. The door was swinging backwards and forwards, no more than an inch at a time, as if gesturing at him.

Joseph looked back to the woman and could see her face had relaxed a little, but she was still shaking viciously and groping at the bloody mess of bone and skin at the base of her leg. He had seen what people here became, what they always became. She was whimpering, her lips trembling. He looked from her to the door, and kicked it closed.

Chapter
Eight

Both Alone, Together

They did not speak for quite some time, sharing only a momentary—albeit, uneasy—rest between them as the storm bashed and begged to come inside. Every catastrophic explosion of thunder sounded as if God himself had fallen wounded.

The woman shifted further back into the wall, but still her eyes wore frenzied panic.

Joseph could see the storm now for what it was, or what he believed it was. The storm was turbulence, tailored just for him. It was unrest. The storm was a reminder that though he might be shut away here, he was never truly safe, not while his living memories stalked the Penrose labyrinth of horrors just outside that door. This was *his* storm; he felt its sentience on him. *Within* him. Most unusual of all, he felt that this woman may be thinking the same.

Joe breathed deeply, allowing himself to look away from the strange woman and glance around at what had become of his shitty, cozy home. His bed looked like it had been dragged from an abandoned asylum, the sheets were dusted with mold and long-dead moths. The roof now sagged so ominously that Joe was sure his head would brush it at the center. He did not need to see the kitchen to know what waited for him there. He could smell it. It was decay, invasive and violent. He imagined that the rotting apple was now a living being, a central mind connecting each of those disgusting, menacing arms of filth and rot. Everything was enhanced to its terrifying potential by the crimson glow of the outside sky and the occasional flash of earth-piercing lightning.

'Why don't you just kill me?'

He might have missed it amidst the hammering of rain against glass, but Joseph had been waiting anxiously for the woman to speak.

'I'm not one of them,' he replied.

'They never are, until they are.'

Joseph couldn't help but chuckle. Wendy had said the same thing.

'Yeah. Yeah I guess that's true.'

They sat in silence for a while more, breathing through the pain almost in unison. Breathing through the anguish.

'I'd get you some ice for that foot,' Joe said, a little louder now, 'but– well, y'know.'

'I'm not sure I feel it anymore.'

'Enjoy it while it lasts. This place—' Joe waved a finger toward the door, 'it won't let you forget for too long.'

'What the fuck *is* this? Why is this happening?'

The woman was visibly calmer. Her eyes fluttered and rarely came to a stop, but she was searching Joseph as a man now, rather than a beast.

'If I knew, I probably wouldn't be here.'

'I saw things— I saw things that aren't possible.'

'Yeah, there's—'

'I saw *impossible* things.'

'I get it.'

Joseph realized he was becoming agitated by this woman; her panic was infectious, and it put him on edge.

'I haven't eaten; they did things to me. I— The things they did, I should be dead,' she said.

'I fucking *know* what they do.' Joseph waved the tattered, blood-soaked sleeve of his arm to illustrate his words. He felt himself getting hot in the face, but something in the way she recoiled in fright made him slacken.

'I know, the things here …' Joseph sighed and swallowed the knot in his throat, 'they shouldn't be. I don't–' The knot came rising again, choking each syllable he searched for. 'I don't want to believe what I saw, but I remember. I remember it all. *God*, I don't want to see what comes next.'

The woman did not need to speak for Joseph to understand, for them both to understand, this was something they were both living.

'What's your name?'

'Taylor D.'

'Your foot—is there anything I can–'

'I told you, I can't even feel it anymore. I can't feel much.'

'I haven't seen you here before. You live in the building?'

'Top floor. I came down the stairs and next thing I know I'm …,' Taylor paused a moment to wipe the sweat from her eyes, 'I'm somewhere else. I could go for a fucking smoke right about now.'

Joseph was about to agree before remembering the somewhat fresh pack of Silk Cuts in his breast pocket.

'I think I might be able to help with that,' he said with a weak chuckle.

She watched in hungry disbelief as Joe withdrew the packet from his jacket and smacked it against his palm. He tossed one into Taylor's grimy lap and grabbed another between his teeth.

'You might find a lighter in that mess behind you.'

'No need,' Taylor wheezed. She flashed a silver object in her hand and snapped it open with a satisfying click.

'That's lucky,' Joe mused, watching as the woman threw her head back and enjoyed the smoke coursing through her bruised throat. She tossed the zippo lighter over to him and gave him a stare that was as close to calm as he had seen yet.

'It was my daddy's. He never left home without it.'

Joseph lit his own cigarette and slid the lighter back, being careful to avoid her foot.

'I used to have something like that,' he said. 'This dirty little piece of string my son gave me. It had a paper clip hanging off it, a little gold one.'

'Your son?'

'He thought it was the only gold paper clip in the world, and he gave it to me.'

Joe blinked through heavy tears. He pushed the cigarette firmly into his quivering lips.

'I'd wear the fuckin thing every day, around my wrist. Then …,' he paused, looking down at his feet and flicking a long, curved tail of ash from the cherry of his smoke, 'Well, one day I just threw the damn thing out, didn't I? A grown man can't be wearing string and paper clips. Not *this* guy.' Joseph angrily stamped his cigarette into the floor and wiped his eyes with the back of his hand.

'Hmm.' Taylor drew the last of the life from her cigarette, savoring every wisp of blue smoke until the red tip faded to black. There was little trace of sympathy in her face, but Joseph found something notably more comforting: understanding.

'Tell you what,' he said, giving the pack of Silk Cuts a shake. 'Tell me your deal and I'll give you another one of these.'

Taylor reclined further into the wall, wincing a little as she moved her foot and then closed her eyes. Smoke dripped from her nostrils in gentle, reaching wisps and her hand trembled as she brought the cigarette to rest on her thigh.

'I didn't always live in this place—this building I mean. I used to live in a house. Six bedrooms, four bathrooms, I shit you *not*. I didn't much think it mattered till I came here. I'll tell you something, mister, you can hang as many expensive paintings as you want, but six walls still feel like you're living in a coffin. It feels like a damn *casket* when you lose what I had.

'My house was down on the riverside of Dawn Valley—you know the place, where all the pompous twits live. I guess I was one of them. Me and Mike, that's my husband … Michael. We lived there, just the two of us. He kept the books for one of these places in the city, I can never remember which one. I worked downtown, helping to acquire new artwork from up-and-comers for the gallery, across from Star Park. Let me tell you something else– uh–'

'Joe.'

'Joe, the world of fine art is total bullshit. You want to know what the secret is to knowing which will sell?'

Joseph didn't say a word; he just smoked and watched. Exhale, nod, inhale.

'It's whichever one we put the highest *fucking* price on.' Taylor laughed, wheezing and hysterical. Joe couldn't help but wonder what she had seen these past few days. What had the storm shown her?

'The people who got to hang their work on the wall were the ones who played ball. Talent didn't fucking matter, not even a little bit. It never does.'

She sniffed hard. She wiped more snot and blood from her nose and took another deep draw on the smoke.

'Who cares, right? Everybody wins. That's what we would say, day after day. Everybody wins.

'Well, one day I come home to find my dear husband had invited his brother to live with us. *Rolph*. Real do-nothing kind of guy. The place was big enough that we wouldn't see him much, but you could always feel him there. It wasn't a big house for a wife and husband anymore; it was a big house for a married couple and a jobless, sackless brother. Sometimes I would see him skulking around when my husband was still at work. *Lucky guy, that brother of mine. Lucky guy.* I can't tell you how sick I was of hearing that.'

Taylor groaned as she shifted her weight from one side to the other, moving her twisted foot further to her side.

'Me and Mike were trying to have a baby at the time. Shit, we were trying to have a baby for years.

'We must have fucked against every wall and on every flat surface in that entire goddamned house. I could barely stand most days at the gallery.' Something of a smile flittered across Taylor's lips, and then it was gone.

'I think it was Mike who said we should see someone, a professional I mean. I didn't want to, because I knew how much he wanted a baby. If I couldn't give him that, I– I just thought he might not … It wasn't me. We saw the specialist and they said I was actually pretty fertile for my age, but Mike, they said he– he was so crushed. Jesus, I never saw him cry like that before … my Mike.'

Joseph did not speak as his guest broke down. She pressed her face into her palms and shook with wailing, uncontrollable sobs. He watched and fought the ache he felt for her, until she began to speak again.

'I was angry. I wanted a baby too, you know, so bad. This woman I worked with had a baby, a beautiful little girl. She would bring her into the gallery on a slow day and you should have seen how everyone would crowd around her. You would think she'd just rescued the thing from a car wreck, the way people spoke about her. She wasn't just Nancy the floor coordinator anymore, she was Nancy the *mom*. You have to understand, I was *meant* to be a mom, since I was a girl. I had the dolls and the nappies and everything. Mike started talking about adoption, but I knew what people would say. What they would think. I wanted my own baby and my husband couldn't give me that. I thought it was his fault. Please understand I was so *angry*.'

Joe knew it was coming; what he had been waiting for. She was about to give him what the raging storm hungered for, the confession.

'I was angry, so one night he was out late and I– oh fuck, I went upstairs to Rolph's room. I went to Rolph.' Taylor ripped another smoke from the packet and sparked it with furiously trembling hands.

'I didn't think it would actually– It was just a stupid one-off, but then about a month later I got sick. I mean I thought I was sick, but I–'

'Pregnant.'

'Yes.' Taylor cried again, collecting herself quicker each time. 'I was *scared*, please know that. Mike never hurt me, *ever*, but I knew he wouldn't want me anymore if he found out. I waited as long as I could, but then it got too obvious. My stomach poked out like I'd swallowed a fucking bass drum.

One day we were both off work, so we went to the pier. It was our favorite spot. We would watch the people walk on by and we'd tell each other stories about them. These complete strangers. We didn't know these fucking people, but I think it felt nice to be creative. Just for a bit. Mike's good at it, better than me; he would say the most unexpected things. I always told him in another life he would have been a great writer, but he isn't as good with words as he is with numbers. When it comes to the page I mean. Anyway, I knew I had to show him my stomach, he was starting to ask about the baggy sweaters. He doesn't know much about fashion that man, bless him, but he's not dumb.

'He– *Jesus* he thought so highly of me that he actually thought it was his. The doctor told him we couldn't– that is that his– the point is he thought it was more likely that we had been granted a miracle than I had cheated. He was crying, right there on the boardwalk. He got on his knees and he was kissing my stomach. He was thanking God. He kept saying how happy he was. I wanted to keep letting him believe that. Christ, it would have been so easy.'

Taylor sniffed quietly, licking at her stained teeth with a pointed tongue.

'I didn't say anything, I just couldn't. I was so scared. I knew Rolph would know. I knew that fucking idiot would tell Mike and ruin everything. Mike told Rolph about the baby less than a week later. He was so excited he just couldn't wait, even though I begged him not to. The way Rolph looked at me when he found out, I– I didn't think I'd be able to breathe ever again. He was going to ruin everything; I knew he was going to ruin *everything*. I had to do something, you know? I thought if it looked savage enough– I thought– I thought if I was smart, it could look like a robbery gone wrong.'

Joseph rolled his jaw, twisting the cigarette between his index and ring finger. This woman, this stranger, did not need to say much for him to remember that feeling of pure, all-consuming desperation.

'I almost did it, you know.' Taylor gave a single weak wheeze that might have been a laugh. 'I was right there in his room with a knife in my fucking hand. He had no idea. Nothing wakes a man who snores like that. I had the knife right up to his neck and all I could think about was raising a baby with Mike, just us, like it should be. But … I couldn't do it. I just– I just couldn't. I was scared, I didn't want to have a baby in jail. I didn't want Mike to– I didn't want him to hate me, you know.'

Taylor looked around the dilapidated room and her lips stretched to form a weak smile, as if to illustrate her understanding of the irony she now bathed in.

'I knew Rolph was going to tell Mike, probably that day. He was going to tell him. I couldn't breathe. *God,* I was scared. I didn't let Mike leave bed that morning, not until I told him–' She bit her lip so hard that a cut on her chin re-opened. Taylor was reaching for these next few words. Her mind was stretching down with clasping, clawing hands, willing her to expose the truth.

'I mean I couldn't tell him the full truth, I– I told him Rolph *forced* himself on me.'

There was a pause between the two in that moment, a calm amongst the thunderous roars of the storm. She was searching Joe's eyes for that familiar, judging disdain that she so often imagined in her peers. She did not find sympathy. She found something far more comforting: understanding.

'It was bad after that. Mike was so angry. I'd never seen him angry. I've never seen him *so* angry.' Taylor flinched a little reflecting on this, as if she had heard her husband's yell. She quickly glanced at the door again. Living memories were waiting for them both; she and Joseph knew this.

'He hurt Rolph—bad. I don't think he meant to. He just lost control. I tried to stop him. I did, I swear, but Rolph fell down the stairs. I saw Mike– I saw him crying. He was angry, but he was so scared of what he'd done.'

The woman sunk her face into her hands again and said almost too softly to hear, 'What *I* did.'

She seemed determined to finish her story now, as if it could in some way absolve her, or perhaps just ease her burden.

'Rolph was at the hospital for a while, and when he came out they– well, they said he had suffered some kind of brain trauma. I thought maybe it was just that he had trouble speaking and walking again, but you could see it in his eyes, something was missing. Mike saw it too. I know he was still angry, still hurting, but he loved Rolph. I felt horrible for a long time, I felt guilty. Then I guess I just felt tired. That wasn't the life I wanted.'

Joseph had ignited yet another cigarette when she stopped speaking and looked sharply at the window.

'Did you hear that?' she asked.

Joseph lifted an eyebrow incredulously and gestured toward the chaotic pelting at the glass.

'That? Yeah, I heard it.'

'No,' she whispered, her voice once again becoming laced with frantic concern. She looked down at her arm and dabbed at some watery blood pooling there. Her eyes searched the room a tenth time before finally relaxing a little and continuing her story.

'I couldn't take it anymore. I was angry at Mike for not taking Rolph to a home, and I was angry at the thing growing inside me. I hated it. I hated it for making me feel so sad and sick. When the baby came, I– I left it. I told the nurse I didn't want it. Jesus, I don't even know if I had a boy or a girl.

'That was it for me and Mike. I think he told me to leave after that. It was all just too much, I– I think I broke him. The truth is we never quite got back to where we were after the ra– ... after I slept with his brother.'

'And now you're here,' Joseph said simply.

'Now I'm here.'

Taylor's head snapped to the window again and her face became painted with confused unease.

'I just ...' she trailed off, looking slowly around the room, and then down at her arms again. She shook them as if they were crawling with ants.

'I know if I ever make it out of here, I'm going to find Mike and make it right. I have to get my life back. I just ...' Taylor paused again, her head lolling back against the wall. Her face was glazed with thick beads of sweat and her skin was almost luminescent in the red gloom. 'I just don't know how much more I can take. I can't survive seven more days of this, I know I can't.'

'Seven days?'

'I think so, yeah. It almost seems like this fucking place won't let me forget how long it's been screwing with me.'

'Seven,' Joe mumbled, quieter now and more to himself than his guest.

Somehow, he was certain that it had been both much longer than, but also not quite, seven days since the storm began. This room, these rooms, operated outside of time—and shit, probably space too. Every step, move or breath felt like it had been before and after the next. But they weren't, that was impossible.

Am I mad? This isn't– this can't be real, right? This pain is real.

This pain can't be real?

Joseph watched the bleeding, crippled woman across from him, wheezing and drifting in and out of consciousness. He felt no sympathy, but he felt something looking at her. Satisfaction?

Better her than me.

No. He did not want her pain, but he wished he could take it away all the same. He saw his hand raise a crowbar high into the air and bring it crashing down on and through her skull. He saw the blood and gore on his hands, he felt it on his skin. He could end her suffering in an instant; it would be so easy. No. There she sat, taking long, tattered breaths. For now, he could give her what little shelter he had. Maybe a few more Silk Cuts too.

'There has to be a way out,' Joseph said.

'Yeah, I think there is, but getting to it is a whole other story.' Taylor looked across at Joseph with groggy eyes. 'It's all the way down.'

'I tried to get there, down the stairs. They just went on forever.'

'I nearly made it.'

'What?'

'I was there, in the lobby. The doors were just a few fucking steps away.'

Joseph leaned forward, narrowing his eyes and pulling the cigarette from his lips.

'What happened?'

'That's the thing, I don't remember how I got there. I was—' Taylor paused, clawing nervously at the tangles of hair above her ear. 'I was watching something … a memory. I couldn't do anything, no matter how hard I tried. I screamed and yelled, and then this thing *helped* me. It looked like me. I've been seeing it follow me around the last few days.'

Flashes filled Joseph's mind, images of his decrepit doppelgänger bashing its face against the glass.

'It pushed me, and next thing I know I changed it.'

'Changed what?'

'The memory, I changed it. As soon as I did, I blacked out. When I came to, I was lying on the floor downstairs and it felt like someone had hit me with their car.'

'So why didn't you get out?'

'I tried, Joe. Don't you think that was the first fucking thing I tried? I got close, like I said, but he stopped me.'

'Who?'

'That big son of a bitch, the security guard.'

The square-jawed security guard, Rick, with fists like bricks seemed a lot less threatening after the past week.

'I was so damn close,' Taylor said through a choked sob. 'He came out with his jaw hanging, talking about how he was gonna smash my head in and fuck my dead body. I only just got away, thanks to that kid. After the big bastard already smashed my foot of c—'

'Wait,' Joseph said. His heart was racing, each pulse a painful thump. 'What kid?'

'That young kid who looks after the front desk, bless him. He tried to pull me inside his flat, but I freaked and went through another door. Next thing I know I'm running down a hallway, being chased by *you*.'

'He's still down there?'

'The security psycho? I would say so.'

'I meant the kid.'

'Oh … yeah.' Genuine sorrow swept over Taylor's face. 'I hope he's okay.'

'We're going to get out,' Joseph said, shuffling forward and resting a hand on Taylor's. She flinched but turned her hand and held Joe's tightly. 'I promise, okay? We'll get downstairs, find the kid, and get the fuck out of here. Together.'

The woman smiled, tears swelling in her eyes.

'Thank y–'

Suddenly, Taylor dropped Joseph's hand and scurried back against the wall like a startled possum.

'What the fuck?' she screeched. She launched clumsily to her one good foot and turned her head sharply and blindly around the room.

'What the *fuck*!'

'Taylor! What's the problem?' Joe had spat out his cigarette and was on his feet too now. He held out his arms cautiously and stepped just a bit closer to the crazed woman.

'No. No, no,' she yelled. She slapped her hands to her ears and screamed.

'I'm right here, Taylor, talk to me!'

The room became utter anarchy in a matter of seconds, the screams and the furious, protesting roars of the storm rendering Joe deaf. The radio too had joined in the racket. It blasted some warped version of what—under different circumstances—might have been an upbeat folk tune.

Well it's all right, every day is Judgement Day

'Help me, *please*!' Taylor screamed.

Joseph lunged forward. He grabbed the woman by the shoulders and tried with all his strength to pull her toward him. She could not have weighed more than sixty kilos, but something was violently pulling her away. He could feel her joints shifting in his hands as the invisible force pulled and tugged from beyond their realm.

Well it's all right, if you've got someone to love

Her skin was wet and cold, *impossibly* cold. Joe's wounded hand retracted before he could stop himself and he felt Taylor arch further toward the window. She was being pulled closer to the howls and the threatening arcs of lightning beyond. Her spine was bending at a horrific, unnatural angle now and it looked as though her shoulders might tear free from the flesh. Her screams were inhuman.

'I've got you. Don't let go!'

Well it's all right, we're going to the end of the line

Her eyes were wide and desperate.

CRACK!

Her left shoulder swung backwards, twisting her spine even more. A flash of lightning illuminated shards of glistening, red bone, poking from every joint. Blood spat from Taylor's mouth in thick strands and still she screamed. Joseph flailed his free hand, reaching desperately but unable to close the distance.

'Taylor! Reach for me!' She was already lost; he knew it was too late.

With a final, sickening crunch, Joseph watched helplessly as Taylor was ripped from his fist. She was plucked through the blackened, red space of the apartment and through the glass. It did not break, she simply passed through it. The storm had claimed her. The last thing Joseph saw was Taylor's terrified, feral-eyed face vanish into the wind and rain.

Those bullshit movies probably wouldn't show you what it's like to be a father, what it's really like. What it's really like for me. I'm sorry but it's– it's bullshit, right? These people, they stop seeing you for all your hard work. All the money, the power, they forget about all that shit. It's all about the fucking kid after that.

'Congratulations, you should be so proud.'

'What a beautiful baby boy. You and Pamela have done a fantastic job.'

They underestimate me when I go into the office now. I see it. It's different when you're a dad. You even see the jealousy leave some people's eyes. The smug sons of bitches stop wishing they were you. They want to be the guy with the forty-three-hundred-dollar suit, but not the guy with a baby seat in his fucking Maserati.

Of course I have love for my son too, what kind of stupid question is that? This counseling stuff is horseshit, I'm sorry.

All right look, it's not a feeling I'm used to, when I'm with Marky I mean. Makes me feel vulnerable, makes me feel guilty for being so ungrateful. Then I end up hating being around the kid *because* I end up feeling guilty. People just don't get it, being a father isn't what you think. That answer your question?

Marcus, please forgive me.

Chapter
Nine

Only the Best

It was impossible to know how much rest Joseph had been allowed this time. *Rest* seemed like a generous word; his brain was still on fire, his body ached. He woke again to the distorted groans of what was once that jazzy Annette Hanshaw song. Rest was not the right word. He could not rest, not anymore.

Joseph rose calmly from the bed and glided through the room to stand at the window. He watched as rubble larger than semi-trailers rocketed through the air and crashed into the street, tossed about by the violent gale. The ominous, blank-faced voyeurs were still crowded by the entrance to the building, far below; there were legions of them now, dotted across every visible inch of asphalt. Each one of them was looking up at him, the man on the eleventh floor. Only a week ago Joseph could never have imagined this. The glowing crimson clouds were domed with a web of blue and white lightning that convulsed and flashed. The thunder and roaring wind were now so thickly layered that they swallowed all other noise and shook the building's foundations. It was a deafening, all-consuming white noise.

The rotting, weeping walls of the room didn't sting his nostrils quite so much anymore. The threatening creaks of the ceiling didn't make his heart race—not like they used to.

What would it mean to die here? Would his mind fade away into the void? Nothing, no one, nowhere ever again? Maybe he was already dead, condemned to this torment day after day for the rest of time. Eternal suffering in the most biblical sense. Joseph pondered on this and decided that he was not sure which he would prefer.

Joseph raised one of his bloody fingers and pressed a nail into the cracks of the glass, curiously picking at the edges. He could feel the building vibrating with the power of the storm, and he believed the floor would soon collapse beneath him. That is if the ceiling did not give out first. He imagined a cascade of black, freezing water, filling his lungs and crushing him against the wall.

'I'm sorry,' he found himself saying.

He breathed deeply as he investigated the tempest outside. He could not see Taylor's face anymore, but he could still feel her calls for help bouncing around his mind. Joseph could not go out like that. So much left unsaid, so much left undone. Wrongs that were not made right. That's how they would remember him, how *everyone* would remember him. Whether this was madness or the hell that it appeared to be, Joe knew he had to survive long enough to be heard outside this place. Not madness, *no*. This was beyond him; this storm had will, influence, and a ravenous hunger. How could he be heard if he died here? Would his soul be torn around in the wind outside, pulled limb from ethereal limb, over and over again for eternity? Would he see Taylor there? Perhaps he would drift into that parasitic, creeping void. Nothing left for him, nothing left *of* him. No light, no darkness, no sound or touch. No thought, just … nothing. Joseph could not be sure which was worse, but he knew neither could be made true until he made himself heard. He *had* to find a way to be heard.

'She said she changed it.'

He plucked his finger from the split glass and stepped backwards.

'Those cracks are real.'

Joseph reached behind him and gripped the back of his favorite armchair. He was fatigued and wounded, but with renewed energy he lifted the seat in both hands and launched it toward the window, as hard as he could physically manage. Just as he watched the chair blink out of existence in the dark, he felt it slide into place behind him again. The muffled racket that should have been music had died out now, and was replaced again with the placid, monotonous tones of Dawn Valley's least memorable radio DJ.

'Day six, ladies and gentlemen, can you believe that? We've been riding it out so far, and the guys back here tell me the storm might be on the way out. Don't get your hopes up, though, folks, they're also telling me that, like most things, this one may go out swingin.'

Joseph sighed deeply. He fell backwards into the chair that should have been a pile of splintered wood and fabric.

'I don't know about you guys, but I like these storms,' continued the radio host. 'Yessir, they have a way of washing away all the shit, mind my French. The storms blow through and yeah, they may leave a bit of a mess, but I tell you what, once you pick up the pieces the place ends up looking a fair dime better. But maybe that's just me, folks.'

'The great fall is soon, so very soon,' Joseph muttered to himself, remembering the words he had heard whispered into his ear. He sank deeper into the armchair, all feeling draining from his limbs. He was no longer just *running on fumes*; he was being dragged and the fumes were suffocating him.

'So what are *you*, Joseph?' called the radio host. 'Are you the crap to be washed away? I think you are.'

'Okay,' Joe said. He relinquished what control he had left. 'Show me then.'

He surrendered himself to the will of the storm, and with a whip-crack of sky-shattering thunder he felt himself fall through the floor.

The room melted back in around him, twice as dark as it had been before.

No, not a room. Am I–

Joseph's fingers clenched shut around the silky, leather steering wheel, so tightly his knuckles burned in protest. He felt his pupils focus in on the beam of light stretched out before him in a wide, bluish-white arc. One thing became immediately clear—he was driving down a stretch of featureless, midnight highway. Of course, it wasn't really *him* driving. Joseph pressed down on the accelerator a little more, coaxing the Maserati Ghibli to growl louder.

Was it him driving? He felt the absence of control—the familiar outer body distance between his mind and his body—but he also felt the desire, the hunger, to go faster, much, *much* faster. He wanted to race into that void beyond the light; he wanted to outrun the blacktop beneath the wheels ... and so, he pressed the accelerator again.

The interior of the car felt silent and still, a stark contrast to the roaring engine and howling winds just outside.

'Where do you want me to go?' was all Joseph could say. He did not dare to look away from the narrow road. Short stripes of white blinked in and out of the light and the wind pushed back on the sleek, cold steel of the car, as if it were pleading for him to stop.

You know where you're going, so drive.

He felt his adrenaline rise as the needle crawled further against the luminous, blue dashboard.

65 mph ... 70 mph ... 75 mph

The danger in each microscopic tilt of the wheels became increasingly evident. Joseph could no longer tell if it was his control, or lack of it, that scared him more. Perhaps dying this way would be better. If he were to be blinked from existence in an obliterating wipe-out, he would at least be spared from whatever was waiting for him at the end of this trip.

'I'm here. I told you to show me,' Joe said through clenched teeth, 'so fucking show me. What do you want me to see?'

More silence.

80 mph ... 85 mph

'What do you want me to see, goddamnit!'

Joseph's hands flinched and he felt his heart skip a beat as the car twitched, threatening to spin off of the road.

'Can you see me, Dad?'

Now Joseph's heart positively stopped; he could feel the crushing stillness in his chest.

'Dad?'

Joe let out a tattered sigh that might have been a sob and looked to the rear-view mirror. He knew what he would see, and yet there was still no way to prepare.

'Marcus?'

The boy's large hazel eyes looked back at him in the mirror from beneath a delicate fringe of black.

'Where are we going, Dad?' Marcus leaned forward a little in his seat, trying to see into the dark outside the headlights. 'Are we going home?'

'Marcus,' Joseph said again, breathlessly. He refused to look away from the mirror; he refused to let his son disappear.

'Dad?'

…

'Dad. You're driving really fast.'

Joseph looked back at the road and swung the wheel left. He had seen the headlights of another car, painting the interior of the Maserati in blinding, yellow light. As soon as he had seen it, it was gone, and by some miracle he managed to regain control before the back tires of his own car began to slide.

The boy squealed, sliding sideways in his seat and gripping the leather with his tiny fists.

'I'm sorry, Marcus, I'm sorry,' Joseph said. He felt a cold sweat on his face and the shakes had gotten much worse. 'I'll be more careful, I promise.'

'Why do you drive so fast?' Marcus' voice was laced with bitter indignation, the way a child might be when crossing their arms. 'Mom says it's really bad.'

Joseph motioned to ease off of the accelerator, but he found that he had no desire to do so.

'There's no point in driving a sports car, son, if you're better off with a Prius.'

Joseph didn't believe that; truth be told, he never had. It was just something he'd heard people say.

'Mom doesn't like it. She doesn't like me going in your car.'

The truth was that Joseph liked the feeling when the speedometer needle arched starboard and disaster was just one second away. He felt powerful being in control of that moment; he felt powerful when he put a cigarette in his mouth or when he locked the clasp on a TAG Heuer watch.

'Mom thinks you're going to drive us into a wall and spray the road with our brains. Is that what you're going to do, Dad?'

Joseph flashed a quick look back at the mirror and saw the eyes of his son locked firmly on his.

'Marcus, I– I don't know if this is real, but I'm sorry.'

'It's okay, Dad. I know Mom is just a scaredy-cat, like you said.'

'No, no, Marcus please. Please listen, I'm sorry. For all of it.'

100 mph

105 mph

'Mom says you spend too much money on stuff, but I don't mind. As far as I'm concerned that miserable bitch can keep crying into those nine-hundred-dollar sheets she wanted so bad.'

Joseph flinched. These were not his son's words, they were his. He remembered stuffing down the brick of guilt as he bragged to a co-worker about his new suit, and the complaints it had solicited from his wife.

'Marcus … Marky, Mom was right.'

'Huh?'

'She didn't want any of this.'

'Dad, but you–'

'I love you, son, and I'm so sorry.'

115 mph … 120 mph

Marcus' eyes glared back through the mirror, contorted and carved with inhuman rage. Something else was there now too, small but growing in size. Two small dots of light far behind them were advancing at a frightening pace, considering the speed they were already traveling at.

'You know what, Marcus?' Joseph's eyes were brimmed with tears and he searched the bulbous, blood-speckled ones in the mirror for some sign of his son.

'Back before you were born, must've been about twenty-something years now, me and your mom used to get around in this little shit-box of a car.'

He chuckled a little, genuine amusement mixed in with the sorrow.

'Old Buick it was. The thing could barely make it down the street without crapping a load of smoke all over the place. Your mom, though … Pam, she loved that thing. It was the car we *escaped* in, that's what she used to say. We would drive all over the damn country. I must have seen a hundred places I didn't give a shit about. I'd get annoyed and bored, but your mom would just keep driving. I'd complain and whinge like a damn kid, but I'd always feel better when we finished for the day. We would find a spot to set up the tent and sleep—she had a way of making it all seem worth it. Then the next day we would be up again, back on the road.'

130 mph … 135 mph

'She still thinks that we made you on the back seat of that damn car, but that's– well, don't worry about that. We had to settle down eventually, especially once you came along. We both got jobs and I'd beg her to let us sell the car, get an upgrade, you know. She wouldn't hear of it. Every time I mentioned the fucking thing she would just say, *No, Joseph, it's the only thing that we've kept.* I didn't think it was that serious really, not until I went ahead and sold the damn thing anyway.'

Joseph blinked away more tears and gave a weak chuckle.

'You know what's funny, Marky?'

Marcus, or the creature wearing his shape, was at Joseph's shoulder now; he could feel the hot, fractured breaths on his neck.

'I almost didn't go through with it. Not just because I felt bad for your mom, but I actually didn't want to give the guy the keys. Can you believe that? The guy was standing there with his hand out and I looked down at this piece of shit car … it was like I was seeing it for the first time all over again. Me and your mom hopping in after school and going down to the park, so she could have a look at the fish. I almost didn't go through with it, son.'

Joseph rubbed the tears from his face into his sleeve, making sure not to lose his grip on the steering wheel. The lights behind them were drawing closer, stabbing at their path with impenetrable, yellow light.

'Your mom was so angry; I thought she might actually leave. I know she thought about it. God, she just looked so *disappointed*, it pissed me off. I couldn't have my wife driving around an old beat-to-shit Buick, so I bought her a Benz, a real nice one. I wanted to get her something she'd like, y'know. I even asked around at work, to see what all the women liked back then. It took her a month before she even started the damn thing. She hated *this* car when I bought it too, always telling me I'd end up crashing the damn thing. I–'

Joseph squinted through the moisture and searched the impossible darkness for some marker. Something, anything, to point the way.

145 mph ... 150 mph

'Fuck.'

Joseph could feel the wheels trembling below, gliding sideways in infinitesimal nudges. He willed himself to take his foot off the pedal; he did not want to die this way. He wanted to go faster, and so harder he pressed.

'Where are we going?' The voice was Marcus, but Joseph knew it was only borrowed now. 'Where are you taking me?' He felt something cold and wet against his neck. It was a tongue, leaving a gelatinous trail across his jawline.

'Stop it.'

'I want to go home.'

'Damnit, stop, please.'

'Where's Mom? Where's my mom?'

'God fucking damnit, I said *stop*!'

Joseph swerved wildly, sending his passenger tumbling into the door and bringing forth a chorus of wails as the car tires struggled for grip.

'Mommy is right here, darling,' said a disembodied, cold voice. Joseph felt a skeletal hand rise from the darkness at his feet and slide to the crotch of his pants. It was crooked, the bones twisted in unnatural ways, and every finger wore a cheap, colorful ring.

Figures were flashing by in the light now, stationed at the side of the road. They were tall, disgustingly gaunt, and as naked as the day they were spat from their abyss. They flashed by in a colorless blur and the lights in the rear-view were now perched directly on the Maserati's tail. Marcus was at his throat again and the hand below was clawing for his zip. It was pure, terrifying chaos.

BANG!

The vehicle behind had barged the Maserati's bumper, causing the back wheels to hop just an inch off the road.

'Get off me, don't touch me.' Joseph swung his knees at the creature below and leaned into the steering wheel to avoid the one behind.

'Get your fucking hands off me!'

'I'll take care of you, don't worry,' hissed the voice at his feet.

'You should do what Mom said—spray the road with our brains, Dad.'

'Marcus, *please.*'

160 mph … 165 mph

'I never wanted this for you, Marky,' Joseph said.

He kicked again at the creature below and braced himself for another blow from the following vehicle. The towering, thin people standing by the road were reaching out for him now. They stumbled onto the road and swung blindly for the strangled rumble of steel that hurtled past.

'Take us off the road. End us, Daddy. *End* us.'

'You didn't deserve what happened. I should've been there.'

'Where were you, Dad?' The boy's voice swung from a demonic baritone to the gentle, inquisitive one Joe remembered. 'You never came for me.'

Small and impossibly strong fingers curled around Joseph's throat. They pressed into his skin and expelled the air from his lungs.

'I tried– I thought I could–' Joseph gagged, searching for the breath to tell his son what he had refused to accept for so long.

The car behind was now pulling up to the side, bobbing back and forth as it tried to become level with the Maserati. Through watery eyes Joseph could see it was a dented and weather-beaten, red Range Rover.

'Such a fancy car, Daddy, and you still can't outrun them.'

The hand below had snaked into Joseph's trousers now and was scratching at his flaccid penis.

'I'm gonna change it if I can, Marky,' was what Joseph would have said, had he been able to speak. The pustular, graying hands at his neck were crushing the sight from his eyes and the voice from his throat. Before he felt the dark completely set in, he found enough energy to throw his hands right. The wheels of the sports car squealed sideways and brought the frame and its passengers into the SUV with an almighty and catastrophic crash.

Having your body hurtle through glass is not the experience you would likely expect. What action film is complete without the muscle-bound hero leaping through a window and landing on one knee, showered by gentle, iridescent shards of glass? They would then get to their feet, dust themselves off, and go back to kicking ass. However, this was no film and Joseph was well past the years of having an action hero's body. He felt every single one of the countless, razor-edged shards of glass as he rocketed through the windshield of the car. He felt them slice through his skin as easily as a propeller blade through water. Like diving through a tunnel lined with needles, he felt himself carried—*pulled*—from one realm to another, infinitely worse for wear.

SMASH!

Every one of Joseph's senses were pummeled as he landed on hard, flat ground. He was blinded by blood, deafened by the storm, and positively engulfed by burning pain. His hands curled into scabbed fists and spit flew from his clenched teeth. His weeping skin felt as though he had been lit in a gasoline-fueled blaze, but a fire was raging within him too. He felt rage unlike any other. It was not blind, intoxicating rage. It was not the same, poisonous emotion that had seduced him into bringing a crowbar down onto an innocent man's spine. It was clarity. It was resolve.

'You want to punish me?' Joe weakly rose to his knees, pressing one hand down onto more glass. 'Then fucking *punish* me.'

A devastating crash of thunder shook the floor and another flash of lightning added detail to the room. The red glow hadn't been enough to confirm his suspicions, but now he could see for sure that he was in the lobby of his apartment building. He turned to look behind him and immediately raised an arm to shield his eyes from the frigid wind. The glass at his feet—some of it still lodged in his flesh—had come from one of the towering windows that kept the elements outside. Joe stepped forward, the powdered glass crackling under his feet.

This was what he wanted, wasn't it? Outside. *Escape.*

The howling roars of the wind seemed somewhat dulled now, as if to welcome him. What had once sounded like screams being carried down the street were now just whistles and sighs. It was soothing, if just for a moment, and then Joe remembered Tyler's deformed body being crippled by the storm. He remembered—he could not *forget*—the way she had been sucked from existence, consumed by the rain and fog.

If I stay, I'll wake up in that room. If I go ... shit, who knows?

Joe took one last look around the cavernous, shadowed lobby. Not much could be seen outside of the dome of crimson light, but Joseph could feel shapes in the dark. He sensed them like a cat with its tail bristled. They were waiting for him; of course they were.

Joseph spat a thick wad of blood onto the ground, as if to spite the specters, and turned back to the window. Strangely, he did not hesitate a moment more before stepping across the threshold and onto the outside footpath. The change was not immediate, and he could not be sure if that comforted him or left him more disturbed by his choice. He felt the world pressing in on him at a creeping, threatening pace.

'What—?'

Each breath became more arduous and what had been a light shower of freezing rain began to press harder by the second. This outside world was somehow more terrifying than it had looked from behind a window, and Joseph felt he was *fading* into it. He had stepped only once but he knew another stride forward would truly bring him into this ... whatever this place was.

'Joseph!' A hiss carried on the wind. 'Come, Joseph.'

A hysterical, frantic laugh echoed through Joe's skull, but he could not see where it had come from. Then he heard pattering, no ... smacking, thumping. Feet on pavement, *hundreds* of feet.

'Who's there?' Joseph yelled, straining to fill his lungs with every breath.

'Hurry.'

'You must hurry, Joseph.'

'Hurry!'

'Come home, you wretched cunt.'

The voices were hushed and laced with fury. The sound of running feet had become louder now, battling the wails of the wind and cementing Joseph in his place. He looked around but saw only mist, rain, and debris being shifted in elegant twists.

'What more do you want from me?' Joseph yelled, collapsing to a knee and gripping his breast in a tight fist. He wheezed and heaved, sucking against the wind for oxygen, for air. Then he saw something. Something impossibly tall, slicing through the haze at least five hundred feet away. It had limbs where a person's arms and legs should be, but the mist shrouded the figure in a veil of black. The ground trembled under each, monstrous footstep.

'My God,' was all Joseph could say, for who else but God could ever imagine such a creature?

'It's time, Joseph.'

'It's time.'

The voices continued to whisper from the fog; their feet continued to run past, some closer than others. There were too many to count.

'We'll take you home, Joseph.'

'We'll take you to Pam.'

'To Pam.'

'Marcus.'

'We'll take you to Marky, Joseph.'

'Is that what you want me to do, huh?' Joseph wheezed, looking around blindly into the gloom.

'Come closer, or we'll fetch them ourselves.'

'We'll bring them here.'

'We'll *fetch* them, Joseph.'

'No,' Joseph said, his lips peeled back in a snarl.

'We'll grab them by the fucking hair and bring them to you.'

'It's okay, Joe, come home. I'll show you the way.'

'We'll beat their skulls into the road and make you eat the mess.'

'Hurry, Joseph.'

'We'll *fetch* them!'

'Hurry!'

'Fine!' Joseph yelled. 'You want me? Then come and fucking get me!' Joseph threw his arms wide and pounded his battered chest. He turned in a circle to face all who ran in the shadows.

'Come on, you sons of bitches! Come and get me!'

There's no way out, the storm won't let me go.

'Finally,' hissed the voices.

'Joseph!' A hand grabbed Joe by the collar and ripped him back into the dark calm of the building's lobby.

Just as Joseph had felt himself being submerged into the storm, he now felt himself plucked from it. It was as if he had been lifted from the deepest depths of the ocean and all of the suffocating pressure had been stripped away. He even gasped for breath the way someone might after nearly drowning. He was as dry as desert waste.

'Are you out of your damn mind? What the hell, man?'

A face hovered above Joseph's and when the air had finally found its way back into his chest, he scurried away as quickly as his legs could carry him.

'Whoa, whoa, hey, relax.'

The lobby was illuminated by the dull glow from the lamp on the concierge desk and after blinking a few times Joseph saw the figure kneeling beside him was a thin, curly-haired young man.

'Daewon?'

'Yeah. What the hell, Joseph?'

Joe felt his pulse ease, but only a little.

'Cut the shit, is it really you or are you one of those things?' Joseph frantically searched the dark corners of the lobby for figures or shapes.

'One of what? What the hell are you talking about?'

'Taylor said you saved her from the security guard—you saw him, right?'

'Taylor? You mean that woman just before? She was standing there screaming like a maniac, so I tried to bring her inside. Her foot was all smashed up, so I wanted to try and call her an ambulance. Next thing I know she takes off, up the stairs.'

'You haven't seen them? Six fucking days and you haven't *heard* them?'

'Six days?'

'Six days this building has been crawling with ...' Joe couldn't finish his sentence.

The boy's confused, and now somewhat disturbed, expression made it clear he wasn't aware of what had been happening above. Was that so unusual? If not for Taylor D, Joseph might have been willing to believe these horrors were for his eyes only. That did not make them any less real; he still felt the deep scratches by his pants zipper, the slice on his palm.

'Joseph, we've been stuck here one night.'

Joseph's heart froze in his chest.

'What?'

'Yeah, I saw you yesterday, remember? Then I think I heard you leave with Mr. Javier or something.'

Joseph crawled to his feet, swaying drunkenly in the dark.

It was real, I know it was real.

'I was just trying to get the emergency power going and I heard the glass smash. I came out and saw you standing there in the rain, yelling to God knows who.'

'You haven't seen anything weird? You haven't heard them?'

'I mean …' Daewon got to his feet and stepped forward to help steady Joseph against him. 'I guess I have heard some weird sounds from the stairwell, and this storm is– I mean what the *fuck*, right?'

Joseph leaned against the surprisingly strong teen and searched the boy's face for any signs of danger.

'I've never seen something like that out there before, that's bloody insanity. I even–' Daewon hesitated.

'What?'

'I thought I saw people walking around out there. Just doesn't make sense.'

Joseph remembered the voices in the mist and cast an anxious glance to the window. There was only the blood-red haze of torrential rain to be seen. He shuddered, remembering the tall creature and the way it had walked with steps like bombshells.

'What the hell happened to you, man? You are beat to shit,' said Daewon.

'I *was* beat to shit.'

'Right ... do you wanna come into my apartment? I have a first-aid kit and I suppose it couldn't hurt to give the ambulance another try.'

Joseph looked down again at the boy's face, willing the monster to show its face and let it be done with him. All he saw was concern and a sincere desire to help.

'Thank you, Daewon,' replied Joseph, allowing the young man to accept a bit more of his weight. 'Thank you.'

Chapter
Ten

I'll Tell You

The silence was thick enough to chew on. Daewon rolled his jaw and gave Joseph another quizzical look as he finished wrapping the gauze around the man's hand.

'I'm going to be real with you, Joseph—that sounds batshit crazy.'

Joseph exhaled deeply and gulped back more water.

'Yeah. I don't blame you for not believing me.'

'I didn't say that.'

Daewon stood up and scratched his head with one hand while admiring his handiwork. Joe resembled a mummy more than he did a man now; every limb was home to a coil of bandage or medical tape.

'That should do it. Until we can get you to a hospital anyway. Good thing too—that was all we had.' The young man kicked a much lighter first-aid kit to illustrate his point. It clattered to the side and spilled a few medical wipes onto the floor.

'How could you believe me? All this … it's impossible.' Joseph was stinging all over from his cuts and the antiseptic sponge bath he had sat through but being in Daewon's apartment somehow felt safe. No, not safe. *Safer.*

'I don't know,' Daewon replied. He slumped onto the floor next to Joseph and sunk his hands into the gray carpet. 'My mom she– she said some weird stuff near the end.'

He caught Joseph's quick, tiny flinch.

'Dementia.'

There was another short silence, one Joe was tempted to break with the often expected '*I'm sorry,*' but the boy started up again as if he had simply lost his train of thought.

'It wasn't easy and all that. She said a lot of strange things. Most of it was random crap, y'know, stuff from her past or maybe she'd just get confused about the date. I think she asked me to get her sister for her a few times, but my aunt died before I was even born. Anyway, sometimes it would get *really* bad. I would sit there next to her bed and she'd go so still, she wouldn't– I mean I could swear sometimes she was barely even breathing. Then bam!' Daewon clapped his hands together, almost in time with a boom of thunder.

'Mom would sit up in her bed like she'd been slapped in the face. She would look at me and say, *The rain is coming for me, Daewon, I hear the rain.* At first I thought it was just more random stuff, but then it happened again and– it was different, y'know? When Mom would lose herself, she would seem confused, like she didn't see us. Like didn't *really* see us, y'know? But when she talked about the storm, she would look right at me. She never sounded confused, just … I dunno, scared.'

'The storm,' sighed Joe.

'Yeah. She kept saying it right until the end, begging me to help her. I didn't know–' Daewon had done quite a good job at playing it cool until this moment. He choked on his last word and a glint of moisture in his eyes had become visible. 'I didn't know what to do, how to help her. She wasn't the best mother in the world, but *shit,* man.'

The young man wiped at his eyes with the back of his arm and cleared his throat. Joseph could feel a knot forming in his own stomach, anchoring him to the floor.

'I never got it then, but something about this storm it– it's not right and it's like I can feel it, y'know?'

'Maybe this is hell.'

'Maybe, maybe not.'

'What else would you call it?'

'Well, my mom said something else at the end. At the very end actually.' Daewon rose to his feet and snatched his phone from the bookshelf.

'What's that?'

'She said she was going to go back and make it better.' He squatted next to the wounded, older man and held out the phone. 'No emergency services are answering, but do you have anyone you can call? I still have service. Ironic, right?'

Joe accepted the phone with his good hand and stared dumbly at the brightly lit screen. He almost couldn't believe it, full bars. Shit, even the battery was at ninety-four percent. It could not be that easy.

It can't be.

'I'll give you a minute. I need to wash your blood off me anyway.' Daewon crossed the dimly lit room and gave one last encouraging smile before disappearing into the bathroom. The young man's apartment was quite spectacular, definitely the nicest Joseph had seen in the building. The perks of being a live-in concierge— that and an obvious eye for smart decorating.

He looked back at the phone and sighed again, closing his eyes with a shudder.

'Come on, Joe, don't fuck this up.'

He dialed digit after digit with a quivering thumb and bit into his lip so firmly that he felt a cut reopen. Would the building let him do this? Was this a trick? It would be more believable now for Daewon to run at him from the dark with a swinging jaw and a raised knife than for him to be able to press that godforsaken green call button.

'All right.'

Joe hit the button and snapped the phone to his ear before it could be plucked from his hand. For a heart-stopping moment there was nothing, and then it rang. It rang once, twice, three times, four ti–

'Hello?'

Joseph gagged, eyes scorching from the heat of his tears and the crease of cut skin.

'Hello? Is anyone there?' Pamela called through the receiver again. She had it almost against her mouth, probably balancing the phone on a shoulder as she cooked dinner.

'Pam?'

'This is she. Who is this, sorry?'

'Jesus, Pam, I can't believe it's you.' Joseph wept openly into his bandaged hand, feeling the weight of his pain—his regret—wringing him dry.

'Uh, I'm really sorry, but who is this?' Pam was audibly concerned now, perhaps even a little frightened.

'It's Joe, hun, it's me.'

'Joe?'

'Yeah,' Joseph felt a laugh escape his lips, tears and spit running down his cheeks. 'It's me, honey.'

'I– I think you have the wrong number, Joe.'

Joseph's laugh turned to an uncertain choke.

'Pam *please*, you don't know what's happening here.'

'I really am sorry, but I don't know a Joe.' Pam's tone was not annoyed or dismissive; it was genuine confusion. Joseph gripped his forehead in his hand and pinched at his temples, every inch of him trembling.

'What do you mean? It's me, Joe. We were married, Pam.'

'Married? Oh Jesus, did Rod put you up to this? This isn't funny, you know, it's creepy.'

'Rod?'

'Rodney, my husband. Do you work at the kitchen too, Joe?'

Joseph collapsed sideways to the floor, still pressing the phone tightly to his ear and groaning. He knew Pam; he knew all of her quirks and the way she would say things when she was happy or sad. They had known each other for more than thirty years and he knew her well enough by now to understand that she had no idea who the hell he was.

'Marcus. Tell me Marcus is with you, Pam.'

The line was silent for a long moment, only heavy breathing being shared between the two.

'That is *not* funny. Fuck you and fuck Rod, if he put you up to this.'

'Pam please.'

'Don't call me again.'

Click

Joseph threw the phone away from him and rolled onto his aching back. He pressed his knuckles into his eyes and willed them to crush the life out of him.

'I'm guessing that didn't go well?' Daewon was rubbing his elbow nervously by the doorway and looking down at Joe sympathetically. 'Sorry, I didn't mean to eavesdrop.'

'It's okay,' Joe replied.

'Want to talk about it?'

'No.'

'Can I get you anything?'

'No.'

'Want me to sit here with you for a bit?'

'Yeah.'

Joseph and Daewon sat for hours, staring at the windows across the room. They were fogged and edged with frost, but the red glow still shone through and every now and then you would see a shape pass by. Maybe just some more debris, maybe something with arms and legs.

'So what about your dad?' Joseph said quietly, not looking away from the chaos outside.

'What about him?'

'He dead too?'

'Hmph, I doubt it.'

'What, you don't see him?'

'Not anymore.'

'Why not?'

'Jesus, Ridley,' snapped Daewon. The young man looked sidelong at his guest and nudged him with his elbow. 'Do you really want to know? You've barely ever looked at me, let alone said more than a few words. Now you're bleeding out on my floor and you want my life story?'

'I just want to know what happened with your dad,' Joe replied, meeting the boy's stare with an earnest one, 'that's all.'

Daewon looked slightly taken aback and felt his face relax back into an expression of indifference.

'Okay, Joseph, I'll tell you. Spoiler alert, we don't talk anymore. I guess you could say he cut me off.'

'Is it because …'

'Because?' Daewon stifled a laugh. 'Because I'm gay?'

Joseph shrugged weakly.

'No, *honey-boo*, it's not because I like peeenis. It's because the guy is a grade-A asshole.' Daewon emphasized parts of his speech with a theatrical flamboyance and puckered his lips to great dramatic effect. Then he let loose a deep-chested laugh and leaned into Joseph with a comical hand flick, making him laugh too. Perhaps modestly at first, but then they were holding their stomachs, laughing simply because they had time to.

'Nope. Old man Achebe knew I liked boys since I could lift a pair of heels, but his big problem with me was that I used up two valuable resources: time and money. Hell, I don't think he ever liked me. Once Mom died, he didn't have to pretend anymore. I don't think he liked her much either, at least not toward the end. I remember the day they wheeled her out, he just had this look. The man never smiled—or frowned for that matter—but that day he sure as shit looked relieved. We lived in a pretty big house and his room was at the other end from mine, go figure, so I didn't see him much after that. You would think that would be sad, right? Like, that's kind of sad, but honestly, I don't think I cared that much then. I sure as hell don't care now. I think I gave up trying to get his attention before I could even start making proper memories.'

'You don't miss him?'

'Not really, no. What's there to miss, y'know? I remember one of the few times we talked, he was drunk off his gourd in the second kitchen. I was popping in because that's where the good food is, and there he was, sitting at the table and staring at me like I was a stranger off the street. I thought he was going to throw the wine bottle at me, truth be told. *Daewon*, he said,' Daewon lowered his voice to a baritone and donned a thick West African accent, *why do you stay here? Why don't you go*? I mean, I knew he didn't like me, but I was only sixteen. I don't know where the fuck he thought I planned on going. I guess a small part of me believed that … I mean, it's kind of stupid.'

'Tell me.'

'Well, I thought that even though he didn't like *me*, maybe he liked having someone around the house, y'know? The old man doesn't have any friends, the rest of our family are gone. He's just alone. I didn't think he *wanted* to be alone. It felt kinda nice thinking that my father wanted me around for something.'

'Are you sure he didn't?'

'Well, let me put it like this, I caught him leaving for work one day and told him I was leaving forever. He didn't even stop to look at me. So, I got in my car and left. I must've made it an hour or two down the highway before I went back. I drove all the way back, went inside and sat in his favorite, stupid fucking chair until he got home, then I cornered the asshole. I stood in the doorway and wouldn't let him leave the study, not until he said something to me. I don't know what I expected. I think maybe I hoped he would at least pretend to care and say bye. I thought he was going to kill me, something in his eyes. That was the scariest part about him, y'know. He could say a lot without moving one muscle in his face, just with a look.'

'Did you get your goodbye?'

'Of course I didn't. He did speak, though. For the first time it felt like he was really speaking *to* me, not just about me. He looked me in the eyes and said, *Daewon, I see you. You think I do not see you, but I do. I see you and it brings me only pain. If I could not see you anymore, I would hope you take my pain with you.* That was it, I can only imagine how long the prick wanted to tell me that. I thought about it the entire drive to Dawn Valley, and I think I figured it out.'

'What do you mean?' Joseph shuffled a little to better see Daewon and raised an eyebrow.

'Well, he said seeing me brought him pain. That explained a lot, at least it explained why he never liked being in the same room as me. At first, I thought maybe seeing me reminded him of Mom, and that was the pain, right? But then, he'd always been like that. He never once hugged me or, hell, even smiled around me. So, I thought maybe seeing me gave him pain because it reminded him of a life he wanted, a life without me. Maybe a life without Mom too. I doubt he would have kept her around if he didn't have to, if she didn't get pregnant, y'know.'

Joseph pondered on this a moment and then felt that familiar, sinking ache in his chest.

The guy couldn't look at his son, it was a painful reminder.

'That's it really,' said Daewon, slapping his knees to wrap up his story. 'I moved to the city, got a small-time job with the roof-over-my-head bonus, and two years later here I am. What about you?'

'What?'

'Well, you told me about those crazy visions you had of your past. You didn't tell me what any of it meant. I still don't understand. Who was the guy in the wheelchair?'

Joseph had purposely left some details out of his frantic explanation earlier, specifically his role in those events.

'I don't think–'

'We're going to be here a while, and it seems like coming clean is far from the worst thing you could do right now, Joe.'

Joseph sunk his face into his hands and felt the tears welling in his eyes again. His mind became flooded with visions of his son in the rear-view mirror, of his wife's voice in the receiver.

'I think you have the wrong number, Joe.'

'I've been thinking maybe this is hell,' said Joe, 'because maybe it's what I deserve.'

'You can be a bit of a cranky asshole man, but *this*? C'mon.' Daewon eyed Joseph's wrapped wounds and his brows wrinkled with worry.

'You don't understand, Daewon,' Joe looked up at the young man, his eyes webbed red and moist from the strain. 'I've done terrible things.'

'You can tell me, Joseph, I won't judge you, I promise.' The boy gripped Joseph's trembling hand in his and gave it an encouraging, gentle squeeze. Joseph took a deep, quivering breath and wiped the snot from his nose.

'When Pam got pregnant, I damn near shit myself, I swear to God. I got spooked real bad, started thinking about all the stuff we couldn't do anymore. I couldn't fucking believe it. I'd just got promoted at this advertising firm too, some real high-level data entry shit. All I could think was, *This is it, the beginning of the end.* I was even angry at her for a while, like it was her damn fault I wouldn't wear a rubber. Jesus, she was so happy I don't think she heard a lick of my complaining anyway. I never once told her how happy I was when I saw little Marky's face for the first time; I don't think I'd felt like that since we were in school and Pam let me kiss her for the first time.'

Daewon smiled, giving Joseph's hand another squeeze and urging him to continue.

'I don't know what happened, but it changed at some point. Don't get me wrong, I loved Pam and I loved the kid; shit, I would go out of my way to flip for the lighter shifts at work just to take them to the park for the day. Pam would put on one of those dresses like she used to wear back when we were kids. Marky would run around until he fell and burnt his knees on the grass. Then he'd come running and wailing back to us with sticks in his hair and boogers on his lip. Mom was always the one to take care of that. I can't remember the last time we did that ...'

'It changed?'

'I guess so. Yeah, it changed. I did. People started treating me differently at work; it really got under my skin. I was running three separate teams and as soon as a photo of my wife and kid goes up in my office, they start getting too relaxed around me. There used to be this way the room would go quiet when I walked in. I used to love that.'

Seems so stupid now. What I would give to see any one of those sons of bitches.

'It's like they knew that one fuck up meant answering to me. Then for some reason, I'm not just the boss anymore, I'm the *dad*. I hated that. I hated the smiles and the whispering. It was like they thought they had something on me, like I couldn't have them packing at a snap of my goddamn fingers. It made me feel so ... exposed.'

'Exposed?'

'Yeah. I wanted them to be scared of me again. I needed them to be. I found out that if I talked crap about my wife and kid around these people, they would realize I could be infinitely worse to them. The more I talked about how much Pam pissed me off, the more I started to believe she did, and the more they started seeing me for my suits again. I didn't even keep photos of them around at work anymore; I didn't want clients getting *the wrong idea*. It just got easier and easier to hate my family and when I think back on it now, I don't know what Pam must have thought. I don't think she understood. How could she have understood?'

'But she loved you?'

'I don't know why she would have stuck around so long if she didn't.' Regret and sorrow dried Joe's throat and tied his stomach in knots. 'Maybe she just didn't want Marcus going without a dad. Some dad I was. I couldn't even hold onto a fucking paper clip for the kid. I think I knew it was wrong, the things I said about Pam and Marky. I would have these episodes where I could barely breathe. I would shut myself away in my office and throw back as many whiskey sours as I could stomach. Sometimes I'd wake up with the moon up outside and drive myself home half-pissed. I knew Pam was pretending to be asleep when I'd get into bed, I always knew. I just never gave a shit. I was drunk when–'

The lump in Joseph's throat had become too big to swallow now. He felt his heart hammering against his rib cage and Daewon's hand was firmly clenched in his first. The young man wriggled his hand free just a little but placed another comforting palm on Joseph's bare shoulder.

'It's okay, I'm still here.'

Joseph clasped his eyes shut and forced himself to breathe in slowly, exhale slower. Panic attacks were not a stranger to the man, but they would usually be quickly remedied by a half liter of anything that burned on the way down.

'I was drunk when I drove Pam home from town one day, and I must have passed out at the wheel. Apparently, my foot came off the accelerator when I blacked out. We went off the road and hit a telephone pole. I barely got a scratch on me. Pam, though, she– her arm got busted up pretty bad. She was in the hospital for a week or two at least, so I had to look after Marcus, you know. I felt so fucking guilty for what I did to her, I kept on drinking. You'd think my stupid ass would have learned its lesson, but no, I kept myself sober just long enough to drop Marky at school and then I'd put that glass on the fucking bench. Pam didn't yell at me. God I *wanted* her to. She would just ask how Marcus was doing, and not say another word. They had her on so many painkillers, thank God. I don't know what she would have done if she'd smelled the drink on my breath. One day I got home from the hospital and I was so pissed at her and pissed at myself, I overdid it. I drank a whole goddamn bottle of aged whiskey and then some. By the time I came to again it was right near nine o'clock. I nearly broke my neck it was so dark; I was still pretty lit up too. Must've taken me a full twenty minutes before I realized I'd never picked up Marky from school.'

Silence. Tense, suffocating silence; Daewon dared not even breathe. They stayed like this for a few minutes. Joseph was no longer weeping; his face was impassive, pale and solemn. This was a detail of the story that transcended guilt or regret. This was mortal, endless dread.

'Where was Marcus, Joe?' Daewon couldn't help but ask. He feared the man might never speak again.

'I– I called the school, but they were closed. There was nowhere else he could have gone, except maybe to the hospital, to Pam. I knew if he was there and she knew I'd left him, that would be it. She would never forgive me for that. I was so fucking scared she was going to leave me that I didn't even consider I could be wrong. I ended up calling her, and she was still doped up, but the first thing she said was, *How's Marcus? I want you to bring him in tomorrow, I got him something from the gift shop.*'

'Holy shit, Joe.'

'I drove right over to the fucking school. I checked everywhere. I drove the streets for an hour and a half, I swear to God. I called the cops, I had to. They wanted to know why I waited till damn near midnight to report a missing kid, but I couldn't tell them I was blacked out all day, could I?'

Joseph began to rock back and forth, burying his face in his arm like a scared child.

'I asked them not to tell Pam. Can you believe that? Of course they fucking did. She came running home from the hospital with her arm still in a sling and her hospital gown tucked into her damn sweatpants. I'd never seen her make a face like the one she had that day, not once. I knew she hated me, *really* hated me. Shit, I hated me too. The cops talked to the school, got some of the security camera footage and brought us in. They had me and Pam sit down in front of this dicky little flat screen and watch as Marky–'

Joe punched the ground and hammered his head against his arm.

'They had us watch Marky get into some fuck's car. A big, bright-red Range Rover. He just walked right over, popped his head in the passenger window, then got in. They caught it on camera as clear as day but couldn't get the motherfucker's plates.'

'Fuck,' Daewon gasped.

'You have to understand, that's all we had: red Range Rover. A million of the fucking things driving across the country, what the hell were the chances a teacher at the school would have one too?'

'What?'

'Yeah, the P.E. teacher, drove the exact same damn car. What the hell was I supposed to think?

We were all thinking it. The cops raided the guy's fucking house, for crying out loud.'

'It wasn't him, was it?'

'He was coaching a football game that day. A hundred witnesses put him there. They had the exact *same* car, don't you see?'

'Joseph …'

'It's my fault, all of it. All of it.'

'Marcus, did he– I mean is he–'

Joseph looked up at Daewon with the stress-beaten face of a man at seventy.

'Marky came home. Exactly one week, almost on the goddamned dot.'

'They found him?' Daewon's eyes widened.

'No. He came home. One day, Pam hears the doorbell go off. She races there expecting to see cops with more news, and she finds Marcus. He was just standing there on the fucking doorstep like a half-dead Mormon. I heard Pam's scream from the other side of the house. Woke me right the fuck out of my whiskey nap. I came down the stairs so quick I fell and busted my ass, then I dragged myself right the hell over and held my wife and kid. I haven't cried like that since–'

Joseph paused, blinking his stinging, raw eyes, and then he gave a solitary chuckle.

'Did they catch the guy?' Daewon asked.

'No one knows dick about him. Marcus hasn't said a word since he got snatched, as far as I know. He wouldn't talk to us, the cops; he wouldn't even draw something for them. He sure as shit doesn't like being in a room alone with another man; he starts whimpering like a beat dog.'

'Oh Marcus.' Daewon bowed his head. He knew what that meant. Anyone who had seen a handful of police dramas knew what that meant.

Joseph pulled at his hair with obsessive repetition. He still had his legs curled into his chest, ignoring the blistering pain from his ribs.

'I wanted to stay, to try to make it right, you know. Pam couldn't even look at me anymore; Marcus wouldn't be alone with me. I knew she was going to leave; I couldn't fix *that*. She had nowhere to go, and I knew that wouldn't stop her, so I left first. I left her a note telling her how sorry I was. God, I was *so* sorry. I told her I loved her, I told her they were my world. I can't sleep some nights wondering if she threw that note in the trash or sleeps with it under her pillow.'

'Is that the last time you spoke to them?'

'Four whole years now—it was right around my birthday when I left. Not that it fucking matters. I miss them so much, I can't– I can't–'

Daewon watched as the forty-something-year-old man covered in bandages curled into a ball and cried. It was not pretty or reserved, like he had seen in the movies; it was red-faced, snotty, and wailing. His heart ached to watch, knowing nothing he could do or say would ever ease this man's pain. Perhaps he had no right to.

'Hey,' Daewon said, pushing Joseph back onto his ass, 'hey! I'm talking to you.'

Joseph looked up at the young man hovering over him and choked back another sob.

'You fucked up, Joe, you did. You fucked up *really* bad. Do you know what that means?'

The large man fought the urge to continue weeping and pushed his knuckles harder into the ground.

'It means you have a responsibility to make it right, or to at least try. You don't get to cry, lie down, and die here. Marcus needs his dad. Maybe not the way he used to, but that's for you to figure out.'

Then Daewon did something Joseph didn't expect—something he did not know he needed. The young man pulled him close and embraced him. They held each other the way a son might hold his father after telling him he's moving to the city. They held each other the way a father might hold his son when he says, 'I'm sorry, I am *so* sorry.' They held each other close and Joseph felt his self-pity and hopelessness melt away.

Chapter
Eleven

A Step Outside

Distorted, stretched groans shook Joseph from his sleep with a jolt. He rose from the comfort of the sofa he had been sleeping on and lunged for the phone. It was still lying in the same spot he had thrown it the night before. The screen was flickering and bending with flashes of digital, rainbow light. He could see a small box flash in and out of view, a media player displaying a song.

Annette Hanshaw – I've got a feeling I'm falling

This indecipherable, howling noise was that song, that godforsaken song.

'Here we go.'

Joseph managed to hit pause before the screen went completely black, and the crackling grumbles were replaced with the thunderous hammering of rain on glass.

'What the hell was that?' Daewon was standing in the doorway of his bedroom, yawning, shirtless, and with one eye still half-closed.

'Don't worry about it,' replied Joe, giving the boy an insincere half-smile. 'You got any clothes that might fit a big bastard like me?'

Joseph pulled the loose, white shirt over his head and looked grimly at the half-dead stranger in the mirror. He found a bittersweet irony in seeing the casually dressed and heavily bandaged man staring back at him.

Much more comfortable than a suit anyway.

Daewon had been fortunate enough to find a box of neatly pressed uniforms stacked away in his storage cupboard. He didn't know how long it had been there, but there were undershirts and slacks in every size, each as musty as the next.

'I could wash it for you, y'know?' Daewon had said.

'No need, they already smell better than I do.'

Joseph knew he couldn't stay here, as much as he wanted to hide from the storm and the shadows that passed by the door when Daewon wasn't looking. He had never looked worse in his life, and yet he felt a bizarre calm when he moved his hand to his shaved cheek, and his reflection did the same. It was as if all of the cuts and bruises had chipped away at his shell, and now he was exposed. No, not exposed … *free*. Except he was not free, not really; he knew this. The storm had plans for him yet. He trembled to remember the pull of the outside wind, the way he had felt himself fading from one world to the next.

'I know what I am. I know this is real.'

He felt his lips move, but the reflection did not speak.

'I know I'm never going home,' Joseph continued.

He leaned in close to the mirror, unbothered by his reflection's motionlessness. Only the eyes followed him.

'I understand it now.'

Then Joseph laughed. Softly, and then hysterically. He laughed so hard the sink groaned under his weight. Still his reflection watched, unmoved. Suddenly, a sound stuffed the laughter back down Joseph's throat and he froze. His head snapped toward the door. It was a knock, not at the bathroom … at the front door.

'Daewon?'

The knocks sounded off again, harder now, three at a time and rapid.

'Who is it?' Joseph heard Daewon call, followed by steps. The young man was passing the bathroom, to the living room.

'Daewon, don't!'

Joseph lunged forward and yanked at the bathroom door. It did not budge, it did not rattle, it did not shake an inch. The door might as well have been made of concrete. The knocking had turned to bashing now, fists against wood.

'What the fuck? Who is it?' Daewon either could not hear Joseph's yells or couldn't distinguish them from the beating at the front door and the relentless crashing of thunder.

'Don't open it, kid! Daewon!'

Joseph punched, kicked and threw himself against the door, heart practically in his mouth. He ignored the pain and barged against the stone like he was being buried alive.

'I've got a knife, so you'd better back the fuck up,' Daewon yelled. His voice was racked with fear and Joseph could sense the boy edging closer to the would-be intruder.

Joe backed away from the door, looking around frantically for something, anything that could get him out before the other thing got in. He found nothing. He spun on the spot and readied for another kick at the door when he saw something new. Painted across the eggshell-white wood in thin, red letters was a message.

USE YOUR HEAD

Joseph frowned and staggered a little.

What the fuck do you mean?

The bashing outside had started to sound more like splintering wood and Daewon's yells had become more like shrieks.

'Joseph? Help!'

'Fuck it,' said Joseph. He ran at the door as fast as his aching feet would carry him, head bowed down like a charging bull. He readied himself for the explosion of black and the pain to come.

'Aargh!'

CRASH!

The door buckled under him like papier-mâché and he went tumbling through the dark and into the wall with a loud slam.

'Goddamnit,' Joseph roared, pulling himself from the dent he had made in the plaster and steadying himself quickly. He looked around just in time to see some movement in the corner of the room. The front door was scattered across the carpet in large shards and a towering, swollen figure was bearing down on a cowering Daewon. The teenager had a kitchen knife raised in his shaky hands and was swinging it feebly.

'Don't you want me?' the figure cackled, ripping at its shirt and leaning closer to the boy.

'Don't you want me to drill your throat with my massive fucking cock?'

Daewon swiped again but missed. The intruder caught his hand and leaned in close, putting the blade to its lips. Joseph stumbled forward, trying his best to hide his footsteps. He searched the red gloom for a weapon.

'What the *fuck*?' was all Daewon could say breathlessly, as he watched the muscle-bound security guard—who he had so often admired—stick out his tongue and lick the edge of the knife, top to bottom.

'Isn't this what you want, Daewon?' The man took the entire blade in his limp, open mouth and flicked his long, skewered tongue this way and that. Then he snatched it from the boy's hands and whipped it down before anyone had a moment to even blink. It plunged into Daewon's thigh and the boy screamed in agony.

'Hey!' Joseph roared.

He charged across the room and lunged at the giant man. They crashed to the floor with an almighty thump. He climbed onto the creature's chest and brought a fist down across its jaw with a sickening crunch. He punched again, and again, and again. His hands and shoulders burned, but still he threw himself down onto the man's skull.

Whack!
Whack!
Whack!

The security guard gurgled blood and laughed, before throwing Joseph off of him as easily as a father roughhousing his child. Joe spiraled through the dark and came crashing down through a row of bookcase shelves.

'There will be no rest,' hissed the security guard, picking up the knife and rising swiftly to his enormous feet. 'I'll bite at your flesh to keep you awake, don't worry.'

The guard took a few steps toward Joseph's motionless body and then once again directed his attention to the teen inching closer to the door, back pressed firmly to the wall.

'Oh no,' the giant croaked, blood bubbling and drooling from its chin in elastic strands. 'We've barely finished with the foreplay.'

He lunged forward, swinging an arm for his prey and missing narrowly. Daewon ducked the grab and hobbled forward into the hallway, gripping his wound tightly and yelling with every step.

'I'm not here for you, but we can still play. You can't leave yet. I'll make you feel better.' The creature's words raged with growing turbulence.

It gained on the injured boy with barely any effort.

'Please stop,' Daewon cried.

The guard lunged forward, knife raised, and grabbed the young man's hair in a bunched fist.

'I can't wait to taste you.'

Out of the darkness a figure barreled into the large intruder, knocking them both into the small bathroom. A single flash of lightning illuminated the strained face of Joseph as he brought a thick, leather-bound book down across the guard's jaw. The knife flashed again and a searing, white-hot pain spread across Joseph's cheek.

'Joseph!'

The yell came from right behind, but it might as well have been a field away for the echo and distance it left in Joseph's mind. The guard swung the knife again. Joe elbowed it aside and brought the book thundering down into the attacker's face with a wet crunch.

'Klng nng,' the intruder gurgled.

THWACK!

The guard cocked his head upright one more time and somehow, despite his crippled jaw, managed to spit one last message before the blood-soaked book finally silenced him.

'So desperate to kill your angels.'

It sounded like it had been whispered into Joseph's ear. He rose groggily and threw the tome aside, looking grimly at the wet, red mess he had left. Where there had been bulging, bloodshot eyes were now only pieces of skull and brain matter.

'Holy shit, it feels good to finally shut one of you up,' Joseph said with a hollow wheeze.

'What the hell was that?' Daewon gasped, before collapsing against the wall behind him.

Joseph rushed to the boy's side, quickly snatching a towel and pressing it to his leg.

'You okay, kid? Stay with me.'

Daewon gave a weak laugh and smiled up at the man. His face was glazed in sweat and one eyelid drooped lower than the other.

'I'm okay,' he said. 'I think I'm okay.'

'You need a doctor.'

'That doesn't seem likely right now, Joe.'

'What do I do?'

'I'm going to need you to bring me that first-aid kit and hold my hand, really fucking tight.'

Joseph looked down at the remarkably sub-par attempt he and Daewon had made at sealing off the wound. Tape, alcohol wipes, and strips of cloth could only do so much, but so far the teenager had managed to stay conscious. There was nothing left for Joseph's face, but luckily it had not been too deep a cut.

'How are you feeling, kid?'

'Cold,' replied Daewon, pulling the blanket tighter around his shoulders, 'but I can handle it.'

They had tried to call the emergency services again, but the phone might as well have been a seven-hundred-dollar brick for all the good it did. Joseph knew it wouldn't work, and looking down at the barely conscious teen, he could not shake an overwhelming sense of helplessness and guilt.

I shouldn't have come here.

'I was thinking,' said Daewon, so quietly it could barely be heard 'if the storm is making you relive all these old memories, maybe you can do it different, y'know?'

Change it, change the memory.

'I'm going to find help,' he said. Daewon raised his eyebrows dumbly.

'You're what?'

'I know what I have to do.'

'What does that mean?'

Joseph got to his weary feet again and took one last look at the battered and bloody boy. Then he took a deep breath.

'Don't fall asleep, and if anyone comes in, you hide.'

He turned and marched toward the apartment's front door, refusing to let his mind give protest. He could hear Daewon groan and try to stand behind him.

'Joe, wait, what the hell are you doing?'

The only way to stop this is to finish it. If it has me, maybe it won't want the kid.

'You can't go out there. Are you mad?'

The only way out is down, right? Down the fucking rabbit hole.

Joseph knew where the storm wanted him; he heard it beckon to him with every roll and crash of thunder.

'Joseph, please!'

Joe heard the teen fall again with a weak thump. Daewon's desperate pleas were silenced in one skin-crawling pop as the man stepped out of the unit.

'I can end this,' Joe muttered. He turned to see the apartment he had just exited was now erased from existence. Where there had been an empty, splintered doorway, there was now only a blank, white wall.

The rest of the lobby was still and absent, illuminated in momentary spasms by stabs of lightning. The door to the staircase he had only just descended sat open, willing him to come home.

No ... I didn't use the stairs, I–

Joseph rubbed his temples with quivering palms and groaned.

'C'mon, you dumb son of a bitch, get it together.'

He looked up and saw a square of dull, red light, surrounded by pieces of jagged glass, the window and the storm beyond. The rain was so heavy now that it traveled almost horizontally and streaks of white and gray screamed past, caught in the gale. Spirits and damned souls perhaps.

'I know ...,' Joe croaked, beginning to laugh into his hands. He stumbled forward, toward the smashed window, '... what is real.'

His shuffling increased to an unsteady run, and before he knew it, he was sprinting toward the window.

'Stop!' Someone, something behind him had sprung from the shadows and was chasing him across the lobby. 'It's not time!'

The slaps of their bare feet on the floor were quick, impossibly rapid, and drawing closer by the second.

'Not yet!' They were close, fingers brushing Joseph's neck.

'Fuck you,' Joe yelled. He threw himself forward, through the window and entirely into the realm beyond.

Joseph felt himself submerged into impossibly cold waters. It was overwhelming and suffocating. He felt every atom of his being swallowed by an icy frost. His jump into the storm felt more like falling; there was no wind to push through, but his stomach dropped the way it might before plunging into a nightmare.

You are cold.

You

you are cold.

You are cold.

The ground is an unknown distance away,
but rushing toward you all the same.
You, reading this now.

Regret

...

anticipation.

A STEP OUTSIDE

WELCOME DESCENT

hello?

Joseph found his body spat into the street, but his mind—his spirit—trailed far behind. He was a passenger as it fell, twisted, and pushed through a moment that spanned a single breath and the rise of a civilization in the same instant. Then he was there, face-down on the road. The sound in his ears, the sight in his eyes, and the taste of blood on his tongue returned slowly.

Joe gasped for breath. He pushed his hands against the steaming asphalt and forced himself to his knees. The terrifyingly familiar feeling of the void was all around him again, as if one false move would be a bottomless drop into oblivion, but he saw the road, he could see the buildings. Whatever tint of red he had witnessed from behind the glass was now gone. Joseph found himself kneeling in a dimly lit, gray street; the only color to be found was in the burnt-orange moon above, positioned firmly in a blanket of empty, impenetrable black.

Maybe I'm already dead.

For some reason the thought made him laugh. What joy it brought him to imagine the look on everyone's faces if they found out the afterlife was real, and this—*this* was it. Those stupid motherfuckers in their godly vestments would shit their righteous drawers. Joseph wondered what people would say. Would they be happy? Would *you* be happy? Would an eternity be better served in torment, or as nothing at all? Would you prefer to be one day forgotten, never to exist within anyone's memory ever again … or would you wish this pain on everyone who ever lived?

'Who fucking knows?' thought Joseph.

The wind was much calmer now, although not completely peaceful. The rain was light and made no sound against the pavement. Joseph could barely feel the moisture on his icy skin. He rose to his feet slowly and looked around, expecting to hear the strangers from the mist once more. There was nothing.

'Hello?' he yelled.

Howls and screams echoed on the wind, but none gave reply. He had never felt so completely and utterly alone, and yet somehow like he was being watched all the same.

The city was a grim reflection of the one that Joseph knew so well. He had spent the better part of a half-decade driving these streets and thinking little of the towering, glass buildings. Now he walked a colorless spread of rubble. Very few of the towers still stood tall, and those that did were bending and flaking away in the wind, bit by tiny bit. Café Olay was now a chasm, as if something monstrous had crushed it under its heel. Perhaps that was for the best.

No more shit coffee at least. Daewon would like that.

Joseph was not unaware that there were shapes gliding through the mist around him, some small, some much larger. He heard the slapping of bare feet on concrete over the shrieks of the storm every now and then as well; sometimes they were moving away, sometimes they came close and stopped, just out of sight. He would fight if he needed to—if he could. However, his heart no longer raced the way it had when Javier had lunged at him with a knife raised above his old, liver-spotted head. Joe knew he had to keep moving. He feared that if he were to stop for a moment too long, he might freeze in place. Then those freaks in the dark could *really* have him.

He walked for what felt like miles, dragging foot in front of tired foot. He knew the streets well—better than most—and he knew he had passed the same demolished storefront more than once, without making a single turn.

'So it's like that, huh?'

Joe turned on the spot and squinted against the spray of rain. Had he not already been so cold, it might have even been refreshing against his countless cuts and bruises. There was a new street before him now, one he did not know. It was a street that did not exist or should not exist. Piercing the haze and gloom, Joe could see a small but bright light in the distance.

Fire?

Warmth.

A way.

The clapping of running feet sounded off again, not far behind, and so Joseph moved forward into the fog.

He had walked for a few blocks when the sounds of screaming began to seem much less like roaring winds and a lot more like people. People in tremendous pain. One of the screams sounded close; it came from one of the last standing stores. Joseph cautiously hopped off the street and did his best to conceal himself in the shadows of the opposite sidewalk. Still he walked, refusing to slow his pace. The source of the screaming became apparent all too quickly and Joseph watched helplessly as a woman ran out onto the street, naked from head to toe. Her chest was covered in blood and one of her arms was twisted in an unnatural way, glistening bone showing through the skin. Some of her scalp had been carved away, leaving only thin, blood-soaked blonde locks sticking to her face. Joseph flinched, longing to help the woman, but repulsed all the same. A tall, skeletal figure emerged from the dark behind the stranger and snatched her by the throat. She writhed under its grip and used every breath left in her lungs to yell and squeal, but it was no good. It appeared the attacker had already had their fill of *fun*. They brought the woman down to the cement in one swift, nauseating crunch and the left side of her face shattered against the ground.

Joseph watched the slack-jawed psychopath as it brought the woman's head down into the concrete again and again. Her screams stopped quickly and were replaced by loud, wet thumps. Even in the dark, Joe could see pieces of skull and glistening slivers of flesh fly away from each impact. The attacker didn't stop until all that was left was a stump of spinal cord and mashed nerve endings. That guttural dread that Joseph had hoped was gone crawled its way to the surface again. He stumbled forward; he knew he must keep moving away from the carnage. The figure looked up from the halo of gore and swiveled its swollen, luminous eyes to meet Joseph's. Joe could not look away. He kept moving, back pressed to a crumbling wall, but those eyes followed him. The figure rose to its full height, standing at least eight feet tall, and took one step toward the man.

No way in hell can I outrun that thing.

It drooled blood and spit onto the road and cocked its vascular head like a confused dog, and then it turned around and walked back inside. What scared Joseph most as he jogged away, toward the distant fire, was not the violence he had just witnessed, but rather the sound of the monster's feet on the ground. It was the same flat blows that echoed all around him, so often stopping just a breath out of view.

The blaze was much clearer now. It was still a few streets away, but Joseph could see it was a modestly sized building in flames, perched atop a small hill between two crippled towers. There were more screams now too, more bodies. Some were laid out in pools of blood, riddled with stab wounds and missing limbs. Some were contorted and twisted in impossible ways, as if they had been tied into knots and released only when the last joint popped out of place. Some were hard to distinguish as bodies at all; they were simply piles of flesh and bone. Joseph could only guess they had fallen from a great height. He was not so sure about his after-life theory anymore, the threat of death here felt very real. Sometimes in his normal life, Joe had felt death looming over him like a shadow, invading and poisoning his thoughts anytime he finished a cigarette or saw his graying hair in the mirror. That seemed so pointless now. Nothing set things in perspective like having a blade scrape your bones.

'*I think you have the wrong number, Joe.*'

Pamela's words still haunted him. How could she not know him? They had been friends until graduation. He had watched through her living room window as she and Rod fucked for the first time—on their second date. He couldn't believe that; it wasn't like her to give herself away so easily. He had even watched from a distance as they said, '*I do.*' Rodney had worn a disgusting, cheap blue suit, probably from some easy fit from a shop at the mall. He was a chef for fuck sake, what was she thinking?

'No,' Joseph sobbed, falling to a knee and clutching the sides of his head. His mind throbbed and felt as though it were spinning in place, tugging against his brain stem and twisting it into knots. 'That's not real.'

He blinked through the freezing sweat and focused his mind, using all his willpower to surface the memory of his son's face. 'You can't take those from me, you can't.'

Joseph did not want to die, and he sure as *hell* did not want to lose what had made his life worth living.

'Get the fuck out of my head!' Joseph screamed, springing to his feet again and running now, as fast as his body would allow.

He passed humming cars with their doors wide open and rubble stacked as high as a stadium. His feet did not come to a stop until he was standing at the base of a narrow, stone stairway. It twisted up a burnt, grass slope to meet what had once been a church. There was no mistaking the arched roof and the tall, blackened doors. Joseph knew this church; he had pulled up here in his employer's Rolls Royce a lifetime ago, to pick up a client. He watched panting, as the flames roared and devoured the rain, creating a nimbus of steam and mist. They reached high into the sky, failing to cast any light on the void above and managing only to cast a weak warmth into the cold. There was something else about the fire, something unnatural. Through the glow of yellow and white, something moved. The belly of the blaze was shifting, wriggling. Black shapes danced against the charred stone, twisting this way and that. It wasn't until Joseph distinguished the blood-curdling screams from the grumbles and crackling of the fire that he saw it for what it was. This was an execution. Bodies were twisting in the flames, nailed upside down to the church walls in some perverse crucifixion. They should not have been able to scream; they should have been dead. Their skin had been peeled away and every hair on their bodies had been consumed in the fire. Still they squirmed and called for mercy. There were no eyes in their sockets. They had turned to vapor and been quickly extinguished, leaving nothing but black holes as empty as the sky. Seeing the woman pulverized in the street felt trivial now as Joseph watched these people who could not die but would not stop burning. He shielded his mouth with a bandaged forearm and gagged, refusing to collapse again. Then something else caught his eye, more shapes. These ones were not inside the fire, they were around it. Joseph ducked behind a small, stone wall and watched as more limp-jawed maniacs crested the peak of the hill. One was taller than the last Joseph had seen, nine feet at least and frighteningly more solid. It dragged behind it a plump man, naked, purple in the face, arms flailing.

'PleaseGodhelpmepleaseJesus!' the man screamed.

The poor man spun from side to side, doing whatever he could to escape the tall man's grip. As much as he struggled, he knew—they knew, Joseph knew—he was already doomed. The pleading turned to unintelligible blubbering and Joseph looked on as the plump man was hoisted into the fire. His screams were agonizing, only adding to the chorus from his ill-fated companions. Two smaller assailants came forward and raised thick, metal spikes to the already bubbling skin of the man's wrists. Joseph looked away, he knew what came next and he couldn't stomach another moment of it.

He sat against the wall for much too long, hoping the screams would die but knowing they would not. The moon glared down, and Joseph began to wonder if it was even a moon he looked up at. It was blank, featureless, devoid of the smears and divots that the human race looked up at every night. Perhaps it was a light at the mouth of a hole, a pit that Joseph was now nestled deeply within. He might have sat theorizing for an hour more had he not noticed a slender shadow block out the light of the fire directly above him. He looked up just in time to see a thin, open-mouthed woman staring down at him with bulging, blood-speckled eyes. Her dark hair hung over her face in thick, twisted knots and every muscle in her body pressed against thin, pale skin.

'A Peeping Tom?' she said, striking forward like a snake. She grabbed Joseph in her strong, wiry fists and threw him over her shoulder. He flew through the air and onto the grass with a painful thump.

'You look like my daddy. I'll make you waAaaArm, DaddyyYy,' she hissed.

She got down onto her hands and knees to be level with Joe as he crawled backwards. She slid one of her knobbled, bony hands under the waist of her pants.

'Screw you,' Joseph said.

He flung one of his feet out and spun the woman's jaw in its place, spraying the steaming grass with blood and bile. He was all too familiar with these maniacs and their fury now; he knew you could kick, punch, and stab, and they would just keep coming. He brought his foot down again for good measure, directly into the center of her face. He heard the bones of her nose crackle under his heel and she staggered backwards. The gruesome woman cartwheeled in clumsy circles, off of the grass ledge and onto the street, muttering excitedly the entire way. Joseph did not need to look behind him to know the others, including that nine-foot behemoth, would be the next to come. He bowled forwards and ran. His feet slid on the slope and wobbled, but he was determined to keep his balance. As he had feared, he saw the demented shadows of at least four pursuers growing in size behind him.

'He's running!'

'Oh I *love* it when they run.'

'Burn him, burn him.'

'No, no, we can play with this one. Cut his belly slow.'

Joseph leapt over the woman he had just kicked, narrowly missing her outstretched fingers. He buckled a little as his feet hit the blacktop.

'Me too, I want him too.'

Joseph heard the frenzied woman calling to her comrades, before being quickly silenced by a number of wet thumps and a chorus of maniacal laughter.

Fucking psychos, they're fucking psychos.

One of them was gaining on him; he could hear the thumping of its feet. It would be the giant, of course it would. Any moment now he would have his feet pulled out from under him, and he would be beaten against the road like a rag doll. The monstrous stranger would bash him until his face was a spiral of bone and pulverized meat. Joseph slid around a corner, gripping a street post and slingshotting himself forward. Judging by the whacks and grunts, the swollen attacker had a bit of a harder time making the turn.

'Sneaky cock sucker, you're sneaky. I'll get you yet, dear.'

Something was positioned in the middle of the road up ahead, a black shape against the weak glow of the fog. A figure, standing by a car. Joseph's heart was pulsing to bursting point now; there was nowhere left to run. If he tried to climb through any of the building debris to his sides, he would be dragged back to the street in an instant.

'Joseph.'

The figure had spoken, and the closer Joe got the more he saw of the stranger. It was a man, tall and naked, but clean. He had a strong jaw and a full head of thick, black hair. It was *him*, his double. The doppelgänger did not acknowledge the hulking figure just a short distance behind Joseph, he simply motioned to the open car with a wave of his hand.

'You are not finished.'

There was something ominous in his tone. Despite the panic lodged in Joseph's throat he knew the figure was not trying to shelter him as an act of kindness. He knew this as sure as he knew his name, but he leapt into the car all the same.

'You will not leave me like this,' said the cleaner, younger Joseph blankly. Then he slammed the car door with a deafening smack.

As soon as the door had closed, Joseph felt the vehicle's frame begin to shake violently. There was no way these doors could keep the horde of maniacs out. They would stick their heads through the glass or tear the steel apart if they had to. He looked up cautiously and found the enormous attacker just a few feet away. The doppelgänger had gone, and the giant was staring at the street ahead with those unblinking, damaged eyes. Something had stopped him; something was making him turn and walk away slowly, as if he had forgotten his wallet back at the fire. Joseph's panting did not relent, his sweat did not feel any less heavy. He turned to see what had steered the monster away and found only more dark mist through the trembling windshield. No ... something was happening. Shapes were emerging from the fog, countless shadows with arms and legs. Joseph watched with a frozen breath as legions of blank-faced people stepped out of the fog and marched toward the car, toward him. They were the same people who had stood outside his building, watching and waiting. He knew this as truly as he knew his name. There were hundreds of them, maybe thousands, and not one of them blinked in the rain. Something else was drawing closer, something infinitely larger. Buildings were toppling over, and a tremendous wind was blowing smoke down the street in a stampede of black corkscrews. It was coming directly at him. Like an earthquake it was sucking the street and everything upon it into the emptiness below. Road fell away, rubble and buildings fell away. Gone, erased. The rumbling crash of the collapsing concrete put the storm's noise to shame; it was deafening, splitting glass in heavy waves. The army of emotionless watchers were swallowed by the billowing darkness.

'Holy shit,' was all Joseph could say. He had watched death beckon him relentlessly the past week, but now it felt much more horrifying. He watched as the world itself crumbled to dust.

He considered whether he should exit the car and make a run for it, but his fingers would not unlatch themselves from the leather seat. There was no escaping this, the void was consuming it all. Joseph closed his eyes as the ground beneath the car gave way. The steel frame lurched forward and fell with one last pathetic creak of metal. Whatever light was left in the world faded to nothing.

Chapter
Twelve

No More Sleeping

Joseph woke with a start. His elbow hit the center of the steering wheel in a wild swing, sounding off the car horn and further shattering the quiet.

'Christ!' he yelled, his eyes clenched shut and his lips curled back over his teeth. He fumbled for the radio dial in a frenzy, desperate to silence the ear-splitting, brass-band notes of Jingle Jangle Jingle.

As I go riding merrily—
CLICK!

Joe rubbed at his temples and let his head fall back against the soft leather seat.

Was I asleep?

He looked up from his lap and shielded his eyes from the blinding sun. It took a few moments and a hundred or so blinks before the memory faded back in. He looked through the windshield at the last of the dawdling children being herded to cars by tired-looking parents. There were a handful of teachers waving half-heartedly, fake smiles painted across their faces from ear to ear. Joe looked at the dashboard clock: *15:42*.

'Shit,' he hissed.

He rolled himself against the door and toppled out onto the sidewalk, catching himself and straightening before any of the teachers could notice. The last thing Joseph needed was one of these sad shitheads telling Pam he had come to the pickup half-drunk. He even gave one of them a wave, returning the fake smile with equal apathy.

'Mr. Ridley,' said one of the teachers, stepping forward. She was a petite woman, her hair pulled back in a tight, fair ponytail.

'Good afternoon, Miss Tenner,' he replied, quickly straightening his tie.

This woman was a real piece of work. She couldn't be a day over thirty-five and yet she had a sharp glint in her eye, the kind you would normally find in some hard-ass war widow. He had only met her twice—the school stuff was Pam's area of expertise—and she had given him an uncomfortable itch in his neck each time.

'No Mrs. Ridley today?'

'No, she's uh– she's in the hospital.'

'Oh my.'

'No, she's fine, she just took a tumble. Hurt her arm something fierce.'

'I see,' Miss Tenner replied, eyeing Joseph with thinly veiled disapproval. 'I didn't see you parked there. You're rather late, aren't you?'

There was that itch again. There was something in the woman's voice that really crawled under Joseph's skin. It was her tone; it sounded judgmental and suspicious, not the kind of inflections a parent would expect from their child's teacher. What the hell did *she* know?

It's always these childless bitches that think they know best.

'I had a business meeting. Marcus knows to wait for me.'

He hated her. He hated the way she seemed so unafraid, so sure that she held the cards in this exchange. She didn't even have to speak, it was in those beady, searching eyes, and the mouth that puckered. And yet, Joe found himself losing concentration and falling into a fantasy. How drunk was he still? He was imagining Miss Tenner's hand down his slacks. He pictured himself throwing her into the back of his Maserati and ripping that slim-fit button-up right off her chest. The thought of hate fucking her made his cock twitch and swell. He was picturing her ankles bouncing on his shoulders, when he found himself pulled back to reality.

'Mr. Ridley?'

'I'm sorry, I didn't catch that.'

Her eyes were even more narrow now, barely slits.

Crap, was I staring at her tits or something? Damnit, Joe, get it together.

She had a wry smile carved into the side of her mouth and the shuffle of her feet gave Joseph a signal he had long since forgotten.

You're shitting me.

Prickles of shame rose in Joe's stomach, but they quickly vanished when he glanced over the woman's shoulder. He had noticed something that replaced those prickles with heavy stones. Marcus was nowhere to be found. There were only two kids left, one girl and one wailing boy, apparently playing tug'o'war over a jumper.

'Say, do you know where that boy of mine might be waiting?'

Miss Tenner went back to looking irritated and looked lazily over her shoulder.

'I don't remember seeing him, but there are a lot of kids that get picked up here.' She turned back and saw Joe's unimpressed expression. 'If he's not out here, he will be inside. I always find him in the music room, playing with the drums. Maybe he's there.'

'Right,' said Joseph with an annoyed sigh. The last thing he felt like doing was playing hide and seek in a school. His whole body was aching as if he had been put through a meat grinder.

Some hangover.

He made sure to give Miss Tenner a wink as he passed, taking great delight in her sharp intake of breath. The other teachers watched him cross the lawn, all three of them looking annoyed. Joseph loved it. He relished that look, the way it trailed behind him and infected all those around. Those low on the corporate ladder despised seeing a man in a six-thousand-dollar suit carve a path through their territory. Teachers were no exception, even teachers at private schools like this. Joseph smiled as he pushed open the plexiglass doors, knowing full well that their jealous eyes were still locked firmly in his direction. He was right. They had watched him the entire way, wide-eyed and seething, and they did not look away until the doors swung shut behind him.

'Marcus, where are you?'

Joseph had walked the length of one corridor before realizing he had no damn idea where the music room would be. This place was huge, by far the biggest school he had ever set foot in. It had been very important to him that Marcus be enrolled in the most expensive school within a forty-mile radius.

'They don't just let anyone in there, y'know. No way my son's going to a public school.'

He never really cared about the rival educational merits of the two; hell, he had gone to a public school and loved it. No, it was just something else to brag about; status is power and when you can reach it, you take it.

'C'mon, Marky, I don't have time for this sh– Just hurry up, will you?'

The silence was uncomfortable to say the least, broken only by the repetitive clop-clopping of Joseph's black Oxfords. It was remarkably eerie to see such a large building so vacuous and still. Joseph imagined these hallways would have been bursting with snot-faced kids just an hour earlier. Fluorescent, white light bounced off the polished floor and cast the endless row of sleek, black lockers in a glow.

'Gotta admit,' Joseph mumbled to himself, 'seems like I'm getting my money's worth.'

He passed a door that led to a small gymnasium, filled wall to wall with expensive-looking treadmills and rowing machines. Their little blue screens blinked out of the dark and what appeared to be a wheelchair was folded against the far window.

'Dad?' the sound made Joe's head spin. It sure as hell sounded like Marcus.

'Marcus,' he yelled back, relieved now but growing more agitated all the same. 'Where are you? Let's move it.'

He picked up his walk to a light jog and threw a quick glance down every hallway he passed.

'Dad, please come get me.'

What the fuck?

Marcus sounded apprehensive, maybe even scared.

'Where the hell are you, son? I can't see you.'

'Dad, where are you?'

'This place is planned like a fucking IKEA,' Joseph growled to himself, his frustration bubbling over. He passed another room and skidded to a stop.

'Jesus,' he gasped.

He peered in on the charred remains of what looked to be a kitchen. He didn't remember Pam saying anything about there being a fire at the school. The acidic smell of burnt plastic and something much more foul punched into Joe's nostrils. He gagged, jumping away from the door.

'Marcus?' he called over his shoulder, struggling to look away from the scorched room. Something about it made his skin crawl. It made the aches in his body tremble. He looked down at his hands and found them bandaged and bloody.

'What?' he gasped.

'Dad?' the boy's yell was louder now, more frantic. Joe snapped out of his daze and found himself looking down at the smooth, pale skin of his palms, and the clasp of a TAG Heuer watch.

'I'm coming, son, just keep talking so I know where you are.' He ran now, panic rising in his chest and fueling his heart in rapid, hard thumps against his frame.

This corridor felt impossibly long; there could be no reasonable explanation for this much space, for this many rooms. Something else was burrowing in Joseph's mind as he ran; he refused to take the time to inspect closer, but some of the doors did not look like classroom doors. They were painted blue and had numbers screwed into their wood like a hotel or apartment building. Some of the doors were even open, and he could swear there were voices coming from within.

'Hello?' Joseph called again.

He called for his son. He called for any of the teachers that were paid an arm and a leg to run this place. The aches in his body had intensified now; stinging pain sang along his arms, legs, back, and face.

'What's happening to me?' he said in a low voice. Sweat poured into his vision and each step became heavier.

'Mom wouldn't have left me,' Marcus said. His voice came from the hallway beyond, the hallway behind. It came from above and below, and still Joseph ran.

'Marky, help me!' Joseph yelled, one of his legs wobbling dangerously beneath him.

'Help me,' the boy echoed.

Joseph threw himself into a side corridor and slid into the lockers with a thunderous boom. There was no exit in sight, only endless white and black, so far into the distance it became a dot.

'This isn't real,' Joseph muttered, taking his head in his hands and pressing his eyes shut. 'I'm drunk and passed out somewhere. Where was I last? I don't remember driving to the school. I was home, on the couch. Was I home? Fuck. How did I get here?'

He opened his eyes again and froze. The bright white had become a dim glow, barely illuminating ten feet of floor in either direction. Directly ahead was another door. It was not a classroom door; he was sure of that now. Not only because of its appearance, but because the room beyond was no classroom. He knew the furniture in the dim, yellow glow of an overhead lamp. It was his living room, his home.

'This isn't real,' he said again, cautiously stepping toward the doorway. 'You drink too much, damnit.'

Joseph shook his shoulders, summoning all of his sober consciousness and tried to collect himself. Deciding that he must be wandering through a dream, Joe charged into the room. Whatever false confidence he had just gathered blew away in one gust as the door slammed shut behind him. It came so close he felt it kiss the hair on his neck. The first thing that reached him was the overwhelming reek of Scotch whiskey; it was as if the walls had been drenched in it. Flickering blue light washed half of the room in its glow. It illuminated an almost empty bottle of Macallan Rare—and a figure crumpled forward in an armchair with his chin on his chest.

'This is a dream.'

No matter how much Joseph chanted his new favorite mantra, he could not shake the feeling that this was too vivid to be an illusion. He felt the floor beneath his feet, the smooth wall under his fingertips. He could feel and see everything with a heightened level of awareness. Could someone be asleep if their heart beat this fast? The adrenaline should wake him up … he felt awake. He attempted to rationalize it in any way he could, but this was all wrong. The fact remained that a moment earlier he had been chasing his son through a labyrinth of private school corridors, and now he was standing in his living room, looking down at himself. His double was snoring into an empty glass, fast asleep.

The imposter in the armchair groaned and made Joseph jump in his skin, then there was more snoring.

Maybe if I wake myself up, then I wake up.

It seemed like solid enough logic. He had heard about lucid dreaming before but had written it off as hippy bullshit. This was uncharted territory for Joseph Ridley.

'Hey,' he said weakly.

Nothing, just more dry snores.

'Hey,' Joseph said again, a bit louder now.

The figure went silent for a single breath, and then kept on sleeping. Joseph knew better than most how deeply he could drift after a few too many drinks.

'Wake up, asshole.' He practically yelled it now, and all it earned him was a grunt and a shuffle to a more comfortable position.

'C'mon,' Joe snarled. He didn't want to be here anymore; he could feel an emptiness around him, like if he made one wrong step he would fall into oblivion.

'Get up you son of a–' He stepped forward and leaned down to give his double a shove. In a flash of motion, the sleeping man shot to his feet and grabbed Joseph by the throat.

'I *am* awake,' the imposter hissed into Joseph's ear. 'Open your fucking eyes.'

Joseph choked, beating and twisting at the man's wrist in a breathless fury. He could feel the blood pooling behind his eyes and his lungs screamed for oxygen.

'How dare you forget.'

The man threw Joseph across the room effortlessly. He spiraled into a sturdy, hardwood cupboard and it cracked under his weight, showering his crumbling body with shards of timber.

'Open your eyes,' the imposter said again.

Joseph blinked through a kaleidoscope of blue and yellow stars. He struggled to regain his grip on the space around him. He heard footsteps advancing closer, heavy and fueled by rage.

'Why are you doing this?' he managed to wheeze before a foot struck him against the cheek, splitting the skin and sending a tooth skittering across the floor.

This isn't a dream. This can't be a dream.

Joe looked down at his bandaged hands. The freshly opened wounds sent a layer of blood crawling through the material.

Bandages?

The foot struck him again, this time in the stomach. It sent a wave of white-hot pain through his body and he heard a crash of thunder rattle his brain. In an instant he saw himself bringing a crowbar down, across the spine of a man with a red Range Rover.

CRASH!

He remembered the perky nipples of a college student, gently gripped between his teeth.

CRASH!

Marcus standing on the doorstep, silent and gaunt. Overwhelming joy and horror as he pulled his son and his wife close.

CRASH!

328

He remembered the apartment and the maniacal neighbors that stalked him. He remembered the gray world perishing in a wall of smoke and emptiness. He remembered everything.

Joseph screamed, what else could he do? The pains of his body had returned in paralyzing waves, but the memories crippled him in a way no impact could. He shook and sobbed and beat his fists into the ground, blowing spit through his teeth. He felt the double lean over him, his breath just inches from Joe's face.

'Now you see, these must *always* be with you.'

'Why don't you kill me?' There was silence, and Joseph felt the doppelgänger move away.

'Please, just kill me,' he wept.

The double said one more thing from the far side of the room, each word fading in volume.

'No more sleeping.'

Joseph knew the man was gone; he had felt his departure in the static vibration across his skin. He pressed his forehead into the wood a final time and rolled backwards onto his ass. The shirt Daewon had given him was now a singed gray and his bandages might as well have been soaked in blood. He knew he should be angry that the memories had returned, that there was

329

truly no escape, but all he felt was despair. In his mind he could see Pam waiting for him outside the Royal Dawn, the storm just a gray smear on the horizon … but he knew that was not his fate. He was going to die here, as punishment for his sins. Perhaps this was what he deserved, but it filled him with dread, nonetheless. Maybe he could survive and somehow return to the world he knew, where people's eyes, however persistent, did not bulge from their sockets. Would it be the life he knew, or would Pam be married to *Rod*? Which memories were real? The more he questioned it, the more he saw Pamela's life from a distance. He remembered a life of loose women and the keys to a brand-new Range Rover. He remembered a chef's son that he wanted so desperately to be his, so desperately that he–

'Stop it,' Joseph clawed at his temples, so deep he drew blood. 'Poison! Lies!'

A sound rescued him from the deafening echoes of memories that he could not believe were his. It was faint, so distant that he almost couldn't hear it over the agonizing pulsing in his head.

Take me home, country roads

'John fucking Denver.'

Joseph rushed to his feet and noticed that the living room was now lit up in golden sunlight. It glinted off the upended whiskey glass in a pearlescent wink. He spun around and saw through the window a view that should not have been possible: a large, green lawn that led out to a busy road. A few people were lingering across its threshold. Two children fighting over a jumper, the boy was crying. A small group of teachers were chattering close by, one of them Miss Tenner. Joseph rubbed the sweat from his eyes and tried to focus, looking for the black-haired child he knew so well.

West Virginia, mountain momma

'Marcus,' Joseph gasped. His face was so close to the glass that it fogged under his panicked breath.

He could see his son walking slowly to the passenger side of a well-used, red Range Rover. There was someone leaning forward from the driver's seat, beckoning the boy forward.

'Marcus!' Joseph slapped the glass and felt his body shake with a jolt of frantic electricity. The boy didn't hear him, he was much too far away, and yet Joe could still hear the music from the motherfucker's SUV.

The radio reminds me of my home far away ...

'Change the memory,' Joe said.

He spun around and grabbed the closest thing he could find, a wood and velvet reading chair that had always been more decoration than seating. He whipped it through the glass without hesitation and launched himself after it, falling to the grass. The shower of glass burned as it burrowed into his existing wounds, but Joseph was already on his feet again. There was no time to lick his wounds, no time for rest. He charged forward in a mad sprint, keeping the large car and his son in his sights. The teachers had stopped talking; they stood rigid now, faces blank and arms at their sides. They watched on swiveling heads as Joseph ran by, making no attempt to block his path or help.

... to the place, I belong ...

The SUV's passenger door swung open and Marcus stepped forward, clearly apprehensive.

'Marcus, don't!' Joseph ran faster, faster than anyone his age should be able to, faster than anyone in his condition possibly could. 'Marcus!'

The world was deaf to his cries and all it gave him in reply was John *fucking* Denver.

... Take me home, country roads

Marcus nodded and climbed up into the car, pausing once more before planting himself in the passenger seat.

'No!'

Joseph was so close now, mere seconds away. The driver leaned across and shut the door, whistling along to the song. He paused as he saw the man sprinting toward them, and then smiled. Joseph could barely see the stranger's face in his blind panic, but he saw the son of a bitch wink from beneath the brim of his cap.

'Marcus!' The boy heard him this time and turned to look out of the window in startled confusion.

'Dad?'

Marcus leaned to open the door and Joseph leapt, arm outstretched. It was too late. The Range Rover roared forward, spewing a cloud of toxic, black smoke. Joseph's palm slapped the steel and he spun, falling to the street in a pathetic heap.

'No, no, no, no, no,' he said.

Joe scurried to his feet and gave chase. His feet burned against the asphalt and the car became smaller and smaller in his sight. He wrenched every drop of energy he could find from the depths of his being, urging his legs to get him closer to his son. His arms swung, his feet smacked blacktop, but the world did not move around him. He might as well have been running on the spot. It was barely five seconds before the Range Rover was gone. Marcus was gone.

Joseph's yell could have cracked the sky. It blinded him. It drained his body and left only pure, visceral anguish in its wake. This was no dream. No man could imagine such misery, no sleeping mind could endure such grief. He had failed his son. He had failed his son *twice*. Had he been a few steps quicker, had he not fallen, he would have climbed through that car window. He would have reached in and strangled the sick motherfucker where he sat. Had he not been sleeping, doused in booze and piss, his son would not have been alone. His son would not have been called over to a strange man's car and gotten inside with false promises of a ride home, or candy, or toys. Had he not been drinking himself through the guilt of being a worthless husband and a worthless father, he would have been able to hold his son in his arms, say 'I love you' and maybe even hear it back. All of this came full circle, back to Joseph.

The storm was approaching quickly. The black clouds flashed with red and the thunderous crashing of rain on asphalt could already be heard. Joseph gave one last, mournful blink at the spot where the car had vanished. He was meant to have changed it; that was the moment. Joseph wasn't sure how he knew, but something deep inside taunted him. A voice far below reminded him that this could have changed everything. If Joe had stopped Marcus from getting into that car, maybe he would have finally woken from this nightmare. He would have rolled over, held Pam in his arms, and called Marcus in for a morning cuddle. Maybe it wouldn't have changed anything, but he would have tried. He could have held his son, if just for a second.

'Out of time.'

Joseph jumped back, startled by the small woman standing barely an inch from his chest. Miss Tenner glared at him, her normally narrow eyes now wide and blank. The street behind her had become blanketed in fog; whispers and running feet hissed and slapped the road just out of view. Joseph watched, waiting for her jaw to slacken, almost welcoming the violence. She simply stared. The remaining teachers on the grass were also advancing on him now, each of them glaring calmly without so much as a breath.

'What other memories could you torture me with?' Joseph said, stepping up to the petite woman and meeting her gaze.

There were only the rising howls of wind and then finally, she spoke again.

'These are the memories you chose.'

Joseph shoved her aside; he had endured his fill of sinister riddles and cryptic idioms. He dragged his feet back toward the doors of the school, wincing with every step. He did not know where he would go next, or to where he would be herded, but for now he was content limping from the storm and mist. At least until it finally consumed him. Only then would he stop fighting it. The next teacher, a burly man with a white goatee, barred his path.

'Nearly, Joseph, nearly at the peak.'

Joe swung his fist and caught the plump gent on the chin. It obviously caused the man little harm but moved him all the same. He marched on, shaking away the blood that pooled between his fingers.

'The storm can wash away the doubt, make things clear.'

'Fuck off.' Joseph shoved the next one aside, a smaller, balding man.

He looked over his shoulder and saw the teachers were following closely behind, increasing in pace and staring through him.

'You must–'

Joseph threw himself forward. He knocked the next woman to the ground and raced forward.

'Joseph!'

They called to him, their steps a breath behind. He could hear other voices now too, emerging from the fog. Voices that spat venom and promises of pain. He lunged forward and burst through the school doors. He stumbled a little as his feet met the familiar, blue carpet. He took a deep breath and strode on, eyes locked firmly on his door at the end of the hall. The home he knew. The voices of the mist and the teachers faded from existence, but a new— perhaps more skin-crawling—sound filled his ears. Nearby thunder rumbled and guttural cries hissed from every door he passed. Some were pleading and agonized, some were trembling with fury. He heard Daewon, taking his dying breath. He heard Pam crying, praying for her son to come home. He heard Marcus begging for help, his throat hoarse from screaming. He heard himself. He was begging to die. The doorknobs all rattled, and the wood flexed as the people on the other side pushed and barged. Joseph saw a figure in his apartment, holding the door open for him. Clean-shaven and as fit as he had ever been, the doppelgänger beckoned Joe closer, unashamed in his nakedness. A door far behind crashed open. The sound of shattering wood spraying the wall echoed through Joseph's skull and he looked over his shoulder, just in time to see a figure walk out into the corridor. The stranger was so tall that he had to bend forward. His limbs were long and thin, giving him the appearance of a horrifyingly emaciated spider. The man's eyes bulged from their sockets, peppered with blotches of broken blood cells and his jaw hung dislocated, pooling with blood and spit. On and on Joseph limped, his double still waiting patiently by the door. He heard more doors exploding to shrapnel and he felt the shaking of bloodthirsty creatures rushing in his direction.

'Joseph, you should see what fun Marcus and I are having. Why don't you come take a look?'

Joseph bit his lip and hobbled ever faster, refusing to look back.

BANG!

'Mr. Ridley, don't you want to come back and fuck me? I'll let you have me anywhere.'

'You can fuck both of us.'

'Mr. Ridley?'

BANG!

'Where is Marcus, Joseph? Where is he? What the hell have you done?'

BANG!

'I can't feel them. M-my legs, I can't– why would anyone do this to me? Why?'

'This is it,' said the double, reaching forward and grabbing Joseph by the front of his shirt. 'Now you choose eternity.' Joseph felt himself pulled through the air, away from the creatures at his heels and into the apartment.

He fell through the red gloom to the floor and looked up stunned. The doppelgänger slammed the door shut, as calmly as one shooing away a salesman. Before the hall was sealed away Joseph had caught sight of the fate he'd narrowly avoided. Enormous men and women with limp jaws and displaced joints had been crowded in the dim light. Their faces were contorted in rage and their bulbous eyes pierced the dark. They were pushing each other violently, screaming and smearing each other's flesh with blood and gore.

The one at the front was a woman Joe knew well. She wore cheap, colorful rings on every finger. Her jeans were faded and held up by a leather belt with a thick, metal buckle. It was a woman he had not seen for a very long time; a face framed in faded blonde curls that he could recognize in any condition. A face that brought horrors of its own.

Chapter
Thirteen

Those Below

Joseph clawed at the bed frame and pulled himself to his feet, groaning with the strain.

'Holy shit,' he said.

He looked around at what had once been his apartment. He had always found it to be a bit of a shithole—especially when compared with his last home—but now it was a portrait of decay.

The walls were peeling, bubbling, and weeping thick, black ooze. It looked more like burned flesh than he could ever remember. The floor was spongey and disgustingly moist; it squelched and sent pools of watery, red mucus to its surface with every step. The smell was the worst of it and seemed to be emanating from the pulsing, black lifeform now spread entirely across the kitchen. It looked like something from a Lovecraftian wet dream; it resembled extraterrestrial bacteria. The rotten apple was gone, buried beneath the convulsing tentacles. Joseph imagined it throbbed there, like a heart.

'Sanctuary can rot, the less it is needed,' said the naked Joseph, not looking away from him. There was something ominous in the doppelgänger's expression, something you could not quite put your finger on, but it set you on edge all the same.

'This is it, isn't it?' replied Joseph, steadying himself against the wall and blinking at his double. 'Soon I'm going to get sucked out that window and chewed up in the storm … like Taylor, right?'

The double did not reply; his face did not even twitch.

'What are you anyway?'

No reply.

'You're me?'

'I was blind. I couldn't speak.'

'Yeah.' Joseph snorted. He reflected on the terrifying, shadowed creature with its eyes sewn shut, looming over the foot of his bed.

'Do you know what this is? This place?'

The double ignored him again. It turned and walked across the room to the window. The world beyond was barely a storm now; it was a vortex of vapor and dust. Rain and debris spun and thrashed, tossed by the wind in relentless spirals and the flashing of lightning did little now to pierce the crimson haze. The sound that filled every space was a deep rumble; the guttural, threatening growl you would hear from a dog with its lips peeled back.

'You saw them, didn't you?'

Joseph's brows creased over, stretching the cut, bloody skin of his forehead.

'What?'

'Marcus. Pamela.'

Joe shuffled closer to the figure by the window, the hairs on his neck at full attention.

'Yeah, I saw them.'

More silence.

'I couldn't save him,' Joseph said, feeling his eyes brim with moisture. 'I couldn't save my boy. I was too slow.'

The double looked back at him; his eyes were drenched with contempt. 'You slept with a bottle in your lap while my son was locked away.'

'I know.' Joseph slouched into his favorite chair but found no comfort there. His face fell into his hands again and he raked at the scratches by his ears. 'All of it was me. It all goes back to me.'

The doppelgänger's face did not soften. There was not a drop of sympathy to be found there. Joseph's body felt too weak to cry; he could feel it losing strength as quickly as the building they stood in. It was all going to come crumbling down; he could feel it in his weary bones. He was out of time.

The front door shuddered under a heavy blow and the furious screams of the attackers grew louder, puncturing the storm. Joseph wondered which would come first—would he be skinned and sliced by the maniacs, or would the storm pull him away, winding his limbs in sickening knots and tossing him to the cold street below? He reached a slippery finger forward and fumbled with the television's power button, hoping perhaps he could bask in its sterile glow before the end.

'God does not cast a light on this peak,' said the doppelgänger.

Joseph hoped he could make some light of his own. The TV buzzed to life with a satisfying click and he watched as a picture expanded across the black surface, flooding the man in flickering radiance.

'My Pam,' he sighed, the faintest of smiles crept across his dry lips.

The freckled cheeks of his wife filled the screen. The sight of her smooth, tanned skin punched through the cold and filled Joseph with a slight warmth. He was watching another memory, through a set of eyes belonging to a much younger Joseph.

'What do you think?' asked Pam, twirling on the spot. Her pale, yellow sundress spun around her waist, flashing the white of her panties and the supple curve of her buttocks.

'You look amazing,' Joseph said.

His lips moved but the voice came from the television. He felt the erotic excitement build in his chest and fire down to his crotch. The suffocating love he had for this woman swept over him in crashing waves. Pamela stopped spinning and stepped closer to the screen. Joseph felt her hands curl around his hips, tickling the skin beneath his shirt.

'I love y–'

The screen blinked static and now Joseph was watching Pam through a window. She didn't seem to notice him. She was pacing back and forth, frantically biting at her nails and pressing the phone to her ear so firmly her skin was turning red.

'What did they say?' She sat down in the reading chair, and then stood again and resumed pacing. 'What are they doing to find him, Rod?'

Joseph saw one of his hands come into view, pushing aside some of the shrubbery he hid behind. He was holding something … a frayed piece of string, laced through a gold paper clip. He had found it when he emptied out Marcus' bag. The boy had stopped crying long enough to say, 'No, that's my dad's!'

The screen blinked again.

'Mommy, Dad!' Marcus rushed across the park green, tears in his eyes. He wiped at the dirt on his little, chubby cheeks and flailed his arms.

'Looks like he fell again,' said Joseph with a small, sweet chuckle, 'poor little guy.'

'I know, I know,' replied Pam. She pushed a curl of dark hair behind her ear, smiling. 'He gets it from me, you don't need to say it.' She stepped forward and caught the infant in her arms, swinging him high and cradling him against her shoulder.

'It's okay, dear, Mommy's got you. I'll make it all better.'

THWNK!

Now Joseph looked in on a dark, dingy space. Flashes of white illuminated the area in quick stabs, arcing out from an old television with a crooked antenna. Joseph watched his view step further into the room, gliding over empty milk cartons and spilled crisp packets. There was a figure curled up on the musty, green couch. Her snores groaned over the sound of the canned laughter from the TV and Joseph could smell a week's worth of cheap booze wafting off of her. Dread boiled in his stomach. He was terrified she would wake, and yet he could not will himself to move. She shifted a little, a tangled bunch of faded, blonde curls falling limp over her face. Joseph had never felt more vulnerable; he had never felt more exposed. He looked down at one of the empty Jack Daniels bottles and wondered if it could split skull. Would it be hard? Would he have to swing it more than once? What if she woke up, what would he do then? The woman snored again, violently. She adjusted her jeans with a groggy hand—each finger wearing a cheap, colorful ring—and her unclasped belt buckle jingled and slapped against the denim. He could end this now, while she slept. How much could he undo if he pushed a blade through her windpipe? How much pain could he erase?

THWNK

He was looking in on the sterile white of a hospital room. A man was weeping in his bed, his thin hands pressed to his eyes and his mouth moist with spit.

'Why?' he sobbed. The small stranger was alone, pawing at the legs beneath his blanket and looking to the ceiling with puffy eyes.

Joseph somehow felt the man's sorrow vibrate through him. He felt the man's overwhelming despair and loneliness. It choked him; it filled his throat like cement and anchored him further into the chair. The stranger looked down to the wheelchair beside his bed and then buried his face in his arms once more.

THWNK!

Almost heaven, West Virginia

'Joseph,' said the doppelgänger from close behind.

Joe was watching now, looking out through the window of his trusty old Range Rover. Pam's son was slowly making his way over.

'Marcus,' Joe called out, waving the child closer. 'I'm a friend of your mom's, she sent me to come pick you up.'

'I don't know you,' replied the boy. His expression was painted with caution.

'Well, it's been a long time, but I went to school with her. We used to go to the pet shop all the time together, to look at the fish. Your mom loves the fish and the turtles, doesn't she?'

Marcus' face relaxed a little.

So, she hasn't changed much after all. That's lucky.

Something else caught his eye, a figure running toward them across the school green. It was a large, wild-haired man, covered in bandages and blood.

'C'mon now, Marky, let's get you home,' said Joe, giving the boy another smile.

'Joseph,' said the double again.

THWNK!

Hands. His hands gripped Pamela's throat. Her face was already turning blue and swelling at the sides. Her eyes rolled up and spots of blood burst across the white of her sclera. Her mouth hung open in a wide, silent scream. Joseph watched helplessly as he raised his crowbar and brought it crashing down, through the front of her face in an explosion of blood and bone. He felt the gore on his hands, he tasted the metallic odor on his tongue.

'No,' Joseph whimpered.

His memories and desires were crashing in on each other. His mind was a catastrophic storm to rival the one outside. He wanted to hold his wife and son and tell them he was sorry. He wanted to see Pam and her piece of shit chef husband suffer, the way he had suffered watching her love another man. He wanted to fuck another woman with Pam watching; he wanted Pam, alone, just her. He wanted to pull Marcus from that two-ton red monstrosity and take him home, keep him safe. He wanted this cycle of madness to end. He wanted his memories with him, the good ones, at least for now.

THWNK!

He was no longer watching through his own eyes. The hands that reached out and picked up the piece of paper were not his; they were slender and feminine. He was not Joseph, he was Pamela. She felt a hurricane of loss and anticipation in her chest; she knew what this was. She had expected this for some time now; her husband had been pulling away for so long.

> *I shouldn't be here anymore. The house is yours.*
> *~~This wasn't what~~ Take care of Marcus.*
> *I'm sorry.*
> *Joe.*

She felt grief cut at her stomach in white-hot swipes. She felt relief.

The banging at the door had intensified even more. The wooden frame bent and warped with each passing second. The voices beyond continued to scream, making their promises of pain and gruesome pleasure. Joseph stumbled forward to the window and fell against it, his face flat against the cold glass. There would be no more running; he doubted he could even fight, should he have found the will.

I'm out of time.

The doppelgänger did not move. He looked completely calm, staring out into the tempest. Joe found it hard to believe that face had ever looked back at him in the mirror, especially now. He did not need to see his reflection to feel the sag of his cheeks, the swollen drooping of his eyes. He was sure he could even feel a decade's worth of thinning to his scalp.

'I must look like shit,' he wondered aloud.

It wasn't until he heard the words that he understood he did not care. The thought of death seemed welcome now, although he found it hard to believe it would come with rest.

'Would you like one?' said the double, raising his hand to show a crumpled cigarette packet. Buried inside were two bent Silk Cuts and a lighter. 'You left it behind.'

'Not sure I should, I've heard they'll kill you,' Joseph said with bitter sarcasm. He was quiet, and then a genuine laugh escaped his lips. 'Thanks.'

He reached out and took the packet, putting the cigarette to his lips and wincing as his thumb struck the lighter's wheel. He felt the warmth fill him from top to bottom, snaking through his throat and creeping from his nostrils in milky blue wisps. It was nice not to feel the guilt for once, the feeling that you were burning away a year of life in a roll of rat-poison-soaked tobacco.

'You should confess, while you can,' said the doppelgänger.

Joseph looked sidelong at the man, almost questioning him on reflex. He knew what the double meant.

'Like I said, all of it … it was me,' said Joseph taking another drag and closing his eyes. 'Every last fucking bit of it, it was my fault.'

The double looked down at him with thinly veiled disgust.

'No more self-pity. Confess. Why are you here? Why are you *really* here?'

'I tricked my best friend into dumping the girl he loved, so I could take her for myself. I tricked Pam into thinking I'm worth the dirt she walks on, then I got her pregnant. I ran her and Marcus through the mud so that people I didn't even like would fear me.' Joseph's eyes could not produce another tear, but they stung anyway.

'I lost my son. I'm the one who put some innocent son of a bitch in a wheelchair. All of it was me.'

'You left,' replied the naked double.

'That was the only thing I did right.'

'You ran.'

'I left for them. Pam couldn't stand to look at me anymore. I can't blame her.'

'Lies.'

'Marcus didn't trust me anymore. He needed me to protect him and I failed. I don't deserve to be his father.'

'You are lying.'

'I know what they thought of me. Drunk, dead-shit loser. There was no coming back from that, I had to leave.'

'Tell the truth!'

The doppelgänger dived forward, grabbing Joseph by the throat and swinging him into the window with a menacing crunch of glass. The glowing cigarette butt flew into the dark, leaving only a trail of thin smoke in its stead. Joseph watched as a reflection of his youth leaned in on him, blank in the face but hot with rage.

'No more excuses, tell me the truth.'

'That is the truth,' Joe choked, too weak to pull at the hand on his neck. 'I couldn't move on, I was toxic.'

'Search deeper.'

'I love my son,' Joseph said. His lip trembled and his vision swam. 'I never stopped loving him.'

'Then why did you leave?'

'Please, I love my son. It's not his fault.'

'Confess.'

'Don't make me–'

'Tell me!'

'I couldn't stand it anymore!' Joseph yelled. It had come from deep inside him, somewhere protected and secret. The room around them shuddered and jets of water began to shoot through the ceiling's cracks.

'You were afraid,' replied the double, never breaking eye contact. The front door cracked, one of the hinges flying into the opposite wall with a clang.

'I'm going to rip the jaw from your fucking head, Joseph,' yelled one of the maniacs.

'Every time I looked at him– at my son, I saw *her*. I couldn't stop seeing it.' Joseph spewed his shame, finally and truly allowing his walls to cave. The room lurched and the black mass in the kitchen shrieked.

'What that guy did to Marky, it– I couldn't stop seeing– it reminded me of what she did to me. I just couldn't–'

'You abandoned your son.'

'I couldn't–'

'You were weak when he needed you to be strong.'

'Yes.'

'When I get in, I'm going to rip your guts through your ass. I'm going to split it wide open.' That one sounded like the drunk neighbor.

'Confess.'

'I destroyed my family, and then I abandoned them.'

Joseph hung his head. He had only enough strength left to keep himself standing. The freezing water was now at his ankles and the blackened walls were melting around him. The creature clinging to the kitchen screamed and twisted, flinging its oozing black arms against the walls in deafening cracks. The doppelgänger loosened his grip on Joseph's throat and gave him a look that might have even passed as relief.

'I'm going to let them in now,' he said, leaning Joseph against the window and taking a step back.

'Okay.'

The double leaned forward, put the last cigarette to Joseph's lips and lit the tip. Without another word he turned and stepped across the room, the water splashing beneath his large feet. Joseph turned to face the window, looking out on the apocalyptic gale. He took a deep, long drag of the smoke. The cracks had webbed out to the window's edges now, twinkling against the blood-red radiance like a spider's web in morning dew. The radio crackled to life and the familiar, droning voice reached through the anarchy.

'Well, folks, this is it. One hell of a doozy, wouldn't you say? How about that wind? I thought the roof would come right off, I tell ya.'

Joseph heard the door crunch open. The sound of rushing feet hammered through the water and stopped close behind him.

'I want him first.'

'Stay back, motherfucker, he's mine.'

'Mine.'

Joe squinted out into the storm, not sure what he hoped to see. The street below had crumbled away to dust, taking with it the blank-faced voyeurs and creatures in the fog. He pressed a hand to the rough glass and felt it flex under his palm.

'Well, it's about time we sign off, folks. It's been a pleasure as always.'

Joseph pushed against the window and felt it slacken.

SPLASH!

They were inching toward him like hungry wolves, tongues lapping viciously at their bleeding gums. He curled his fingers into a fist and swung it at the glass, watching in mild surprise as it crumpled and shattered. The cloud of twinkling glass was sucked from the room in an instant, in its place a powerful, rigid vacuum. It sucked water, blood, and pieces of ceiling from the room in dangerous currents.

'And to my pal, Joe, out there, don't forget to– don't forget–' the radio stuttered and crackled.

Joseph did an about-face and pulled the cigarette from his mouth, blowing smoke from his nostrils. He looked across at the crowd of blood-soaked psychopaths that formed a half-circle around him, each of them frozen in place and twitching. They were completely intoxicated with anticipation.

'Don't forget to welcome the fall.'

The radio growled into silence and clicked off, leaving only the wailing of the storm. The doppelgänger watched from the far wall, completely passive.

'It's okay, honey,' hissed the woman at the front. Her faded, blonde curls were stuck to the corners of her torn mouth and she stepped forward, closer to Joseph and the pull of the wind. Elastic strands of blood and foam clung to her lips and reached out for the void. 'I won't let them hurt you, baby. I'll take good care of you, young man.'

'Shut up,' Joseph replied calmly. He pinched the cigarette between his teeth again and drained the last of its bounty. 'You can't have me, not anymore.'

He gave the double one last look—an exchange of indescribable understanding—then he flicked the butt of his smoke at the intruders and threw himself back. He watched as all of the deformed attackers leapt forward, clawing at the space where he had been. They roared and wailed, some seemed to laugh. Joseph felt himself carried out into the cold and then thrown down. The jagged window frame of his apartment faded from view, swallowed in the mist. He closed his eyes and breathed deep as his senses dripped away. He thought of Pam, the way she had looked when she came down the aisle toward him, dressed in white. He thought of Marcus, purple-faced and screaming as he entered the world, reaching his tiny fingers out for Joe's. If there was anything he could take with him from this life into oblivion, it would be those memories. He knew they were real. He could not have fantasized a life so perfect, and so perfectly wasted. The emptiness he dreaded was around him now, seeping into his mind and loosening his grip. He had fallen so far and now he was simply fading.

You can forget me, it's okay. As long as the pain I gave you dies too.

Joseph hoped there was a world, a time, where he had loved Pam the way she deserved. Maybe in that world he had also been the father he sometimes dreamed of being—forgiving and supportive. Perhaps there was a world where Pam married a modest cook, and a kind-hearted gym teacher could still walk his dog. The thought made Joseph smile.

Chapter
Fourteen

The Other Side

The evening news anchor continued her bleak announcements as Pamela Byrnes stacked freshly washed plates into their proper home.

'Three cars were involved in the collision, killing five adults and two children. The cause of the pile-up is still being investigated, but it's believed that one of the drivers may have been under the influence. Next up, a grisly suspected suicide–'

Pam hummed to herself, tapping her leg and singling along to Fleetwood Mac who was softly playing from her phone, oblivious to the droning from the exhausted-looking woman on the TV. She wasn't much of a fan of the news nowadays—it was too depressing—but she did find comfort in there being another voice in the room. Even one as miserable as that. She grabbed a handful of cutlery from the dish rack and started sorting them into the drawer. It was soothing to see the glinting steel fall neatly, one after the other, exactly where they needed to go. Cleaning was one of the few, more shameful delights she took pleasure in now. It wasn't good to think about that too long; it's a bitter feeling to realize how boring you've become.

Something caught her eye in the window above the sink, a flash in the dark. Her heart beat faster, harder, and she froze with a butter knife tightly gripped in her hand.

What the hell?

She squinted through the dark, searching for a shape but hoping for nothing. She found only the swaying, slender shadows of the oak tree's branches in the neighbor's yard.

'Damn,' Pam hissed.

She threw down the knife and ran her hands over her face. She pulled down on her cheeks and fought at the fog in her mind. This was not the first scare she had had recently; it was not even the first today. It was as if she could feel something hanging over her and breathing down her neck. She was sure the hairs there had been bristled for days.

'That's it for tonight but tune in tomorrow for updates on this and more.' The news anchor signed off and the television blasted its obnoxious chorus of trumpets to signal the end of *Raven's Crest News at Eight*.

DING!

Pamela jumped again, just as she picked up another knife from the rack.

'Oh my God,' she said. Her cheeks were flushing darker and her eye twitched.

Who the hell would be coming around at this time of night?

DING!

Pam stormed from the kitchen to the hall, getting angrier with every footfall. She reached out for the doorknob and froze. Who *would* be coming around at this time of night? She heard a sound on the other side of the door, shuffling of feet. There was no peephole on the door, but Pam could look out of the window. If she did, her visitor would most certainly see she was home. The feet shuffled again and Pam's breath caught in her throat. Then came a knock, three loud raps.

'Who is it?' Pam had tried to sound assertive and failed spectacularly.

There was a tense pause, and then the visitor replied.

'Pam? Hello?'

The voice was familiar, albeit generously slurred.

'What the h–' Pam wrenched open the door and found herself looking at a swaying, broad-shouldered woman of at least forty.

'Thea? What's the matter with you? It's after nine.'

The woman slapped a hand to her mouth and staggered again, handbag swinging wildly in her fist.

'Oh *shit*, sorry, hun. I didn't know it was so late. Did I wake Marky?'

Pam looked over her shoulder at the dark space at the top of the stairs, still visibly frustrated.

'I don't think so, but what are you doing here?'

'Oh come on, I knew you would be up,' Thea said, immediately forgetting her transgression and casually strolling into the home. She pushed back a thick bunch of red, wavy hair and gave Pam a badly aimed kiss on the cheek.

'That doesn't really answer my question, Thea,' Pam replied. Her tone had ultimately softened, and she closed the door behind the woman gingerly.

'Well, as you know I went out to that bar with Clint and his friends. They wanted to keep the fun going at the Diamond Strip, like a bunch of fucking teenagers, so naturally–'

'Naturally, you said yes?'

'Of course I did,' Thea said. She gave Pam a devilish smile and sat clumsily on one of the kitchen stools.

Pam grabbed a freshly polished glass and began to pour some cold water for her friend, when the woman regained her train of thought.

'I said I would at least try and get you to come along first, though, so here I am. I knew you wouldn't hear me out on the phone.'

'You know I'm not going out to the Diamond Strip, Thea, come on.' Pam laughed, genuinely amused at the thought of ordering a drink, deafened by thumping music and surrounded by perky twenty-somethings. 'You shouldn't either—you're too damn old.'

Thea feigned indignation before laughing as well.

'You don't get it, Pam—his friends are actually pretty cute.'

'Last time you said that I ended up across the table from greasy Fred.'

'Greasy Fred?'

'The truck driver. He was literally wearing overalls—I didn't even know they made them anymore.'

'Oh, greasy Fred!'

'You're not cupid, Thea.' Pam smiled as she handed Thea the water, sitting on the stool opposite.

'I swear- *hic* it's different this time, hun. There's this one guy named Walt. He's a real *free spirit* kinda deal. Just your type.'

'Free spirit?'

'Well, I mean he wouldn't shut up about how much he hates the boundaries of monogamy, but he's kinda cute. Maybe a bit short.'

'Pass.'

'There's another one who would be absolutely *perfect* for you. Charming, handsome, hard worker. Barely said a word but seemed friendly enough. One hell of a smile.'

'Oh yeah?' Pam raised her eyebrows. The longer she kept Thea talking, the more chance there was that she could get her into the spare bed, safe and sound.

'Yeah, Tony something-or-other. But he's married.'

'What a shame.' Pam didn't even try making that one sound authentic. Still, she smiled.

'Oh come on, Pamela,' Thea said, slapping the countertop and rattling the glass of water. 'You need to get out more, and don't give me that *I'm too old* rubbish. I look like your damn mom and I still have enough fun.'

'I don't doubt that, sweetie, but I actually *am* a mom. I can't go running off in the middle of the night to chat up married men.'

'But I miss you.'

'I miss you too, but you're here now. Why don't we put on a movie and get out the secret stash of sugar? I don't think Marky has found it this time … yet.'

Thea froze, staring at her friend dumbly like she was an old computer booting up. She was clearly enticed by the idea of Hugh Jackman and chocolate. After a short moment she came to her senses again and shook her head defiantly.

'No way, the boys are still waiting. *Please,* Pam. Marky will be okay. He'll sleep right through the night. He'll never know you were gone.'

Pam's face went blank, the smile melted away instantly and she sat back.

'I'm not leaving him alone here, Thea.'

Thea looked startled by the change in mood, and then realization dawned over her. Her mouth twisted into a guilty grimace and she looked down anxiously.

'Sorry, hun, I didn't mean ... that was stupid.'

'It's okay,' Pam replied. She got to her feet again and made herself busy getting Thea more water.

The red-haired woman had been sobered drastically by the exchange, and her playful, wandering gaze was replaced with concern.

'How're you doing, Pam?'

'I'm okay.' It was almost convincing, but not quite.

'I know it can't be tonight, but you do need to get out of the house.'

'I do get out, Thea.'

'Yeah, and then you lock yourself up again for months on end. I really do miss you. I'm worried.'

Pamela sighed deeply and turned back to Thea with a weary look.

'I know, you're right,' she said. 'Between work and looking after Marcus, it's just a lot.'

Thea nodded and reached across the counter to hold Pam's hand in hers.

'What can I do?'

'No, it's okay. I've just been having these weird *feelings* lately.'

'Feelings?'

'I don't know how to describe it. It's like when you wake up from a bad dream and you can't remember what you saw, but I've been getting it a lot. During the day too.'

'I think you need to see someone, Pam. Really talk this out, y'know? Get an expert opinion and all that.'

'I keep feeling *him*. It's like he's walking past every time I turn my back.'

'Him? You don't mean your piece of shit ex-husband, do you?'

'It's stupid.'

'It's not stupid, but he's not here. That's why you moved, to get away from that house and all the memories.'

'Yeah, I know. It doesn't always feel bad, though,' Pam continued. Her eyes were quickly moistening as old, buried emotions crept to the surface. 'Sometimes I wake up and it's like for a few seconds I forget all of the bad stuff. Just for a moment it feels like he's there with me, just us and Marky, y'know.'

Thea got to her feet, still swaying a little but holding the bench for balance. She wrapped Pam up in her arms and kissed the top of her head. It was not the first time they had done this, and it was unlikely to be the last. Suddenly, Pam's phone stopped playing the chorus of *Dreams* and began to ring. The harsh, loud chirps broke the quiet and shook the women from their trance.

'Do you want me to–'

'It's okay,' said Pam, reaching out for the phone and wiping her eyes. She cleared her throat and swiped to answer.

'Pamela speaking?'

'Hello, I'm terribly sorry to call at such a late time. Am I speaking with Mrs. Pamela Ridley?'

'It's okay, and yes, that's me.'

'Thank you, ma'am, my name is Constable Dunham. I'm calling from the Dawn Valley Police Department.'

Pam gave Thea a confused, concerned look and she returned it with a quizzical tilt of her head.

'Oh, how can I help you?'

'I'm sorry again to do this over the phone, ma'am, but I'm calling about your husband.'

Chapter
Fifteen

You Are Here

Sleep released its grip on Joseph Ridley just long enough for him to gasp for air. He opened his eyes gingerly and immediately cringed against the harsh, fluorescent white.

Beep. Beep. Beep.

He looked around slowly, paralyzed with panic. A cold sweat was quickly building on his brow. He found himself surrounded by flashing machines and plastic bags on hooks. It was a full half-minute before he realized he was in a hospital bed, and a minute more before he remembered what came before. The room was small and brightly lit, decorated wall to wall with medical posters and tightly sealed supplies. He was just about to pull the tube from his left arm when the door opened and a woman in blue scrubs came rushing in.

'Hey! Don't do that.'

Joe pulled away from her as she advanced. He reached wildly for something that he could use to defend himself. The woman noticed his alarm and took a step back, raising her hands.

'Woah, I'm not trying to hurt you, buddy. I'm here to help.'

'I was out. It was over,' Joseph said. He felt woozy. The aches in his body were subdued but his joints were as heavy as steel. 'Please God, it was over.' He slumped backwards, desperate but exhausted.

The woman inched closer and eyed the man cautiously. 'I'm Doctor Myers,' she said, gently touching Joe's arm and leaning over to inspect his EKG machine. 'You've been asleep for a few weeks. Can you tell me your name?'

Joe blinked groggily, one eyelid out of time with the other. He tried to focus on her words, but it felt as though his mind was still waking from a deep sleep.

'Joseph, my name is Joseph,' he replied.

'Very good, Joseph. Would you tell me what you meant by *it was over*?'

'I was out,' he repeated half-heartedly, feeling himself sink further into the mattress.

'Out of where?'

'All of it. Everything.'

'I see.'

Dr. Myers carefully lifted one of Joseph's heavily bandaged arms and checked the IV line. 'You just relax, okay? You've had one hell of a fall.'

'What?'

'Truth be told, it's a miracle you're even alive, let alone awake.'

'Fall?'

'Just relax, okay?' she repeated. 'We'll take good care of you. See if you can get some more sleep and I'll go fetch the head surgeon. He'll want to do another check-up.' The woman gave Joseph an earnest, sympathetic smile and marched from the room quickly, closing the door behind her.

He did not want to sleep; he feared where he might wake up. There was a stillness in the air that he had forgotten existed; it was a calm. Somehow it made him even more uneasy. He sensed the allure of peace.

It's a trick. It's another illusion.

Every squeak of rubber on linoleum made him twitch. Any moment now a crowd of drooling, slashing, humping maniacs would come crashing through that door and he would be well and truly fucked. What would he use to fight them off? The IV stand? He could not even lift his arms, let alone take a swing at a one of *them*. No. If they came, he would die here. He would die bloody and screaming.

'I was done,' he said, pushing his head further back into his pillow. Joseph fought the urge to sleep. He felt his mind drifting again, fading into the black. 'Don't make me go back.' His voice trailed off and his strength failed. His head collapsed to the side and he exhaled deeply.

'I've never seen anything like it.' The hushed voices woke Joseph from his sleep and he jolted upright, pushing against his sheets.

'Hey, hey, take it easy.'

A short, bald-headed man with snow-white stubble rushed forward. He placed a strong hand on Joseph's shoulder and pushed him back down onto the bed. The hospital room faded back into Joseph's vision and the sight of a figure looming over him brought a new wave of panic.

'Joseph, relax,' Dr. Meyers stepped forward, trying to help her colleague calm the man. 'We spoke just before, remember?'

Joseph relaxed just a little but did not become still.

'Don't touch me,' he said, spit flying from his teeth.

'Okay, okay,' the man jumped back. He raised his hands high and the woman did the same. 'See? We're not trying to hurt you, my friend.'

'This is Doctor Maroun, the surgeon I mentioned. He was the one that kept you alive when you were brought in.'

'You may be giving me too much credit,' the man chimed in, giving Dr. Meyers a warm smile. 'You are quite the fighter, Mr. Ridley. There were a few moments I was sure we'd lost you.'

Joseph looked from doctor to doctor, trying to wrap his head around this and entertain the possibility it was real.

'How did I get here?'

The doctors looked at each other grimly. Dr. Meyers shuffled her clipboard from one armpit to another.

'When the paramedics brought you in, you were in a critical condition,' she said. 'Apparently, you were found on the street outside your apartment building.'

'The street?'

'You don't remember what happened?' She stepped forward and gave Joseph a genuinely concerned look. 'You fell, Joseph. You fell eleven floors.'

'Your being alive and speaking is nothing short of a miracle,' added Dr. Maroun, 'but you are not out of the woods yet. You've had some severe internal bleeding and—well, I suppose I should tell you about your leg.'

Joseph shook his head, trying to clear the haze in his skull. None of it made sense.

This is another trick. I remember falling, but …

'Wait,' he said, snapping back to reality, 'my leg?'

Doctor Maroun stepped forward and took a seat beside Joseph's bed. He released a depleted sigh and nodded toward Joseph's feet.

'With your head trauma and the cuts from the glass, you should have bled out within the hour. You were very lucky, Joseph, you should know that. You're going to feel intermittent pain and have some trouble controlling your movement for a long time, perhaps forever. There was no avoiding that. The impact caused a lot of internal bleeding and your ribs punctured your lung. However, you are alive. The point is we could save almost all of you, except for your right leg; the damage was too extreme.'

Only when the words processed in his brain did Joseph become aware of the tingling in his right knee.

'We were forced to amputate. I'm very sorry.'

Joseph lifted his sheet with trembling hands and looked down on one leg—swollen and bruised from thigh to heel—and a stump, thick with padding and tape.

'Wow,' was all he could say.

The doctors shifted uncomfortably again, and Dr. Meyers said something they had both obviously been waiting to wade into.

'Was the fall an accident, Joseph?'

The memory flashed before his eyes—his hand pushing the glass away in an explosion of sparkling mist, the bittersweet joy he had felt as he let the storm take him. Before he could answer, Dr. Meyers spoke again.

'It's okay, we're going to have a resident psychologist come speak to you when you're ready. You've got a long recovery ahead of you, so we just want to make sure you're as comfortable as possible.'

'Why don't we get out of your hair?' said Dr. Maroun, nodding to his colleague. 'Here, I'll put some music on for you.' He reached across to the clock radio, fumbling for the dial.

'No!' Joseph snapped. Dr. Maroun looked taken aback and got to his feet.

'Very well.'

They turned to leave, and Joseph sighed.

'Hey.'

The doctors turned to face him again. They were visibly concerned about what further inquiry was coming.

'Thank you. I don't– just thank you.' Joseph attempted a smile and the doctors returned the gesture in tandem.

'Oh,' said Dr. Meyer's skipping back into the room, 'you have a visitor. We let your emergency contact know you're awake, so I believe your wife is here. I'll let her know you're ready.' She gave one final nod and left again, clipboard tucked firmly under her arm.

Pam? Pam is here?

Joseph found it hard to breathe. He gripped the crisp sheets and flexed his fists. The machine to his left beeped with increasingly rapid repetition. The spikes of his heartbeat cut through the dull green screen, one after the other.

My wife ... Pam. Is Marcus here?

Joseph's mind raced. He gasped for breath as he drank up everything he had just heard. His leg was gone. He fell from his apartment? No, he had jumped. He had to. He had *wanted* to. Was it real? Had he been chased through a nightmarish landscape of blood and rain and agony? Or had he simply jumped through his eleventh-story window, driven mad by years of guilt and booze? He closed his eyes and let his mind run in reverse. He had stood by the window with a naked, younger version of himself. Or had he been alone …? It was hard to say. He remembered looking back at his apartment and throwing his cigarette, then he jumped. He definitely jumped, that much was certain. The emptiness had embraced him, suffocated him. Not darkness, not black, just … nothingness.

'Joseph?'

Joe's eyes shot open, his chest heaving. Had he been holding his breath? Pamela stood in the doorway, not a day older than the last time he had seen her. She was wearing black jeans and one of her signature, oversized sweaters. Her eyes were bloodshot and puffy; she'd been crying.

Joseph was speechless; he was not prepared for this. Pamela stepped closer, looking over Joseph's pile of bandaged limbs and becoming moist in the eyes again.

'Joe,' she said softly.

'Pam,' he replied with a choke, 'tell me it's really you. Please, tell me it's you.'

She rushed forward to the side of the bed, throwing her purse to the floor.

'It's me, Joe, I'm here.' She rested a hand on his and smiled with trembling lips.

Joseph wanted so badly to reach out for her, to take her face in his hands and feel her skin on his fingertips, but he was too weak to move. Whatever medication kept the pain of his wounds at bay also rendered him paralytic.

'I can't believe you're really here,' he said, tears pooling on his top lip.

Pam stroked the side of his face, running a finger along the stitches in his cheek. Her face flinched with each new cut she saw.

'Joe, why?'

Joseph knew what she was asking but could not bring himself to speak with her hand on his face.

'They said they found you on the street, they said–' the breath caught in her throat. 'Joe, did you jump?'

'Pam, I–'

Joe didn't know what to say. He would not lie and yet there was so much she didn't understand, so much she couldn't. He would not have ended his life in spite, not if it would hurt her like this. His pause gave her all the information she needed. Her face crumpled and her cheeks flushed. She brought her hands to her face and wept. Joseph did the same.

They sat in silence for what might have been a minute or an hour. Joseph was too scared to speak, lest it scare Pam away. She looked the way he remembered her, except for a few white hairs hidden throughout the brown. She even smelled the same; it was intoxicating, almost painful.

'Marcus.' The word escaped his lips before he could catch it.

Pam looked up from the flat space where Joseph's right leg should have been and met Joseph's eyes with a glassy distance.

'He's okay,' she said. Her voice cracked, hoarse and worn from the crying. 'He, uh,' she dabbed at her nose with a tissue again, 'he talks to me sometimes, but he still doesn't say much. I'm home-schooling him for now.'

Joseph smiled, imagining Marcus with his books spread across the countertop. He would be blasting his music no doubt, some soft pop classic from well before his time. His music taste had always been inherited exclusively from his mother—a lot of Duran Duran and Hall & Oates.

'Are *you* okay?' Joe asked. He finally found the strength to brush her arm with his fingertips. He felt her quiver under his touch.

She nodded, a little too quickly to be convincing.

'I'm a manager at the aquarium now. You remember how I love fish?'

'Of course I do.'

'I get to spend every day surrounded by them. I know you were never much of a fan, but Marcus loves them.'

The words were true, but they stung, nonetheless. Any time Pam had wanted to take a trip to see the fish and the turtles, Joe had made a show of it being a chore.

'Of all the animals to become obsessed with Pamela, I don't understand it. They're the most boring fucking creatures on the planet.'

'They calm Marky down. I can see it when he comes into work.'

'He always was more of you than me,' Joe said with a weak laugh, 'thank God.'

'I heard you're a driver now?'

'Well,' Joseph said, throwing a glance down at his stump, 'I suppose I was.'

Pam flinched, visibly guilty.

'Pam,' Joseph said, touching her hand with his again. 'I need to tell you–'

He hesitated. How could he possibly find the words to express his regret, his guilt. How could he make her see that he finally understood? And that none of it was her fault?

'Joe–'

'Pam, I'm sorry.' His tone was earnest, racked with shame. It was a side of Joseph that Pamela had not seen for decades. It was a side of her husband that she had all but forgotten.

'I will never be able to show you how sorry I am, but I need to tell you that.'

'Joe, I– I don't–'

'Everything that happened, all of it. It was my fault.'

Pam sniffed through more tears and hesitantly held Joseph's hand between both of hers.

'Joe, is this why you did it?'

'No– I mean yes, but–'

'You son of a bitch,' she said, pressing her face into the bedsheets. 'You can't do that to us, not after everything.'

'I know,' replied Joseph desperately, 'you're right Pam. You've been right this entire time.'

'I don't understand.'

'I don't expect you to forgive me—you shouldn't. But please believe me when I say that I'm sorry. I should have been a better husband, a better dad.'

'I don't know what I should say.'

'You don't need to say anything. It's okay.'

Pam blinked through burning tears, feeling her foundations crumble and give way to something long buried. She looked up at the man she had spent the last four years loathing, regretting, and aching for. She was consumed with the death of the man she loved and the memory of the monster that replaced him … but now she saw *him*. Joseph, the *real* Joseph. Pamela saw her husband again, holding her hand in his. This man looking back at her with watery eyes was not just the boy she had fought the urge to kiss in high school, for fear of breaking her boyfriend's heart. He was not just the young man she made love to in the back of a rusted, old Buick decades ago. He was something more; he was a person she had not yet met. He seemed … *exposed*, his soul stripped naked and laid bare. It was as if that concrete shell she was so often crushed under had finally been cracked and torn away with bloody hands.

'It's okay, Joe, it's okay now.'

Joseph winced as he pulled the shirt over his scarred chest. It felt remarkably freeing to finally get out of that hospital gown, even if it was into some clothing that he would not have normally worn. He looked down at the black band tee and smiled. It was Pam's, one of the baggy ones she would wear on a slow day. She would sit in the sunlight with a book just inches from her nose, feet crossed over the arm of her chair. It would have been tight on Joseph not too long ago; it probably would have bunched up around his gut. But he was now at least ten kilos lighter; losing a leg and eating through a tube for a few weeks will do that.

Pam had been coming into the hospital almost daily for the last two weeks, bringing him magazines and food that he shouldn't have been eating. They spent hours reminiscing about school, their road trips, and Marcus' babyhood. They would talk and laugh with their mouths bursting with chocolates and sweets. It was like they were teenagers again; it even felt like they were friends. The gifts were wonderful, of course, but it was seeing those freckled cheeks scrunch up in a smile—it was smelling that familiar scent of vanilla and jasmine—that really brought Joe's mind back to earth.

He had decided quite early on not to tell her how he would flinch whenever the doorknob turned, how he was so deathly afraid of the radio that he had asked for it to be taken out of his room and be put far, *far* away. He especially wouldn't tell her about the dreams. Every night, against his better judgment he would feel his eyes close and then his body would fall through the bed. It fell through the floor and the concrete foundation of the hospital. He would watch the world melt into black and feel the eternally empty limbs of darkness pull him down, *down*, into the void. When he woke from the dream he was standing in the corner of a dark room, looking down on a sleeping figure. His eyes were sewn shut, but he could see. His mouth hung open and his throat was swollen with bile, but still he groaned. Then the man in the bed was sitting, tangled in the sheets and glazed with sweat.

'Why are you here?' said the shadowed figure.

Sometimes in the dream he was holding the door open and watching a beaten, bloody reflection of himself limping closer through the hallway. Sometimes he was weak, so weak his bones popped and ground against each other with every step. Other times he felt strong, stronger than he had ever been. One thing was always the same—the storm: the rolling crashes of thunder from the other side of the glass, and the lightning that cracked the glowing, crimson sky.

'Easy does it,' said the small, female nurse with the buzz cut. 'We'll take it nice and slow, Joe.'

'Yes, ma'am,' said Joe. He gave the girl a cheeky smile and let her prop the crutches under his arms.

He had gotten out of bed a few times so far, but usually only to hop over to the bathroom— almost always falling into the walls. Today he was leaving, he was going home. A *new* home. Pam had helped him put his apartment on a listing, and then to lease out something a bit more accessible; a place she had described as, *cozy, modest, not at all your style*. Joseph couldn't be more excited.

Clack

Joe grunted as the crutches hit the floor and he swung his foot forward, finding himself a step closer to the door.

'There it is,' said the older, male nurse, 'what'd I tell you? Piece of cake.'

'Why don't we chop off your leg then, Greg, have a race maybe?' Joe replied, taking a deep breath and chuckling. He swung forward again, finding a rhythm but nearly slipping.

'Tell you what,' said Greg as Joseph passed into the hospital corridor, 'if you can catch me, I'll let you take my leg and give it a go.' Greg passed by and crouched into a phony runner's start. Then he laughed over his shoulder and marched into the belly of the hospital with his clipboard pressed to his chest.

'So remember, Joe, try to get lots of rest and be back here next week for your checkup,' said the female nurse. She gave Joe one last reassuring squeeze on his shoulder. 'Are you sure you'll be okay to get to the exit? We can still get you a wheelchair.'

'Gotta get used to these things eventually. You leave me be, before the other patients get jealous.'

She smiled and turned to leave, unsnapping the pager from her waistband. 'Oh, by the way, Pam is at the front waiting for you. I think she wants to see you off.'

Joseph grinned, giving the girl one last two-fingered salute as she rushed off, looking immediately busy again. He looked around the astonishingly white hallway and breathed in the cocktail of sterile, chemical odors. The space was buzzing with frantic energy as doctors in blue scrubs rushed this way and that, some of them leading a small group of anxious-looking residents. A round-looking man in a—much too loose—patient's gown wandered toward the vending machines. He dragged a squeaky IV stand behind him and stroked his magnificent red beard.

The longer Joseph stared into the corridor the more he began to see beneath the coat of eggshell paint. He saw pale, yellow walls, lined with doors that had numbers nailed into the wood. The polished, white floor peeled away to reveal starchy, blue carpet. An elevator dinged and he watched the door at the end of the corridor swing open. *His* door. All that could be seen in the darkness beyond was a faint, red glow and the occasional flash of white.

'No.'

Joseph shook his head violently and breathed deeply, trying to calm the hammering in his chest. He heard the chaotic chatter and mechanical beeping fade back into reality and the light bore into his closed eyelids. He found the luminescent, green rectangle that could only be an exit sign and began to limp toward it, smiling and nodding at the people who met his gaze.

'This ain't so bad,' Joseph mumbled to himself, crutches and leg swinging past each other in a pendulum of motion.

Clack Thud Clack Thud

He could already feel himself tiring. He turned every corner to find more busy, white space. The lump in his stomach grew heavier. Joe puffed and felt the sweat bead on his forehead as he increased his pace, chasing that accursed green exit sign through hallway after hallway. He dodged doctors, patients, and sobbing visitors. The smiles felt less friendly now, they mocked him. The excitement turned to panic, and a tight pulling pain pierced the center of his chest.

'Pam,' he gasped.

He turned another corner and felt a familiar, terrifying darkness creep into his vision. Then he saw them. On the other side of the lobby, Pam was kneeling in front of a dark-haired boy in a chair, tightening his laces. The boy stared blankly down at his mother and pushed away a long, black curl. Joseph's grip finally failed on his right crutch and it slipped away with a tremendous squeak and crash. He fell into the wall and with the help of a passing doctor, managed to steady himself. He never looked away from his wife and son. Pam and Marcus had heard the noise and were staring back at him now, the woman's face painted with confused concern. She said something else to the boy and then rushed over, grabbing Joseph around the waist.

'Jesus, Joe, are you okay?

'I'm– I'm okay, I just slipped.'

'Are you sure you should be checking out?'

'I'm sure, Pam.' He gave her a reassuring smile, but his eyes were still looking over her shoulder.

Pam seemed to notice and shifted from one foot to the other nervously.

'I had to bring him with me. I hope that's okay.'

'Of course it is,' Joe replied breathlessly, 'of course it is.'

'I don't like leaving him home alone and the babysitter is off on some trip.'

'Pam,' Joseph said, looking back at her with a quiet desperation, 'can I talk to him?'

Pam froze for a few seconds, then looked back at Marcus, chewing her lip.

'I don't know, Joe, it's been a long time. You have to understand, we didn't think we'd ever see you again.'

'Please, I just need to tell him I love him.'

Pam scanned Joseph's eyes and saw the pain there, the anguish.

'Just for a minute, okay?'

'Of course, thank you, Pam, thank you.'

She looked down at the faded Thompson Twins shirt he was wearing, and a small smile spread across her lips.

'It's weird seeing you out of a suit again. I started wondering at one point if you'd stitched them to your skin.'

'The ties started feeling more like a noose, so I thought I'd try something different,' Joseph replied. 'I like it. Much more comfortable.'

They crossed the lobby slowly and Pam pulled a chair across to face Marcus. She knelt in front of him again and spoke in a quick, hushed voice. Joseph carefully slid into the seat and leaned his crutches against the arm. He flexed his hands and his breathing became heavy. Pam looked over her shoulder and gave Joe one more hesitant frown, before exhaling slowly and getting to her feet. She stood behind the boy, anxiously tapping her legs and bouncing from foot to foot. It was a long, agonizing moment before Joseph found the courage to speak. He looked up from his quivering hands and found his son's emotionless, hazel eyes staring back.

'Son,' he said. His voice was a weak, hoarse croak. Joseph cleared his throat and tried again. 'You've gotten big, son. I can't believe you're eleven now.'

Marcus didn't move, he didn't speak. He just watched as his father picked the thread from his sleeve like a nervous child.

'I just want you to know, Marky, I love you and– God, I'm sorry, son. I'm so sorry.'

Shit, here come the tears.

Joseph's eyes burned and misted over as he fought to keep his voice from trembling.

'I've messed up a lot in my life, a whole damn lot, but failing you and your mom is my biggest regret. I should have been there for you, Marky.'

Pam looked like she wanted to interrupt, to wrap Marcus up in her arms and run, but she couldn't. She too found her eyes glossing over and every fiber of her being wanted Marcus to speak, to say something, *anything.*

'That day,' Joseph leaned forward and cautiously reached a hand out for Marcus' elbow. He pulled back when he saw the boy twitch. His stomach twisted in agonizing knots, drenched with guilt and longing. 'That day, son, I should have been there for you. I shouldn't have left you and your mom, but I did. I can never make up for that, and I'll understand if you can never forgive me for what I did.'

Marcus' expression remained unchanged. Joseph searched the boy's eyes, searching for any sign of the child he had picked up and swung around in a fit of laughter, so long ago.

'I know I can never really be your dad again, Marky, but if you remember anything about me, let it be this; it's not your fault. None of this is your fault, it's mine. All of it, every last goddamn bit … it was all my fault. You and your mom, you deserve the world. You deserved better, better than me.'

Marcus moved ever so slightly in his seat, then looked up at his mother with complete calm.

'Can we go home now, Mom?'

Joseph felt his heart fall through the pit of his stomach and land flat on the ground. He felt the hole that traveled through his core glue him to the chair. Pam looked both relieved and disheartened, all in one instant.

'Of course, baby, let's go get some lunch, yeah?'

She ran a hand through the boy's thick hair and blinked away the tears in her eyes. He promptly hopped to his feet and strolled toward the hospital's sliding glass doors with his hands in his pockets.

'I'm sorry, Joe,' said Pam, helping Joe up onto his foot again and handing him his crutches, 'he just needs more time.'

'I get it. Seeing him here today, it was already more than I deserve. Everything you've done for me, Pam, it's *all* more than I deserve.'

Pam's mouth curved into a quivering, lopsided half-circle and she gave his hand a gentle squeeze.

'It's not too late for you, Joe, there's hope for everyone. I believe you can be the man you used to be. I believe you can be even better.'

She wiped her wet, freckled cheek with a palm and turned to leave.

'Pam.'

'Yeah?'

'I know– I know we can never be what we were, but do you think I could see you again sometime? Maybe be friends?'

'Yeah, maybe,' she said softly, 'you have my number. I'm only a call away if you ever need to talk.'

She took another step toward the exit and jumped back when she saw Marcus standing just an inch away.

'Jeez, Marky, you scared me half to death. Let's hit the road, okay?'

Marcus nodded and let his mother step past, before looking up at his father again.

'Goodbye, Marky,' Joe said, 'I love you, son.'

Marcus turned to follow his mother and paused.

'You were there.'

Joseph's heart stopped in his chest. He was sure he could feel the blood freeze his joints in place.

'What?'

'That day, you were there. I saw you.' Marcus spun around to face Joseph again, his face now carved with fear.

'You ... saw me?'

'When–' Marcus' chest began to rise and fall a little faster, 'when I got in the car, I heard yelling. I heard a yell and when I looked out the window, I saw you.' His eyes traveled over the pale scars that speckled Joseph's arms. 'There was blood, lots.'

'You saw me.'

Joseph's mind raced. Visions flashed before his eyes, images of his bloody, bandaged arms reaching out for his son. Marcus' shocked face staring back from the passenger seat of a red Range Rover. He saw the SUV pulling away around a bend, never getting closer, no matter how hard he ran.

It's not possible, is it?

'Change it. Change the memory.'

'You were trying to help me?'

'Of course I was, Marky, I wanted to get to you more than anything else in the world.'

Marcus looked up at his father and twisted his mouth, as if he was deciding on an item from the McDonalds menu.

'Okay. I believe you, Dad.'

Joseph did his best not to collapse as he watched his son run into the open arms of a concerned and confused-looking Pam. He could have sworn he'd seen Marky smile.

Chapter
Sixteen

Just One Week

The city street looked much the same as it did when Joseph had stood here just three months ago, smoking a cigarette and waiting for his last day of work to begin—though he had not known that at the time. The pavement was still crowded with people rushing from corner to corner, arms stuffed with shopping bags, their eyes glued to the smartphone in their hand. Joe used to hate the city, the crowds, the suffocating stench of exhaust fumes and smog. Had he not been so repulsed and bored by the countryside, he might have chosen to live somewhere other than a bustling metropolitan area. The truth was that he hated the way strangers could stare, like they had you figured out. He despised being watched, but, boy, did Joseph *love* being seen. He had been quite content hiding away with a bottle of whiskey and a TV remote, but every now and then you had to get out and remind people you had money and power; everything they did not have. He saw people as a virus, one that he would never truly control. They were unpredictable, dangerous.

That is how Joseph used to feel, but now he walked amidst the swarm happily. His right leg fell just a bit heavier than the left as he stepped. The metal and rubber of his prosthetic leg compressed and expanded, hidden away beneath faded denim. It had taken a while to get used to, but now Joseph could go hours without remembering the missing limb. The quiet moments were the worst for a multitude of reasons.

The phantom itch is a real son of a bitch.

Joseph strode the sidewalk, hands in his jacket pockets and Bob Seger blasting from his headphones. It felt good to be immersed in the vitality of the city; it filled his chest and face with warmth. All these people were alive, right now, and so was he. That was something they shared. They would all be dead one day too, another thing they had in common. They all walked with the same planet beneath their feet and, for the first time in a long time, Joseph didn't feel quite so alone.

The soft pretzel almost refused to finish its journey down Joseph's throat as he stood, looking up at the Royal Dawn. It towered over him, reaching so high that he felt the ground spin slowly under him. It made his skin crawl. It charged life into a feeling that had been resting just beneath the surface of his skin since he woke up that first dark, stormy night. Dread crept through his body, threatening to paralyze him. The window he had jumped through—*his* window—was hidden in shade, reflecting only the black-shadowed stone of the building opposite. Joe finally brought his eyes to ground level again and tried to regain control of his balance. He saw himself in the reflection, standing tall on an identical, darkened street beyond the glass doors. His spine shuddered as a cold breeze blew through him. It guided him toward the entrance. Before he knew what he was doing, he watched a shaky hand reach out for the long, brass handle.

'Joe?'

He snapped out of his trance and spun around to see a curly-haired young man looking up at him.

'Daewon?'

'I thought you'd moved,' said the teenager, his face becoming lined with rapidly increasing grief. 'I saw your apartment go up on the listing. I didn't know if I should reach out. I was scared that– I didn't know if you re–'

Joseph pulled the boy into a tight embrace, no longer able to contain the urge. He held Daewon close and fought the fresh tears forming in his eyes.

'I didn't know if you made it, kid. I couldn't bring myself to check.'

Daewon hugged him back, pressing his face into the large man's shoulder.

'No one believed me, Joe. Please tell me you remember. Tell me I'm not crazy.'

Joseph pulled back and gave the young man a grim look, 'I remember. I remember it all.'

'Oh thank God,' Daewon said with a gasp, pressing his wet face into Joseph's chest. 'I thought I was going insane. I nearly stabbed Rick in the fucking eye when he came in for work.'

'Rick?'

'The security guard, built like a bloody cement truck.'

'Oh.'

'He came up to say hi like he usually does, but– but all I could see was the blood.'

'Your leg, how did you– is it okay?'

'I don't know, it's weird,' Daewon stepped back and looked down at the spot where Joseph had wrapped the knife wound. 'I passed out after you left that night, everything went dark. When I came to, I was on the floor and the cut was gone. All the blood, it was all just *gone*. I thought I dreamt it, but then I felt the pain. I could still feel the pain. It hurt so bad I could barely breathe, so I called an ambulance. They were so angry. They thought I was pulling some sick prank.'

Daewon rubbed his eyes and linked his hands behind his head. He was bouncing anxiously on the balls of his feet, clearly disturbed.

'I still feel it sometimes, especially at night. It's like it's happening all over again.'

Joseph knew the torment that dreams could bring. Just that morning he had woken with his blanket twisted around his body, drenched with sweat. He had seen himself, watching through the dark and the flashes of lightning as his gaunt reflection broke the window and jumped. He had watched peacefully as his doppelgänger's body fell away, swallowed by the storm.

'I'm sorry, kid, you never should have been involved.'

'Oh piss off. You would have been dead without me. Remember?'

'Yeah. Yeah, I sure as shit would've been.' They exchanged a genuine smile. 'So the others ... Javier, Wendy ... they're all okay?'

'Like I said, no one remembers a damn thing. There was one, though … one of the tenants went missing. Her family came around and her apartment was empty. I think they're still looking for her. It was all over the news.'

'Taylor D?'

'Yeah. Yeah, Taylor sounds right.'

Joseph sighed. Deep down he knew that part wouldn't have changed. Taylor was still in the storm. He had hoped maybe she didn't exist at all. That would have been better.

'Hey, listen. All the tenants are saying the storm blew over in one night, Joe, *one* night.'

Joseph had heard that too. The doctors had told him how lucky he was that the storm blew over so quickly, otherwise he never would have been found in time.

'It doesn't matter anymore, kid. It's over.'

I hope it's over. I really do.

'Tell you what,' Joe said, 'why don't we go down the street and grab one of those sugary coffees we both hate so much.'

'All right. You sure you don't need a walking frame or something? Don't think I didn't notice the limp.'

'Shut your mouth.' Joseph gave the young man a playful shove and they both laughed again, ignoring the pissed-off glares of the pedestrians jostling past. Joseph noticed something over the boy's shoulder and gave him a gentle slap on the back.

'Hey, give me a few seconds, will ya? I'll be right back.'

'Uh, okay?'

Joseph stepped onto the road and weaved his way through the beeping, cursing traffic jam until he was standing on the opposite side of the street. Daewon watched with confusion as he stopped beside a towering, powerful-looking old man in an expensive, midnight-blue suit.

'Good afternoon, Joseph.'

'Mr. Bub.'

'Please, Samuel will do fine. I'm not your client anymore, am I?'

Joe met the man's piercing gray eyes and felt that familiar tingle of awe run through his body.

'Would you like a cigarette?' Joseph looked down at the packet in the man's enormous hand.

'I'm trying to quit.'

Damn, Silk Cuts …

'But I don't want to be rude.'

Samuel's lips curled into a wry smile and he plucked out two tailors from their sheath. There was a moment of respectful silence as the men lit the tips of their smokes and inhaled the warmth. A white and pale blue halo of wispy smoke circled them and faded into the wind.

'I can't say you seem the type to be out here walking the street. Where's your town car?' said Joseph.

'I like to walk sometimes.' Samuel blew smoke from his nostrils and waved a hand lazily toward the tops of the surrounding skyscrapers. 'You spend enough time up there, you begin to forget what things are really like down below.'

'Wow. They should get you on daytime TV, that was pretty good.'

There was a tense silence, and then Samuel laughed. It was deep and guttural, with the bass of thunder. Joe laughed too.

'Quite the storm that day, wouldn't you say, Mr. Ridley?'

'Yeah ... quite the storm.'

'I'm glad to see you're well.'

'You sure about that?'

'Of course.'

Samuel Bub crushed the cigarette butt in his palm and Joseph stamped his beneath his boot.

'Not everyone can enjoy a good spot of rain and lightning, but I would like to believe everyone can appreciate what comes after.'

'What's that?' said Joseph.

'Everything—' the tall man replied, moving a hand slowly from one end of the horizon to the other, 'washed clean.'

Samuel put his hands into the deep pockets of his black overcoat and gave Joseph what was clearly a parting smile.

'I'm not going to see you again, am I, Sam?'

The tall man bowed slightly and squinted, staring through Joseph with an intense focus.

'Time will tell.'

Samuel turned on the spot and strode into the mob, vanishing almost immediately among the rabble. He had been humming something familiar, something that sounded a lot like a John Denver song. Joseph smiled again and made his way back across the road, waving to Daewon to indicate he hadn't forgotten him. The young man tapped the back of his wrist theatrically and joined the man's side as he walked past. Not so long ago he would not have seen himself going for lunch with—and paid for by—the grouchy old bastard in room 1102. It was not the same man he walked with now, or the same man that had saved him from a hulking, bloodthirsty maniac. Perhaps, despite what his father had unconsciously taught him, people really could change. Maybe all it took was one bad week, and one *hell* of a storm.

Epilogue

Rays of sweltering, afternoon sun beat down on the endless stretch of blacktop. Waves of heat snaked off the dark asphalt and obscured the horizon in a winding, dancing mirage. Either side of the highway was peppered with rain-starved scrub and the occasional ominous sign.

LAST FUEL
FOR 100 MILES

Tony tapped the steering wheel in an offbeat rhythm as his car roared down the road, pushing 90 miles an hour with no signs of slowing. There was not a car behind him or in front, as far as the eye could see. It was perfect.

There is a house in New Orleans
They call the Rising Sun

Tony sang along until the tune died out and the radio DJ's slow, bored voice flooded back into the car's interior.

'Well, that was The Animals, folks, but I'm sure you know that. I tell you what, it's a hot day today, ladies and gentlemen. I'm sittin here sweatin buckets from head to ass crack.'

Tony knew how the mopey bastard felt; his air-con had died out in a weak hiss an hour or two earlier. Now he felt the dark patches on his gray shirt growing larger by the minute. He had put his windows down of course, but he might as well have been driving a fan-forced oven for all the good it was doing. He was used to working in the heat, but he didn't like it any more than he had on his first day thirty years ago. You would be hard-pressed to find a mechanic who hadn't spent countless hours with their face mere inches from the ass end of a hot engine. All those years turning bolts and now here he was, looking down the barrel of a five-hour drive in the blistering sun, in a car with busted air conditioning.

Just my fucking luck.

The bored DJ crackled out and Jim Morrison sung the opening lyrics to 'Break On Through,' much to Tony's delight. He had been driving for some time now and felt a pleasurable tingle down his spine imagining the bed back home. Suddenly, his phone began to chime and the screen illuminated to show the face of a smiling woman with pale, blonde hair.

'Ah shit,' Tony hissed. He quickly turned the volume knob and snatched the phone from the passenger seat.

'Hey, honey,' he said into the phone as he pressed it to his ear. The edges of his mouth curled into an insincere smile.

'Yes of course, I'm on my way now … I'm still pretty far away, maybe five or six hours, I don't know. It looks like there may be some rain up ahead … I slept in, Jill, sorry … Of course I know that's tonight. I said I'll be there, didn't I? … Like I said, I slept in … You know how this works, Jill. I had to pick up parts for the garage; there's no fuckin way I was paying postage for all this. You should see it. I've got boxes to the damn ceiling in here. I can't even see out the back window … It was good. I gotta go, okay? I'm drivin. I'll tell you all about it when I get home, if that's what you want … I'll get there when I get there. Why don't you grab some takeout for yourself and Dee? … Yeah, all right, see you soon … Love you too.'

Tony threw the phone over his shoulder onto the empty back seat, shaking his head.

'Fuckin bitch, quit nagging me, damnit.'

He turned up the radio again, just in time to hear the opening jingle of the evening news, a sound that always gave him an excited, terrifying rush.

'Hello and welcome back to B107 news at five. Breaking news today as a man comes forward claiming responsibility for a brutal assault in 2015 that left one primary school teacher paralyzed. The man's identity has so far remained protected, but an update from the Dawn Valley high court is expected soon.'

Tony shook his head and ran his tongue over the front of his teeth, fighting back a bitter chuckle.

There's some real psychos out there.

'Come on, you piece of shit,' he said, giving the air vents another hopeful slap. He knew better than most how little good that would do.

'How the fuck does a grease monkey like me end up with so many piece-of-crap cars?' he asked himself.

He felt his temperature rising, this time not because of the climate. His temples throbbed and he knew another one of his debilitating migraines would be bending him over the hood if he didn't get his temper under control, and quick.

'Daisy never gave me trouble,' he grumbled over the chattering of the news anchor. 'Dear old Daisy.'

Daisy had been his prized possession for many years. She was not easy on the eyes, but any mechanical issues were usually fixed with one well-placed whack from the wrench. He had driven that machine to hell and back and loved her almost as much as he loved his wife. *Shit*, maybe he loved the car more. It wasn't an easy decision to take Daisy apart; he had pulled her apart, panel from panel, down to the foundations and sold her as scrap. He had shed more than a few tears about it, but what could he do? He'd changed the plates of course, but it was still too risky. All over the news they were talking about the bright-red Range Rover; it wasn't worth the gamble. It had been a monumentally stupid decision to take that car that day. God knows he had beat himself up about it. Truth be told he hadn't even planned on stopping in that neighborhood, or even on that day. He was just driving past, as he liked to do. The kid was sitting on his own, looking lost as all hell at nearly four o'clock in the damn afternoon. How could that not be fate?

'It's safe to say a lot of people are still very concerned about the tension between the United States and North Korea, with Kim–' The radio continued through the political segment of the evening news and Tony felt his mind wandering back to that week, four years ago now.

417

Which one was that? George? No, Mick ... Mark? Hmm.

He had hightailed it out of Dawn Valley and back to Blue Rock Falls as soon as he had let the kid walk. He always let the kids go; he wasn't a *monster*.

Michael? Marcus?

Sure, sometimes they would cry when they realized you weren't taking them home, but he always took good care of them. They got ice cream, cable TV, anything they wanted. He always did his best not to hurt them. Then when the fun had run its course, he always took them home. *Always*. He wasn't some kind of psycho, like those sick bastards that snatch kids and leave their half-naked corpses lying by the side of the road. Just the thought of it made him sick; it made his blood boil.

Damnit, breathe, Tony. Breathe, idiot.

His head throbbed menacingly, migraine cresting the horizon like the swirling, crashing thunderclouds up ahead.

'Now we go to the weather. Paul?'

'Thanks, Christine. It's looking very sunny for the Dawn Valley area, but we do have a bit of a situation forming along the coastline toward the northern, rural areas.'

Tony turned the dial up a little more, frowning at the expanding, dark mass in the sky. It was swallowing the cloudless blue like a black fog and the lightning had started to look a darker shade of red.

'To put it bluntly, there's one *hell* of a storm coming, folks, and if you're in the area, woo boy, do I hope you're ready.'

'You gotta be fuckin kidding me,' said Tony through clenched teeth.

'Hunker down somewhere sturdy if you can or go ahead and try your luck. See if you can shoot through to the other side. Some folks have been lucky enough. Can't say I'd recommend it, though, Anthony.'

Tony turned his head sharply from the storm to the weak, green glow of the radio. His foot eased off the pedal and his throat expanded with a breath that wouldn't surface.

'What the fuck?'

'You heard me, Anthony. This storm is a *big* one ... one of the biggest I've ever seen, and guess what?'

Tony's heart bashed against his chest and he jumped as rain started pattering the windshield. The scorching heat outside had been replaced with a brisk, chilling wind and an all-consuming shade. It was as if all sound except for that voice in the speakers had been sucked from the world. A violent shiver ran down his spine. He felt as though he were the only person left on the planet.

'This one was made special, Anthony. It was made just for *you*.'

The weatherman's voice faded out with a distorted sizzle and then a pop. The storm clouds had already blacked out the sun and left the highway desert in a colorless, dark fog. Tony gripped the steering wheel with sweaty hands, flexing his fingers and muttering frantically.

'You're imagining shit, Tony, get it together.'

The radio blasted to life again with an explosion of static and a jazzy, crackling tune bounced across every surface.

I'm flying high but I've got a feeling I'm falling

There were no other cars for at least fifty miles in either direction when Tony's car disappeared into the storm. He was utterly alone.

Note from the Author

I want to give a big thank you to my family, friends, and viewers on Youtube for all the support during the writing of this story. I know the expression is well used, but it truly would not have been possible without you.

I especially want to thank you, the reader. Thank you for taking a chance on an indie Author like myself, I hope you found Joe's *journey*—should I be so generous to call it that—worth your time.

While Welcome Descent is not short on action, I wanted to tell a story that preys on your mind. A story in which you may find yourself sympathizing with a truly deplorable man. A story where you question what is real. I'm not claiming to have written anything substantially profound, but I encourage you to reflect on what happened to Joseph and why—that's where I always found value in these types of books anyway.

From the bottom of my heart, **thank you**. I can promise you I have plenty more stories in the works.

- C.W

About the Author

Cam Wolfe has had a morbid fascination with
the grim and the macabre since the day he first
picked up a Goosebumps book.
Through his life he has nurtured a passion for
writing: a joy passed down from a mother who
loves reading, and a father who loved to tell
stories.

You can also find Cam over on his Youtube channel
(Page Nomad) where he makes videos about the
highs and lows of being a writer.

'Welcome Descent' is Cam
Wolfe's debut horror.